CHANCE MEETING

A Story of Life and Love

A Novel by
Sid Rich

PublishAmerica
Baltimore

4/10/2007
To Earline
with all good wishes
and very best regards.

ISBN: 1-4241-6612-8
PUBLISHED BY PUBLISHAMERICA, LLLP
www.publishamerica.com
Baltimore

Printed in the United States of America

If you want to know more about Sid Rich, his family and future literary projects, consult his web site www.sidrichonline.com

OTHER BOOKS BY SID RICH:

Standing on the Promises
Men in War
Picking up the Pieces
Two Tigers from Texas
Manila Gold

Chapter 1

May 1997

AS CLARE CLOSED her journal, her memory of that last night in Nairobi was crystal clear. She always wondered what, if anything, was behind Marshall's question. And after such an experience, she was taken aback by his rather flippant and shallow impression. She had to always remember that Marshall could have access to the journal and she had to be careful about making any compromising entries. Although she didn't tell him that night, the trip had heightened her resolve to become a less dependent person; to become her own person—instead of the pitiful, obedient, mindless, reticent to a fault woman she had become. With that resolve was also the commitment to make their union work in spite of her growing sense that she had made a terrible mistake. And she remembered the excitement and anticipation of seeing her new home, meeting new people and settling in Johannesburg, one of the great cities of the world. And she remembered that she needed to see a priest.

Chapter 2

Friday, February 25, 2000

MORGAN MASON SAT in first class and would be one of the first to deplane the crowded flight. He retrieved his garment bag from the overhead, pulled out the roll-bag from the first class bin and headed for the forward exit. The flight deck was open and the captain was greeting passengers. "Thanks for flying with us."

The head flight attendant echoed his sentiments, "We enjoyed serving you, Mr. Mason, and we hope to see you again soon."

"Frequent flier miles, Sue Ann. You'll see me soon, I suspect. The flight was nice. Thanks for everything."

"You know him?" the captain inquired.

"Oh yeah, he's Morgan Mason, a *New York Times* best-selling author. Everything he's written has been a hit. He goes to New York City and Dallas quite a bit and always flies with us."

"Seems like a nice enough fellow."

"Yes, he's a gracious gentleman," said the flight attendant with a sigh. "And I'd like to take him home with me."

The captain laughed and bumped her playfully, "Down, girl."

Morgan reached the end of the jet-way, turned toward the main concourse, and caught sight of a shapely woman with coal black hair arranged in a French braid. He paused to take her in. Her jeans were starched and clung attractively to her shapely legs. Even her dark blue blazer couldn't disguise her well-shaped derriere. All that loveliness was perched atop her attractive dark-blue high heel stilettos. That look never failed to capture his attention. He smiled as he approached but remained wary, cognizant of the many times he had seen a similar sight only to be disillusioned by the complete specimen.

Walking slowly, he tried not to be too obvious when he looked back to satisfy his curiosity. Her looks stopped him dead in his tracks and several people grumbled as they tried to get around him. She was stunning. Morgan liked women, beautiful women, but very few women really made him look twice. This woman was an exceptional beauty, olive complexion and voluptuous. She rummaged in her purse in front of the public telephones: her dilemma for change was apparent.

Morgan piled his luggage against the wall, reached in his pocket and extracted a handful of assorted coins. Approaching her with a grin he said, "Here, take whatever you need."

She looked up, startled momentarily. Realizing what was being offered she smiled and said, "Thank you. I feel so stupid! I don't have much change at all, but I couldn't..."

"Please take what you need," insisted Morgan.

"You didn't have to, but I'm too desperate to argue," collecting the exact amount she needed.

"Will you be okay now?"

"Yes, thank you so much."

"I'm pleased to be of service."

Morgan collected his belongings and walked toward the terminal. *She is so beautiful, just my type,* he thought. Morgan's type was brunette, not too tall, not too skinny, and well built. As he talked with her, he took note of two other attractive features; perfect porcelain white teeth and piercing green eyes. *I cannot bring myself to let it end this way.* As the concourse turned right he temporarily lost sight of her. He put down his bags, leaned against the wall and waited. Soon she turned the corner and almost ran into him. He gently caught her and said, "I hope you made your connection?"

Surprised to fall over him, and surprised to see him waiting, see took a moment to decipher his meaning and said, "Oh yeah, thanks; I did reach my party."

"Good. Listen, I was thinking maybe I could buy you a quick drink."

"Oh, I don't know," she glanced at the slim gold Rolex that Marshall had given her. She didn't quite know what to do, or say, to this stranger. But she thought to herself, *I shouldn't, but he helped me, and he's gorgeous.*

"Okay, sure, why not? I've got a few minutes."

"Great, there's a little bar right down here on our right. Let me take your things."

"Oh, I can get them."

"I insist," said Morgan, with a playful but definite tone of authority.

"All right, thank you very much."

"How about over there?" Morgan suggested, pointing to a small table for two by the wall. "Does that look okay?"

"Sure," she said, taking a chair. Morgan borrowed an unused chair from another table and carefully placed their things on it.

He took his seat, rubbed his hands together, smiled, and asked, "What would you like? Maybe we could decide before the waitress comes over."

She pondered the question, but when she offered no definite selection, Morgan said, "I think I'll have a cold beer."

"You know, a beer sounds just right to me."

"Great, beer it is," said Morgan, "I love Mexican beer. In fact, I don't drink any other kind."

"Really?"

"Actually, I don't drink beer very often. I always have it in the refrigerator at home, but a six-pack might last me several months. But when I want it, I really want it. And when I want it, I don't want light beer. I want the real stuff. Actually, red wine is my favorite drink, a nice Merlot."

"I'm partial to red wine myself."

"Not Zinfandel?"

"Oh God, no, I can't stand the stuff."

"Believe it or not, I'm like you with the beer. I don't drink it much, but sometimes it tastes sooooo good. And like you, I want a full-bodied beer."

"My favorite is Bohemia," said Morgan.

"Well, if they have it, order me one as well."

After a few minutes of small talk, the waitress appeared, took their order, and soon placed two chilled bottles of Bohemia on the table. Morgan touched her bottle gently and said, "Here's to smooth flights and pocket change."

She laughed and took a long swig of the golden liquid. Morgan followed suit.

"Isn't that nice?" Morgan asked.

"Wow. It's very smooth. Good choice."

He extended his hand, "My name's Morgan."

She laughed as they shook hands, "I'm Clare."

"Well, Clare, it's very nice to meet you, and do you have a last name?"

She tapped her chin with her index finger and smiled at him, "I think Clare had better do under the circumstances."

"Look, I understand; I'm a perfect stranger. But what the heck? I thought I'd ask." He paused a moment and tried again, "I guess your phone number would be out of the question?"

She laughed for a few seconds and then said, "Yes, I'm afraid it would be."

"I can't believe I'm sitting here; it's not something I would ordinarily do," Clare confessed.

"It's not like me to pick up women in airports."

Taking another satisfying swig of beer, Clare inquired, "So what kind of work do you do?"

"I'm in the book business."

Like Morgan, she has done her share of checking him out. *Let's see, he appears to be around six-feet tall—black eyes, jet black wavy hair, broad shoulders, and tanned. Very nice.* He was also dressed casually; faded jeans with heavy starch, a blue T-shirt, and a dark-blue blazer. His highly polished boots were a beautiful copper-like color. They looked to be alligator. She liked the look; she liked his looks.

"The book business? You have the look of a professional athlete."

"Well, I played college football, and I was in the fitness business for a few years."

"Yeah, I thought something like that."

He smiled and took another swig of beer.

"Just exactly how are you in the book business?"

"I'm in production."

"Oh, you work for the publisher."

"Something like that," he replied with a chuckle.

"What's your line?" Morgan asked.

"I'm in sales. I've been in Atlanta for training."

"I landed there once, changed planes, and flew out. That's about it for me and Atlanta."

"It's a nice city."

Glancing at her watch she said, "Morgan, this has been nice. Thanks for coming to my rescue, for the beer, and the nice conversation. But I really must go; my ride will be waiting."

She gathered her things, paused, and before leaving observed, "Morgan, you look familiar. But I don't know why. I can't put my finger on it."

"Join the club. The majority of people I meet tell me the same thing. I don't get it. But I live in fear of being dragged into some police station and someone swearing that I was the one who robbed their convenience store." They both laughed.

Clare moved in close, bent down, and gave Morgan a friendly kiss on the cheek. "Really, thanks again for everything. Good luck in the book business, and maybe our paths will cross again somewhere."

"I certainly hope so," said Morgan with quiet resolve. "Be careful."

Chapter 3

CLARE BOLTED INTO the house to grab the insistent telephone. "Hello," she gasped.

"Clare, it's Peter. How are you, love?" Wilson was calling long distance from his wild-game ranch near the Botswana border.

"Peter, it's so wonderful to hear your voice and so nice of you to call." Her breathlessness was replaced with excitement.

"I've had you on my mind and had thought I would write, but I never got around to it so I decided I'd just ring you."

"Peter, I'm so glad you did. How is business?"

"It could be better, love. I need a beautiful Texas girl to help me promote it."

"You give me too much credit, Peter; I can sell my hotel but I doubt if I could promote a wild-game ranch or safaris."

"You don't give yourself enough credit. You could do it all right."

"I'm doing well here. I'm at the premier hotel in town, and business is booming. I'm bringing in my share of it, and they seem to be happy with my work. And I do so enjoy interacting with the people. And Peter, since I do have to work, it's a fabulous place to come to each day."

They rattled on for a few more minutes. Clare spoke about her new house, the springtime, her sister, April, and the painting she was working on. He told her about Zimbabwe and the Mugabe government, the growing battle with aides, hunters, his house servants, and the animals.

"I'd better ring off now. Stay in touch."

"Sure thing, Peter; we'll always stay in touch. Goodbye for now."

"Yeah, goodbye, love."

Chapter 4

Friday, March 10, 2000

"MR. MASON, IT'S so good to see you and such an honor to have you with us today," said Virginia Johnson, the Executive Director of The Texas Writer's League.

"I'm very pleased to be here. And I'm always taken aback when someone thinks I'm important or have something to say. And please call me Morgan."

He put his arm around her and gave her a friendly squeeze. "How many folks you got registered for the conference?"

"The count is over twelve hundred. It's a record for our annual conference. The fact is, Mr. Mason, uh Morgan, you have contributed with your money and time. You are a super star in the literary world and now the movies and all; still you remain a member of the League and consider yourself a local boy. The luncheon, the panel yesterday, the breakout session this afternoon, and the book signing tonight after the reception—it means so much to the participants."

"Well, that's fine. I'm one of you, you know; we're family." Johnson smiled warmly.

Morgan, at the insistence of Virginia Johnson, had agreed to the book signing as an extra appearance, although his publisher objected. It wasn't an occasion to sell books, but was an opportunity for League members to bring in any of Morgan's books for him to sign. He wouldn't just sign his name as many do, but he would take time to talk briefly with each person and then write a short, meaningful greeting on the inside of the cover. Although Morgan could be abrupt at times, he was really a gracious man and virtually unchanged by his success. He was loyal to the people who had been loyal to him.

League members began to file into the large ballroom for the luncheon. Virginia and Morgan were observing the scene, when a striking, raven-haired beauty suddenly appeared. She noticed Morgan immediately and they made eye-contact. She smiled warmly, and spoke to Johnson first. "Virginia, how is the meeting going? Is there anything the White House staff can do for you?"

"It's going great, thank you, but I appreciate your checking with us. Not all hotels are good about that. Clare Casey, may I present Mr. Morgan Mason, our featured speaker for our luncheon today. He's a local boy but also a *New York Times* best-selling author."

"So it's Mason, is it?" beaming as she extended her hand.

"And you're Casey," replied Morgan with a grin.

"Mr. Mason and I have met."

He noticed that her hair was up and that she was wearing a suit, very businesslike, very professional, but nonetheless stunning.

Morgan's pale lavender shirt and white tie stood out against his perfectly fitting black suit. You could see yourself in his plain-toed black shoes. She remembered how shiny his boots were when she saw him at the airport. *Shoes are important*, she thought to herself, *but how incredibly broad his shoulders are!*

"You told me you were in the book business. Production, I believe that's how you characterized it. Why not tell me you were an author?"

"If I'd told you, it would have seemed…"

"Yeah, I guess so," said Clare, cutting him off. They laughed again.

Virginia Johnson looked confused by their cryptic conversation.

"So what have you written?"

"Well, I've done a few things; *Manila Gold, Ramblin' Rose, The Promise*, but maybe you'd be familiar with *Picking up the Pieces.* It sold several million copies," he said, matter-of-factly.

Before Clare could answer, Virginia chimed in excitedly. "They made a movie of it. It was about this…"

Clare raised her hand. Her face lit up and she clasped her hands together. "Yes I did see that movie. It was great. I cried a lot. It had a wonderful happy ending. No fooling, you wrote that?"

"I'm afraid so. I didn't write the screenplay, but I consulted on the script, and they followed the book closely."

Clare seemed genuinely excited. Smiling, she clasped her hands, "What do you know? You wrote *Picking up the Pieces.*"

Morgan laughed. He was amused at Clare's excitement. He had never taken himself too seriously and it always surprised him when others did. Perhaps it was something about being form Austin, his Southwest upbringing, he didn't know.

"I'm so delighted to see you again, Mr. Mason. Really, this is a thrill. You wrote *Picking up the Pieces.* How about that? Well, I've got to go now. I must get back to my sales-manager duties."

Morgan delayed her departure, "Well, tell me, Clare, what exactly does a sales manager do, and how do you measure success?"

"We book meetings and conferences like this one. Actually, it's about the rooms."

"The rooms?"

"Yeah, we measure success by keeping our hotel full."

"I believe you did mention during our earlier meeting that you were in sales. If this meeting is any indication, you're a success."

"We have our good days. This is one of them." Clare smiled and took her leave.

"Morgan, you have a definite twinkle in your eye. Could it be that Clare Casey has gotten your attention?" Virginia asked.

"Clare Casey had already gotten my attention," he replied, taking a moment to explain how they first met. "She's my type."

"Are you sure it wasn't about her rather giddy reaction to learning she was talking to a famous writer?"

"Nope," patting his chin with his right index finger, "I was pleased, but that was incidental. I definitely need to see more of this young woman. Looks get your attention, but you move past that pretty quickly to the personality. Yes, I think I need to follow up with her."

"It's time for us to take our seats. Are you ready?"

"LADIES AND GENTLEMEN, it's an honor and privilege for me to present the best-selling author, and Austin, Texas, product, Mr. Morgan Mason!" As Morgan made his way to the podium, the entire gathering stood and gave him a lengthy ovation. Morgan, embarrassed, tried to get them to take their seats. Clare Casey slipped quietly into the back of the ballroom.

Chapter 5

Monday, March 20, 2000

MORGAN WAS UP by 6:00 a.m., an hour earlier that his customary rise-time. He called himself a "night bird," not because he was out partying but because he usually stayed up until midnight or later. He read or listened to music. If there was a sporting event of interest he would watch. A movie buff from childhood, he had taped over 1,000 movies. He was particularly fond of the ones from the 1940s including the big Hollywood musical extravaganzas. A movie from his collection provided him time to relax. He always found time to play with Bogart, his playful five-month-old black and white Shih tzu.

He showered, shaved and ate breakfast, then ascended the stairs to get on the clock and write. He was deep into another romance novel and his publisher was pushing him for completion. The words flowed easily for Morgan Mason. He hit the power button and the slumbering computer awoke with sounds and flashing lights. But instead of attacking the keyboard as usual his mind wondered. The constant barking of Bogart, sitting impatiently beside his director's chair, made matters worse. A demanding little cuss, Bogart wanted Morgan's constant attention. So he picked up the little "dust mop" and gave him a hug, patted his soft belly and briskly rubbed his shaggy back. The little fellow looked longingly at his master and warmly licked Morgan's bare chest. They were a beautiful pair. But not even Bogart could end his preoccupation with a certain brunette girl at a prominent Austin hotel.

IT WAS HARD for him to believe that he had been single for sixteen years. Morgan had had lots of women in his life but none with whom he would seriously consider marriage. He had been busy writing, touring and complying with all the demands that accompany a successful literary career. Writing could be demanding with the publisher and the agent pushing for a finished manuscript or a demanding promotional tour. Still, there was plenty of time for him to pick up and go—anywhere in the world—thanks to eight consecutive best-selling novels with movie rights to several of them. How many women could just pick up and go at a moment's notice for a man with an itch to wander?

He put Bogart down, picked up the telephone, and dialed.

"Information, may I help you?"

"Yeah, I need the number for the White House." A moment of silence on the other end on the line was sufficient for Morgan to clarify his request. "Sorry for the confusion. I was referring to the hotel here in town in the Arboretum area."

The operator laughed and instructed him to wait. The electronic response provided Morgan the seven numbers he was seeking. He scribbled them down on a yellow pad and then transferred them to his handy Rolodex.

"White House, how may I direct your call?"

"Clare Casey, please."

"It will be my pleasure to connect you, sir, and have a good day."

Morgan's heart beat faster with every ring of the telephone. He couldn't believe how excited he was. It seemed like forever until she picked up.

"Clare Casey, may I help you?"

Morgan froze for a moment and then gathered himself, clearing his throat, "Clare—this is Morgan Mason. You know, airport, Texas Writer's Conference."

Clare laughed at Morgan's explanation, "Hi, Morgan, how are things in the literary world?"

"It ruins you for real work; I know that."

Clare laughed again; she was thrilled that he called.

"Listen, I was wondering if I could take you out?"

"What did you have in mind?"

"Dinner, for openers."

"When?"

"Friday night."

"Let me pull up my calendar here on the computer. These calendar programs are really neat."

"I guess I'm behind the times. I still use a monthly planning guide. I like to see the entire month at a time, and I just feel more comfortable penciling in my commitments."

"Well, Mr. Mason, you're in luck—I'm open Friday."

"Great. I hope this was enough notice?"

"Absolutely," said Clare. She thought to herself, *Fifteen minutes would have worked for me.*

"Are you picky about what you eat?"

"Not in the least. My momma raised us to eat everything on our plate whether we liked it or not."

Morgan chuckled. He liked this girl. "I was raised the same way. Okay, well, let me give that some thought, and I'll make a reservation. If I picked you up at 7:30 would that be okay?"

"It would."

"Wonderful. Tell me where you live."

"Actually, I live in Round Rock. But I have a late meeting at the hotel with some prospects from out of town. We should be finished by seven. I wouldn't go home. Just pick me up here at the hotel. In fact just come to the sales office and fetch me."

"All right, I'll do that. Incidentally, do you want to be surprised or do you want to know where we are going?"

"If it was just lunch, I wouldn't care. But since it's dinner, I would like to know so I can dress appropriately."

"That makes sense. I'll call you when I decide."

"Fine, I'll look forward to your call."

"Clare."

"Yes, Morgan."

"I'm looking forward to seeing you."

Morgan could not see the smile on Clare's face or know that her heart was beating faster than usual. Like Morgan, she hadn't been able to get him off her mind. She wondered if he would contact her. She had even contemplated calling him. Although a modern girl, she was pleased that he made the first move.

As soon as they hung up, Clare called her sister April. They had always been close. Even now she lived in the other side of Clare's duplex. "Southwest Airlines, may I help you?"

"Jan, this is Clare. Is April available or what?"

"They don't fly for another hour. She is actually standing in front of my desk as we speak. I'll have her pick up."

"Hey, sister, what's going on?"

"April, I just got off the telephone with Morgan Mason. He asked me for a dinner date."

"Oh, wow, Clare, that's exciting."

"April, my heart is still racing. I don't know if I can wait until Friday night."

"Listen, sis, I have to run. But we're doing a quick turnaround to Dallas, and then I don't fly again until 10 o'clock tomorrow morning. You can tell me all about it tonight, okay? Hey, I'm really excited for you."

"Thanks, April. Tonight: we'll talk tonight. Bye."

Chapter 6

The Evening of March 20, 2000

THEY TALKED FOR quite a while—mostly about men—and one man in particular.

"I've laid five outfits on the bed. Tell me what you think," Clare asked her sister.

"I think the black; yes, definitely the black."

"You know, that's what I was thinking. Well, that confirms it. Okay, what do you think I should do with my hair? I don't know anything about Morgan Mason. You know, what he does or doesn't like." She paused for a moment and then reasoned, "First dates are very important. I want to look my best. I want to blow this man away."

"Just go with your gut, and be yourself," said April impatiently. "See you later, sis."

After putting up the clothes on the bed, Clare decided to get ready for bed. She checked to make sure the Venetian blinds were closed before she undressed. Turning out the bedroom light, she entered the bathroom, tossed her bra and panties in the hamper and her dress in the pile for the cleaners. She intended to wash her face, take off her makeup and brush her teeth. But she uncharacteristically found herself looking at her body in the full length mirror behind the bathroom door. She turned to look at her back side. Firm buttocks are important, she was certain of that. Hers could use some work but all in all, not so bad. She mashed her stomach, analyzed whether it was flat and firm enough, then sucked it in for effect. She examined her thighs and ran her fingers up and down her calves, looking at the back of them as best she could.

What would Morgan Mason think about my body?

Actually Clare had a good body, but like many a female, she was never satisfied with her weight or her looks. She had a small waist and ample breasts, and recalled, as a budding teen, how the other girls teased her. She smiled when she remembered that day in the girl's rest room when, on a dare, she opened her bra to prove to the jealous little twits that they were real. She shuddered at the thought of Sister Angelica walking in at that moment. *Oh God, that would have been horrible.*

I want to look good for Morgan. Weight Watchers worked for me before. I'll get back on the program and I'll start exercising.

She returned to her bedroom and turned on the nightstand radio to her favorite FM easy-listening station. Nat "King" Cole was singing *Unforgettable.* She lay back on the bed, stretched her arms over her head, then brought them down by her side. Her thoughts were of Morgan Mason as she drifted pleasantly off to sleep.

o o o o o

CLARE CASEY had carnal knowledge of only one man—her ex-husband. Well—except for that one incident. Her parents had kept a tight rein on Clare: mass every Sunday, confession on a regular basis, Catholic school and no dating until her senior year in high school. She attended a Catholic college and stuck close to her dorm and her studies. April, on the other hand, was the wild child. When they forbid her to date, she met boys at the mall and even slipped out of the house late at night, swearing Clare to secrecy. April was frivolous, squandered money, lied if it benefitted her and barely made passing grades.

Disappointed by her first marriage, Clare had only dated a couple of times since returning to Austin. They were boring events and she wondered why she even went. She wasn't interested in those men. Perhaps, for once in her life, she would just throw caution to the wind. Maybe a fling was just what she needed.

Chapter 7

Friday, March 24, 2000

"I WANTED TO say how pleased I am that you chose *Siena*," said Clair. "I have heard good things about it and have wanted to go there in the worst way."

"Well, I hope tonight won't be the worst way!"

Clare grinned and shook her head back and forth. "You are quick, Mr. Mason."

"Well, after all, I am a writer. Words are my stock in trade." He smiled at her as he drank her in. Her cole-black hair was in a French braid, like he had first seen her at the airport. She looked great in her black dress. She had just the right amount of jewelry. *This lady is gorgeous and pure class.*

"Clare," said Morgan, "I love French-braided hair. That's the first thing I noticed about you at the airport."

"No kidding. Well, I'm glad I decided to wear it like that for our first date."

"Not as pleased as I am," Morgan said, with a coy grin.

"Tell me, Morgan, how did you come to be a writer?"

"I couldn't get work at my usual profession."

"Which is what?"

"A shepherd." Morgan stared straight ahead, expressionless.

"Maybe you need to do 'stand-up' in addition to your writing," she laughed.

"You think so, do you?" he responded with a smile.

She liked this man. He made her laugh. *That's important in a relationship*, she thought.

"Well, here we are," Morgan announced, as he pulled into the parking lot.

As Morgan opened the front door, another couple was coming out. The man smiled and spoke to Morgan. "Hey, how's it going?"

"Everything's lovely," said Morgan.

"Did you know him?" Clare inquired.

"Never saw him before."

Clare looked puzzled. "Why did he speak to you?"

"I have no idea. This happens all the time. Perfect strangers are always speaking to me. I don't understand it."

"Interesting," Clare observed.

"I'm Morgan Mason. I have an 8:30 reservation. We're early so we'll just go to the bar, and you can fetch us when our table is available."

"Yes, sir."

"This is a really nice bar area," Clare observed.

"Yeah, I think so. I hope you don't mind. I thought a drink would be nice before dinner, and I enjoy talking to you."

"I couldn't agree more."

"What would you like, Clare?"

"Well, there a couple of things I like, but a nice red wine is always in order. What are you having?"

"A champagne cocktail," he declared.

"Okay, that sounds good to me."

"That was easy."

"No Bohemia tonight, Mr. Mason?"

"Not tonight," he declared with a smile. "Not here, and not with you looking like you do."

Morgan touched Clare's glass and proposed a toast. Looking intently into her eyes he said, "*Nuca mas que tu. Nuca menos que tu. Pero siempre a tu lado.*"

Clare looked bewildered. She had no idea what he said or how to respond. "That's an old Spanish toast," Morgan explained.

"Really, what does it mean?"

"It means, 'Never above you, never beneath you, always by your side.'" He paused to let the words sink in.

"Oh, Morgan, that's beautiful. I'm touched."

The moment was interrupted by the sudden presence of the young hostess holding Morgan's most recent romance novel. "Mr. Mason, when I saw your reservation, I got very excited. I love your work. I know this is terrible of me, but would you autograph my copy?"

Morgan was irritated, but he didn't let it show and was gracious. "Sure, what's your name?"

"It's Ellen." Morgan signed the book and handed it back.

Ellen left, clutching her book.

"I'm sorry, Clare. I hope you'll forgive the interruption."

"Of course; think nothing of it. You were gracious, and that speaks well of you. Does this happen often?"

He sighed, "Well, not very much, actually. People recognize me, I guess, but most of them would never approach me. You and I are just getting started; I wouldn't want this to be…"

"Morgan," said Clare, reaching over and putting her fingers against his lips. "It's not a problem."

"You promise?"

"Girl scout's honor."

"You'll have to find out for yourself, but I'm pretty much like I was before the books. I am grateful for this crazy, somewhat unexplainable ability to put words on paper that people want to read."

"And buy," Clare quickly interjected.

"—Well, yes—and buy. Anyway, it's enabled me to have freedom and a lifestyle like you can't imagine."

The manager came over to their table. "Mr. Mason, I want to apologize for the intrusion a while ago. We do not condone this kind of behavior from our staff. I hope you will forgive us. To show our appreciation for your indulgence, the drinks are on us. And I want to buy you and your lady a bottle of our finest wine. Just tell the waiter what to bring from the cellar. Now, if you all will follow me, I will personally take you to your table."

Morgan stood when Clare went to the powder room…and when she returned. He poured her wine and was completely attentive. She was pleased. "Morgan, no man has ever stood when I left the table and again when I came back. Guys don't do that very much. In fact, you are quite the gentleman."

"Well, thank you, Clare. I like women, and I like to show them the respect they deserve." He laughed.

"What's funny?"

Oh, I was thinking about a situation that happened once at the Four Seasons Hotel. I was having dinner in the main dinning room when I noticed a young couple come in. They were seated close by. He walked in front of her and didn't pull out her chair or help her to be seated. He just plopped down and buried his head in the menu." Morgan took a sip of wine and continued, "Anyway, the young woman had to visit the powder room, I suppose, and he hardly looked up from his food. When she was gone I engaged him in conversation. I suspected that this was a special occasion, maybe an anniversary dinner. I asked him if the lady was his wife and if this was an anniversary. It was their first, he told me. So I said to him, 'When you see your wife coming back, I want you to stand, and remain standing until she reaches the table. Then I want you to help her be seated and push in her chair. After you are seated, I want you to tell her how beautiful she is and that you can't think of another woman on the planet that you'd rather be with on this special night.'"

"What did he say?" Clare inquired.

"He listened intently to everything I said. He was nodding as if he understood. Pretty soon he saw her coming and he did what I suggested. Clare, you should have seen her reaction when he stood and helped her to be seated. She smiled and said something to him. Then I saw him lean toward her and I presume he repeated what I had said."

"Did she react?" questioned Clare.

"Did she ever! She got up from her seat and went over and kissed him. Later on he caught my eye and grinned."

"Morgan, that's a great story."

"Yeah, isn't it? I bet he got dessert!"

Clare laughed. They both did.

"Clare, you asked about writing. What is it you're interested in?"

"Well, first, I've always wondered where you get your ideas?"

"When I first started writing I drew on people and things I was familiar with. As time passed that all changed."

"Changed how?"

"It's kind of like the insurance salesman who, in the beginning, sold to his friends and family. But after the well runs dry, he had to do real prospecting. After a writer draws on his immediate pool of people and things he's familiar with, he has to come up with ideas that may very well have no real reference point."

"So how does that work?"

"I have no idea—I can't explain it. The thoughts came to me right out of the blue. Take *The Promise*, for example. Why I would think of a Marine in Vietnam, who, thinking he's mortally wounded, promises God that he'd dedicate himself to the priesthood if God will save him. And that decision would torment him for twenty years and change his life."

Clare stared at him, thinking about what he'd said.

"And here's another interesting thing. I can start writing a scene, not knowing exactly where it's going, and it will come to me as I'm typing—as if someone was dictating to me through an ear piece."

Clare smiled and slowly shook her head.

"And here's one more interesting thing that I can't explain. Words will come into my head at the exact time I need them. Most of the time they are words that I never use, and sometimes I'm even unsure of their meaning. I'll look them up, and they'll be perfect—the exact word for the situation."

"Morgan, that's a gift you've been given. I don't think it's any more complicated than that."

"I think you must be right."

"Are there times when you draw a blank? You know, you just can't think of anything to put on paper."

"What you are referring to is 'writer's block.' They mention it in our trade journals and give us tips about how to overcome it. But it's never happened to me."

"Really—not ever?"

"No. When I'm writing a book it's like standing under a waterfall. The words never stop coming. And I've written for ten-twelve-fifteen hours at a time on many occasions. But what I try to do is work like everyone else. I get on the clock about nine and work until noon. I come downstairs, eat lunch, relax, let my eyes and fingers rest a bit and play with Bogart. Then by one o'clock I'm back at it. Then I knock off at five and go to the gym for my workout. I'm home by about seven, and Bogart and I eat supper and play. I may not write again until the next morning. You see what I mean. I want a normal work routine because there are other things in life."

"Tell me about the other things; I'd love to know more about you. You know, family, school, that kind of thing."

Chapter 8

"I'M FOURTH-GENERATION Austin. I'm the only child of Eugene and Irene Mason. As I understand it, Dad dropped out of college and bummed around a while, working at one thing and then another." Morgan chuckled, "Dad finally got steady work. He joined the Marine Corps when World War II broke out."

"Here's your ticket and credit card, sir. It was a pleasure to serve you."

"Morgan, the meal was superb."

"I'm glad you enjoyed it. I think they do a nice job. Listen, let's give them their table back. We can go back to the bar and continue our conversation in there."

"That sounds like a plan."

They found a secluded table and took their seats. Morgan caught the waiter's eye with his raised hand. "Grand Marnier, two times, when you get a chance."

"Where were we?" asked Morgan.

"Your dad, you were talking about him."

"Yeah, I was. Okay, after the war he came back home to Austin and joined the police force. He was a good cop; he took to the work. I guess after war in the Pacific, nothing much frightened him."

"I like Grand Marnier," he reflected, taking a sip.

"Mom got a degree in music. She taught choir in high school. She had a decent singing voice, and so do I. I guess I got it from her. She was always a calm and stabilizing influence on both Dad and me when we got too flying too high.

"They married in 1958. Both had been married before, and I was born in 1960, August 23 to be exact. So if you were wondering about how old I am, I guess you can do the math.

"We were a happy family. I was loved—and that gift of love is about the most important thing a kid can receive from his parents. I was a good student and enjoyed school. I played high school football and was a decent running back. I went off to Texas A & I at Kingsville to play tailback."

'"So you were pretty good?"

"Good enough to get a football scholarship. Two other boys from my school went there as well."

"You were a Javelina!"

"You know about the Javelinas?"

"Yeah, my uncle went to school there."

"I got my knee torn up pretty bad and eventually had to give up football. Since that was the only reason to be in Kingsville, I decided to come back home and finish up at the University of Texas."

"Wouldn't they honor your scholarship?"

"They probably would have, but I wanted to be in Austin. I could live at home, and everything I earned went toward tuition and books" Taking another sip of Grand Marnier, Morgan continued. "I almost forgot to mention a pretty important part of the story. I married my high school sweetheart. In fact, we never dated anyone else. That wasn't very smart, but you can't tell kids anything. They think they know it all. It lasted six years. Two years after I graduated from UT, we were done. As we grew up we grew apart; we became different people from when we started out. And that's a very real risk you take when you marry too young. It was a fairly amicable parting. And we didn't have any assets or any children. Actually, as I look back on it, I think it's a miracle we didn't get pregnant."

"Did you guys have a big wedding?"

"No, it was modest. We had the reception at the church to keep costs down and make it easy on everyone. I'd heard lots of people talk about how exciting Acapulco was, so we went there on our honeymoon. Actually, we flew to Mexico City and saw the sights there. Then we went to Acapulco and then back to Mexico City before we came home. My wife got sick in Acapulco. You know—Montezuma's revenge."

"I've heard of people getting sick in Mexico. It's the water, isn't it?"

"The water is a problem, for sure. Most people drink bottled water or beer. I'm not exactly sure what it was, but she was really sick. She threw up until she was too weak to function. She got the bug while we were in Acapulco, and she was sick when we flew back to Mexico City. That night there was an earthquake. That took her mind off her stomach."

"An earthquake?"

"That's right. They have a lot of them down there. And it was about two in the morning. You've heard the term "Chinese fire drill." Well, that fit the situation perfectly. People didn't know what to do. They came running out of their rooms, in all kind of attire. It was pretty funny when it was over, everyone standing in the hallway looking at each other. Fortunately for us, and for everyone else, it was a new hotel and very well built. It held up just fine. But there was a lot of devastation in and around the city. Anyway, we were young and felt indestructible, so the next day we were off to the pyramids, the canals, and the bull fights."

"Pyramids?"

"Yeah, the Mayan pyramids. They're impressive. I bet you've seen pictures of them. I'm certain of it."

"And you saw bull fights?"

"Yeah, at the Plaza Mexico. It's the largest venue in the world except for the ring in Madrid. Clare, I loved it. I was screaming and yelling, *'Ole'* along with the locals and drinking Mexican beer in the hot sun. My wife thought I was crazy. Anyway, I've loved Mexico ever since and have been all over the country. They treat you like royalty—foods good, great hotels, great beaches, great deep-sea fishing, great shopping, and great scuba diving. It's beautiful and inexpensive. I mean, what's not to like?"

"Montezuma's revenge!" suggested Clare.

"Yeah, okay. That's not too good. Funny thing, I've never gotten it, and I've traveled extensively in Mexico for years."

"What was your degree in?"

"Kinesiology."

"I guess you are going to think I'm really dumb, but I don't have the vaguest idea what that is."

Morgan chuckled, "Yeah, you and most everyone else on the planet. It's the study of the principles of mechanics and anatomy in relation to human movement."

"Wow," said Clare, "that's a mouthful. What did you plan to do with that?"

"I thought about working for a professional sports franchise. I could teach or become a personal trainer, which is what I decided to do. Even after receiving a degree you have to be certified, and that's like going back to school. But my prior studies made it pretty easy." A smile crossed his face as he summed it up, "In a mundane sense, you get paid pretty well for hanging around a gym. And of course, we get to work out as well. I enjoyed it."

"I still don't quite get how it works," Clare frowned.

"It isn't complicated. Trainers pull regular shifts in the weight room, supervising the activities and helping people with various exercises or how to work the machines. We get paid a salary for that. But when we're not on duty, we can take appointments with people who want or need special attention. You're their personal trainer and paid very well for that. I think some people consider it cool to say they have a personal trainer."

Morgan took another sip of his drink. "You've probably heard professional athletes or celebrities talk about their personal trainers. We design specific programs for people based on their age, health, and goals. And then we work the plan with them. I enjoyed it. But there's no silver bullet. You have to work hard to make a difference in your body. Most people have never exerted themselves very much physically, so they struggle and complain that it's too hard. We get all types of people, as you can imagine."

"I bet you had lots of women flirt with you."

The enormous grin on Morgan's face gave him away. "Yeah, there was a considerable amount of that. But I'd just laugh it off and stick to my job. I learned to handle it in a way to not hurt their feelings or bruise their egos. And that's what it is. We can't get involved with our clients. Well, at least we shouldn't."

Morgan was grinning again as if there was something else he wanted to say, but was hesitant. Clare urged him on, "Out with it, Mason; I know there's more to this tale."

"Well, there was this trainer we had for a while. She was from Estonia."

"Estonia?"

"Yeah, it's on the Baltic Sea and borders on Russia. Anyway, she had a bunch of degrees from the University of Leningrad. She didn't speak English well, just enough to get by. I'm not sure what the story on her really was, but I got the idea that she had married an American so she could get to this country. Anyway, she was pretty good; she knew what she was doing. She was a personal trainer like me and had a stable of male clients. She was a blond and had the best body I've ever seen on a woman. I kid you not. And I think she bought her outfits a size too small, because she was poured into them. Her clients were always hitting on her. I know because I heard it. I don't know if she was going out with any of them, but one day she was gone, and management was very silent about it."

"Did she hit on you?"

"Oh, yeah. One of the members heard her tell me she liked my buttocks. I thought I would never live that down."

Clare felt comfortable with this man even though it was a first date. She felt as if she'd known him forever. "You know something? I've been checking you out, and you do have nice buttocks. Girls notice buttocks, especially the firm ones."

Morgan roared with laughter. They both laughed. They talked about various subjects and were oblivious to the man who approached their table. "Mr. Mason, it has been a great pleasure to serve you and the lovely lady this evening. You two look like you've had a good time," said the manager. "But you see, the kitchen's been closed since ten o'clock and it's eleven thirty. You guys are the last customers in the house. We have to close."

After a pleasant drive, the Boxter pulled into the White House parking lot, and Clare pointed Morgan to where her car was parked. He opened her door and followed her as she climbed into her Miata. With the door still open, she smiled warmly and motioned for him to bend down. "This has been a perfectly marvelously evening. We should do it again sometime." And with that she kissed him tenderly, the kind of kiss that meant, 'I like you, I had a good time, and I'd like to see you again.' Morgan took it as such.

Clare was highly tempted to be totally spontaneous, to do something completely outrageous, but she thought it wiser to take it slow. She was afraid to be too aggressive for fear of sending the wrong signal, of putting him off. She would do nothing to dissolution Morgan Mason. Perhaps nothing would. Perhaps he wanted her as much as she wanted him. But she would take no chances with this relationship. She was excited about this man, a feeling of exhilaration and euphoria such as she had seldom experienced. As much as she hated to leave him, she was confident that there would be other opportunities, many more opportunities.

He closed her door. "Call me," suggested Clare.

"You can count on it."

Clare's excitement had no bounds. She pondered the unlikelihood of their first two meetings, the perfection of their first date, the possibilities of this relationship—all of it was exploding within her brain like a Fourth of July fireworks celebration. She had never been with a man like Morgan. She shamelessly wondered what it would be to like to make love to him—a strong man, a confident and self-assured man, a highly masculine and virile man. As the little red Miata took her north toward her home, her thoughts turned to the next time she would be with him. *Soon*, she hoped, *very soon.*

Morgan stood in the parking lot until Clare's car was out of sight. He liked this girl. He liked her a lot. She had looks, smarts, class—and a sense of humor. He could hardly remember when there had been a woman of substance to capture his fancy.

Morgan was a man who was patient with relationships. He was willing to take his time and was not prone to make his feelings known too soon. As he drove away from the White House, he had the feeling that this was the start of something that could be very special. He couldn't help but recall the *chance meeting* that had set the whole thing in motion.

Chapter 9

Monday, April 3, 2000

"CLARE CASEY, MAY I help you?"

"Clare, this is Morgan Mason. Do you remember me?"

"Vaguely," she replied. They both laughed.

"Clare, one of the other things I do pretty well is cook. In fact, I'm a regular little ole gourmet. I'd like to fix dinner for you at my place Saturday night if you don't have a commitment."

There was a moment of silence. "I can hear you on the keyboard. I guess you're looking in the computer at your calendar, right."

"How did you guess? Oh Morgan, I can't. I'm going camping with one of my girlfriends and my sister April. She's bringing one of her friends, another Southwest Airlines flight attendant. I'm so sorry, but this has been planned for some time. April and her friend are always flying so it's been tough to find a weekend where all of us can go."

"Camping?" asked Morgan, trying to hide his disappointment.

"That's right, camping. You know—tents, campfire, bugs, all that stuff. I'm looking forward to it. And I'm taking a fresh canvass to start a painting." She laughed.

"What's so funny," Morgan inquired.

"Oh, these girls I'm going with. I've made all the arrangements, got the food and supplies together, so they'll have no excuses."

Fearing that Morgan might be put off, she quickly sensed that she should offer an alternative in order to firm up their next date. She liked this man and she wanted to see him again. "Let me look at the computer. I could come the following Saturday night, if that's okay."

"Uh, I can do that."

"Great," said Clare, "you're not mad about this Saturday?"

"Why would I be angry?"

"Well…"

"Clare, I have no right to be angry. Anyway, don't give it another thought. Now, we'll probably talk before then, but is there anything you don't eat?"

"I don't much care for octopus, but that's about it."

"What a bummer," replied Morgan, "that's what I was planning. I have a tremendous recipe for it. Okay, well, I'll come up with something. You can come early, but be here by six-thirty, and come comfortable."

"Can't you be a little more explicit about the attire?"

"You can figure it out."

"Do you need directions?"

"No. I looked you up in the telephone book. I know right where you are and how to get there."

"Well, I guess that's a done deal then," concluded Morgan.

"You want me to bring anything?"

"Just an appetite and that wonderful smile."

"See you, Mason."

"See you, Casey."

Chapter 10

IT WAS AFTER 10:00 p.m. when Clare finally arrived, exhausted, at her Round Rock home. Monday's were always rough. She worked all day and then there was choir practice from seven until nine-thirty. It's wasn't practical to go home after work, and she didn't like to eat right before singing, so she usually worked late and went directly to practice. She kicked off her shoes as she entered the back door of her duplex. Tossing her keys on the kitchen table and her blue blazer over a chair, she poured herself a glass of red wine, walked into the living room and plopped down of the comfortable floral covered couch. She massaged her feet and then slowly removed the restrictions of her panty hose. She took another sip of wine, laid her head back and closed her eyes. "Whew," she sighed and thought to herself, *For two cents I'd just curl up here on the couch and call it a night.* After a few minutes she decided to get ready for bed. *Mail—I should probably get the mail.*

She thumbed through the envelopes and was struck by the enormous amount of junk mail. She wondered if she was being picked on or if everyone got as many of the throw-a-ways as did she. As she closed her front door she was energized to see an envelope from *Petica Safaris, Inc.* She hurriedly tore it open, plopped down on the couch once again, and pulled her legs up under her.

Greetings from the bush.

I wish I could report that everything was great but I've got some bad news, Abula has been killed. Let me explain.

Clare bit her clinched fist as tears streamed down her face. She knew Abula, knew him well. She gathered herself and continued to read.

It was the Safari from hell. It was two very wealthy aristocrats from Atlanta. The woman didn't want to be there, and I don't know why she came. She complained from morning until night. It was too hot, it was the food, it was too noisy. You know, we don't think about the noise because we live here, but Africa is really a noisy place. You know what I mean, Clare, the animals are always reminding us of their presence and maybe a subtle reminder that they were here first. And one night, love, the man passed out from too much vodka and she came to my tent and tried to seduce me. That really made the rest of our time quite uncomfortable. They are a pretty sad pair I guess.

He wanted to get a lion. So I took them to where I thought we might see one and sure enough, we'd been there about 45 minutes when a very big boy came strolling slowly out of the brush toward the water hole we had staked out. The fellow had a dream shot, about 75 yards, completely unobstructed. When he wanted to shoot from the vehicle, I should have known we were in trouble, but we're paid very well to see that these fellows get the animals they came for.

Anyway, I finally coxed him out and he and Abula crept forward about twenty feet. His wife questioned me, thinking the lion would see our vehicle and spook. I explained to her that the lion, if he looked our way, would probably think the vehicle was a rhino. And the wind was favorable, I explained, blowing into our faces so he couldn't possibly smell us. My client waited, and waited and when he finally decided to shoot, his safety was on.

He was obviously nervous, because his first shot missed and he hurriedly fired two more times. The second bullet missed, but the third round hit the lion in the gut, I was certain of that.

I told him that we'd have to wait a few minutes before going in after him, so we lit up a smoke. I informed him that the lion was in a bad spot, in that the bush was so thick we wouldn't be able to see him until we were right on him. These things can get real dicey, but I didn't elaborate because the fellow was a bit jumpy anyway.

After a bit we moved forward and saw blood, where the client first hit the lion. As we continued forward he asked if we couldn't just set fire to the brush and force him out. I told him we couldn't and wouldn't do that. I was trying to keep my composure, love. This man was really such a cowardly sort, but I decided that it was in everyone's best interest to level with him about what we were going to encounter. I told him we could drive an unwounded lion. In other words, the animal would move ahead of the noise. But when one is wounded, he's eventually going to charge. He'll lay down in there and take cover. He won't show himself until he's ready to come out.

My reluctant warrior nervously asked for water and another cigarette, his ashen face relieving any doubt as to his state of near-panic. He raised his hands in front of his face, as if shielding himself from an impending blow, as he pleaded his case. He wanted no part of our incursion. You know, going in after the lion. I told him I wasn't all that keen on it myself, but I was experienced at it and paid to do it. He didn't have to go. He's scared you know, but he doesn't want his wife to see it. He doesn't want to lose face, so now he's stubborn. But he has one final suggestion in order to avoid the inevitable. He suggested we just leave the wounded lion and just forget about it. I explained that it wasn't done, that I could lose my license for something like that. Besides, the lion was suffering, and I couldn't just leave him. Not only that, I explained, someone else could wander up on him and be accidentally mauled.

I told him he should lag to the back with his gun barer, and Abula and I would be out front. I figured the lion would growl or make some kind of noise to let us know where he was. When he hesitated I suggested that he return to the vehicle and sit with his wife, but he would have none of that. Well, we walked forward slowly and finally we heard him growl, just like I thought, and then he came. He was huge, and he was barreling through the brush looking for restitution. As soon as I could see him, I cut loose, fired twice, and dropped him. I put a third slug in his head to make sure he was dead.

There was so much excitement at that moment that I didn't realize what had happened. Love, when that lion growled and he heard that bloody noise in the brush, that jerk panicked and fired. He hit Abula and killed him instantly.

We'll that was it, Safari over. He had already gotten an eland and a water buffalo. And with the lion, that was all he paid me for anyway. There was an investigation when we got back. There always is when something like this happens. But I was not sanctioned, and the incident was officially recorded as an unavoidable accident.

Oh God, love, it was bad when I had to tell Abula's wife.

It was awful, and she's pregnant. And they already have four kids. I seriously thought about quitting this business. You knew Abula, and I knew you would want to know.

I miss you. Love,
Peter

Chapter 11

"CAN YOU FIND an author's books by putting his name in the computer?"

"Yes, we can do it that way or by the name of the book. Who are you looking for?"

"Morgan Mason."

"Oh, are you a fan of Mr. Mason?"

"Well, I don't exactly know how to answer that. But I may become one, at that." Wanting to see how that would play she added. "He's fixing dinner for me Saturday night."

"Wow, for real?"

"For real. Under the circumstances, I thought I should get familiar with his writing. I saw a movie based on one of romance novels but I haven't actually read any of his books."

The girl at the information desk looked stunned, like Clare had committed heresy. "I have all his books pulled up on the computer. Now, which ones do you want?"

"All of them."

Chapter 12

April 21, 2000

MORGAN SAW CLARE'S car from the kitchen of his town home where he had been prepping their dinner for several hours. When she got to the door she glanced through the big front window and Morgan motioned for her to come in.

She pitched her bag on the eggplant-colored couch and began to look around hoping for a tour of the tastefully decorated dig. Clare observed the fresh flowers on the table also set with fine china. A single red rose lay across one of the plates.

She picked it up. "Is this for me?"

"You're a perceptive woman. That could spell trouble for the ole scribe."

They laughed as she moved around the corner and into the kitchen, smelling her rose. "Here, try one of these," he said, pointing to a tray of attractive hors d'oeuvres.

"I've got something for you first."

She moved in close to him until their bodies touched. She gave him a long, slow, tender kiss. He smiled and said, "That beats what I had for you."

Morgan wiped his hands and fetched a bottle of champagne from the refrigerator. He mixed two champagne cocktails in long, slim, green-tinted glasses that had been chilled, and dropped a sugar cube in each. She noticed that Morgan was always quick to offer a toast, and before he could do so she smiled, tipped her glass to his and said, "To the pleasure of your company."

"Well, how very nice."

"I'll tell you what, Mason; this is a quality cocktail. It's better than the one we had at the restaurant, and that one was very good. My compliments."

"Thank you so much," Morgan said, with an over-done British accent.

"Can I do anything?"

"Perhaps another wee kiss for the master of the manor would be in order."

She laughed and proceeded to give him a wee kiss, and playfully pinched him on the derriere.

"I'm hungry. Are we going to stand around kissing or what? I want you to feed me?"

"All in good time, my lady, all in good time."

"So what are we having?"

"We are starting with chilled cucumber soup. Then we have poached grouper with tropical fruit salsa. The vegetables are coconut cilantro rice pilaf, broiled tomatoes, and black sesame asparagus. I have some wonderful ciabatta bread warming in the oven. For dessert we have mango sorbet with raspberry drizzle. And last but not least, we have fabulous Maui blend coffee."

"Heavenly days, Morgan, I'm really impressed."

"Wait until you taste it before you get too impressed. Okay, we can eat now," declared Morgan.

He seated Clare and then carefully plated the food and brought it to the table. Clare stared at her plate for a moment,

"Morgan, this is a beautiful presentation. Really, I'm very impressed."

"Thank you, Clare," said Morgan, as he took a seat beside her.

"Wow, is this ever terrific! I find it truly remarkable that a single man can cook like this. I thought you'd probably eat out most of the time or pop something in the microwave."

"Well, I've had an interest in cooking for quite a while; it's become a hobby of sorts. And the more you do it the better you get at it. And the more gourmet cooking you do the more you learn about food. I've been a work in progress, but I think I'm beginning to get the hang of it. And I like to give small dinner parties for my friends, so I get quite a bit of practice."

"Well, at the risk of being redundant, you are quite accomplished. This meal just blows me away."

"Well, the reward for the chef is when the guest is satisfied."

"I'm a happy camper."

"Listen here, Casey, you know quite a bit about me. What about you? It's time you started to fess up. Let's have it."

Before she could begin, she was distracted by barking and scratching at the back door. "What's that?"

"That would be Bogart."

"Bogart?"

"Yeah, my little Shih Tzu puppy."

"Oh, I love dogs. Can we let him in?"

"Sure. He got bathed and groomed today so he looks and smells good."

As Clare opened the back door, Bogart bolted inside. He was spinning and jumping. As she reached down he playfully licked her hand. He had a colorful bandana around his neck and did look cute. Clare picked him up and cuddled him in her arms. She giggled as he licked her ear.

"Bogart doesn't take to very many people. You should feel fortunate."

"Well, I guess I am. Morgan, he's adorable."

"Yeah, he's a sweetheart. I take him with me when I run errands. You know, the copy place, the bank, the post office. Everyone just loves him. But our food is getting cold, and we need to get back to the Clare Casey story."

"Shucks," said Clare, "I thought you'd forget." She put Bogart down.

"Oh, no."

"Well, let's see. My parents divorced when we were small. I was ten years old and my sister April was eight. Our father, Arch, was a career air force officer. Apparently Mom got tired of going from one base to another. We were constantly being uprooted from school and our friends. The story is that she gave Dad an ultimatum: military or us. He chose the military. He never married again. Mom moved us back here to Austin, and we moved in with my grandparents until Mom could get a job and we could get our own place. Dad didn't fight the divorce. She got custody, and he paid child support. Mom got a job with a bank, and that's where she met my stepfather, Burt Brown."

"Why didn't Burt adopt you and April?"

"Oh, I think he would have, but Mom never pushed for it. My dad was a good man. She didn't want to try and take his name from us. Anyway, Burt was a vice-president of the bank, and I guess he made pretty good money. At any rate, Mom quit work and stayed home with us."

"Did you mention your Mom's name?"

"I don't think I did. It's Marge."

"Sometimes second families are a mess. I hope your situation was positive."

"Well, first of all, my sister and I were never used as a wedge between my biological parents. They had a good relationship. My stepfather loved us, and we learned to love him. He treated us like his own. April and I were loved, and we knew it. And my real dad loved us, too, and we saw him as much as we could."

"I'm so glad to hear all this. Divorces can really wreak havoc with kids. Many times their welfare is not a high priority."

"You're so right about that. Anyway, I'm a good Catholic girl, and I went to Catholic schools. I graduated from Saint Mary's University, a Catholic college in San Antonio, with a degree in music and a minor in voice. I'm classically trained," she declared with pride. "I was part of the group that backed the *Three Tenors* on their first performance."

"I'm impressed. Tell me how that came about?"

"It was in South Africa, Johannesburg; I lived there about two years."

"Ah, come on, really?"

"Really."

"I sure want to hear about that."

"I've got to go back a ways in time to explain it."

"I've got the time if you do," said Morgan. Clare laughed.

"Okay, I met my husband Marshall at our church. My mother and his mother were determined to put us together. I was nineteen. He was a good Catholic boy, and that was important to me. He was 12 years older and doing pretty well as a lawyer, and I was impressed, I guess.

"Well, anyway, we dated until I graduated from the university. I was twenty-three when we finally got married. We went to England on our honeymoon. I'd never been much of anywhere, certainly not to Europe. I loved it, and I got hooked. Marshall had been working on an African deal before we got married. It wasn't very long after we returned to Austin that the job in South Africa opened up. We took it and moved to Johannesburg. It was fun and exciting at first, but it soon got complicated, at least for me."

Clare took a sip of wine and continued, "His friends were all ten years older than him, which made them more than twenty years older than me. I really got bored being with them so much. And security was a big sticking point. We lived in a secure, gated compound, with all the other corporate families. Marshall kept cautioning me about going anywhere without him. I felt trapped. And the thing was, most of the other women seemed to come and go without any trouble. That was strange, and I wondered if he just wanted to control me. Anyway, I didn't like the situation, and it kept getting worse. We argued about it all the time."

Clare stared out the front window, thinking back and gathering her thoughts. "Most of the time when Marshall and I went out by ourselves, it was dinner and right back home. I mean, that was his idea of a big evening. That really bugged me, and it didn't help matters.

"I made friends with a couple of young women my age, and I enjoyed them immensely. They went out all the time, but Marshall still gave me grief about it in the name of security. He didn't like me going out with them either."

"Clare, he was clearly controlling you."

"Yeah, and that became obvious. Anyway, my two girl friends were planning a two-week trip to England. They invited me to go along. It wasn't easy, but I finally persuaded Marshall to let me go with them. We had a great time, and I felt liberated. I felt like a bird finally able to fly. I saw how happy my young friends were. I wanted to be them!" She stared at Morgan, expressionless for a moment, and then said, "I wound up staying a month."

She sighed and took another sip of wine. "Both my girl friends said that when we returned to Johannesburg, I was a different person. We vacationed in Italy the last year we were together. Actually, my parents came over, and I met them in Rome. Marshall was delayed by his job, and we didn't hook up with him until Pompeii. The time I spent with Mom was great. I really needed to get some stuff off my chest, and she was a great listener, wise but not judgmental."

Clare paused a moment, thinking about her mother. "I have always been close to Mom, more so than April. And she has always depended on me. She had my respect as my mother, but she was also very much a friend. You know, someone I felt completely comfortable with. As I already said, not judgmental.

I know that someday I will lose her, but I can hardly entertain the thought of it. I honestly don't know how I would handle it."

"It was like that with me and my dad," said Morgan.

"Anyway, she told me, 'Clare, I'm so sorry I pushed you into marriage with Marshall. I thought he was a good catch and that he would take care of you. I didn't know him as I should have.'"

"But I didn't try to lay it all on her. I married the guy."

That was not a pleasant subject for her and suddenly her thoughts turned to Italy. Clare lit up, clasped her hands and explained, "Morgan, I fell in love with Italy. And my fantasy is to own a bed and breakfast in Tuscany."

"I know what you mean about Italy. It affects most people in a positive way, me included. It's probably my favorite country, and I've traveled extensively." He paused a moment, grinned and said, "Tuscany, is it?"

"Yes, oh, yes."

"Well, hold tight to your dream; it might come true someday."

"Funny thing," said Clare. "I fell out of love with Marshall and in love with Italy."

"Lucky for Italy."

"If I ever marry again, I'd dearly love to honeymoon in Italy," she confessed. "Anyway, it lasted two years in all, but after England it was never the same. And it was very strange. Marshall's remedy for fixing our marital problems was for us to take dance and tennis lessons."

"How does the Catholic church feel about divorce?"

"They definitely teach against it. Without a dispensation, one could never again marry in the church. But I got an annulment."

"Really," said Morgan. "You were married two years, and yet the Catholic Church can just invalidate the whole thing. I don't get that."

"Well, I'll try to explain it. The church looks at marriage in a totally different way than civil law or popular opinion. They try to determine if there was a covenant between the man and the woman. If there was not, then they can grant an annulment. Let's say a woman married a Catholic boy, a soldier, stationed over seas. They came back to the States and soon after divorced. It's very possible the church would grant an annulment if they determined that the only reason she married him was to get to this country. There was no covenant."

"I don't know," said Morgan, suspiciously; "it still sounds goofy to me."

"Well, it's not an easy thing. I had a long conference with my priest, who thought I should apply. Then I had to fill out a thirty-six-page questionnaire. They interviewed Marshall, and they required four witnesses to testify at a tribunal in the Bishop's office. If the diocese that governs Austin agrees to the annulment, then it is sent to another diocese for review, and they must concur."

"Does it ever go all the way to the Vatican?"

"If the two dioceses don't agree then it's sent to the Vatican."

"Well, couldn't this take some time?"

"It takes about a year or so if everyone agrees. If they don't concur, and it gets kicked to Rome, it could take years. I'm grateful that the church did this for me, and I'm relieved that it's over."

"So you can marry again in the church, with their blessing, like nothing ever happened."

"That's correct." *Like nothing happened.* Morgan's statement struck an ugly cord, and she wondered to herself, *If Morgan Mason knew the whole story, I wonder what he would think of me, his good Catholic girl.* Only three people in the entire world knew the truth. One was in England, and the other two were in Johannesburg. She knew there was no chance that her secret would be found out. But that would not take away the pain and shame she carried alone. She sighed, *Maybe someday I will tell Morgan, depending on the future of this relationship. But then again, maybe not, maybe never.*

Morgan shrugged. "That's incredible."

"Anyway, I came back to Austin and had to move in with my parents. I didn't have a job, money, or a car. It was humiliating enough for me to have to admit that my marriage had failed. Moving in with my folks and being dependent just made it worse. But I was determined to get myself straightened out. I got a job at the Heritage Inn. They took a chance on me, but I worked hard and learned fast. Once I got some money I moved into an apartment and bought an inexpensive car. When I got a chance to move over to the White House as a sales manager, I jumped at it. Then when I began to make more money I bought a better car and the duplex."

"Well, I'm proud of you, Clare."

She smiled at his approval. "Since I've come back, I've grown up as well. When I was with Marshall I became what he was. He was interested in scuba diving. That scared me, quite frankly, but I learned along with him and forced myself to dive. He liked antiques so I liked antiques. He liked clocks so I liked clocks. I was so subservient that it makes me ill to think of it now. I was so afraid to be myself."

"Clare—why are you telling me all this?" Morgan asked a bit bewildered. "Are you warning me that you're now your own person and not to tread on your independence?"

She didn't answer for a moment. She sighed and said, "You know, I'm really not. I feel comfortable with you, and I guess I just wanted to get it out. You see, I never told anyone about how I felt."

Smiling now, less bewildered, he said, "Well, I'm glad you're in a comfort zone with me, and if it helped to get it out then I'm even more pleased. And Clare, we're just getting started, you and I, but you can talk to me. I don't judge, and I don't tell— never have, never will. So there it is, for what it's worth."

"It's worth a lot, believe me."

"Clare, when you told me about the camping trip, you mentioned a painting. What's that all about?"

"My mom is a talented artist. I guess I inherited it from her. She has a degree in art and taught high school before she married my stepfather. Naturally she encouraged her daughters, but April never took to it. I always loved it, and she encouraged me. I'm always working on a canvas."

"It's kind of funny. My mom has a degree in music, but I didn't follow her direction. Your mom was an art teacher, but you got a degree in music. Do you think it's a coincidence?"

"I do indeed."

"Painting is a wonderful talent and diversion. I'm glad it's working for you. I'd like to see some of your work."

"I can arrange a private showing."

Morgan smiled and nodded. "So tell me, is Casey your married name or your maiden name?"

"It's my maiden name. My married name was Splitgarber."

"Splitgarber," Morgan repeated in wonder. Then he laughed. "I'm sorry. Splitgarber: it just doesn't work for me."

"Well, it didn't work for me either." They both roared with laughter.

Chapter 13

"AFRICA IS ON my list of places to go. Since you lived there, why don't you tell me about it," said Morgan.

"Although I traveled over quite a bit of the continent, I know the most about South Africa, since I actually lived in Johannesburg for two years."

"Please do."

"Well, it's the southernmost country in Africa. Geographically, it's bordered on the north by Namibia, Botswana, Zimbabwe, Mozambique, and Swaziland; on the east and south by the Indian Ocean; and on the west by the Atlantic Ocean. Its really beautiful and has a diverse landscape. Most of the interior is covered by high plateaus, which are separated from the country's long coastline by chains of tall mountains. South Africa is rich in gold and diamonds, and its industrial base grew up around the mining industry. Blacks comprise three quarters of the population. The remainder are a combination of Caucasians, Coloureds, and Asians."

"I'm sorry, Clare, Coloureds?"

"Oh, that's the term used to describe people of mixed race. And the Asians are mainly Indians. There are numerous ethnic groups and eleven official languages; English, Afrikaans, Ndebele, Northern Sotho, Southern Sotho, Swati, Tsonga,

Tswana, Venda, Xhosa, and Zulu. Of these, English and Afrikaans, which is South African Dutch, are the most widely spoken."

"Do so many different languages hurt them in terms of global development?"

"That's a good observation. Yes, I think it does."

"Go on."

"Let's see, where was I?" said Clare. "Okay, even though apartheid ended in the 1990s, the country is still recovering from the racial inequalities in political power, opportunity, and lifestyle. But the government is stable, I believe, and since 1994, it's been a nonracial democracy based on majority rule."

"Clare. I'm impressed. You really know this country."

"Well, with my less-than-active social life, I had a lot of time to study about it."

She smiled and continued, "It's divided into nine provinces and has three capitals."

"Three capitals?"

"That's right. Cape Town is the legislative capital, Pretoria is the executive capital, and Bloemfontein is the judicial capital."

Clare stroked her chin, deep in thought. "The thing that struck me the most was the imbalance between opulence and abject poverty. The living conditions of the very poor are indescribable. We had them living right next to our corporate compound. It just tore me up."

"Marshall was into big-game hunting. He hooked up with an Australian named Peter Wilson, who owned and operated a wild-game ranch."

"So you hunted on his ranch?"

"No, we had to go elsewhere for that. But, the ranch supported 23 species of plains game and 280 species of birds."

"Wow," said Morgan, "that's impressive."

"It was quite an operation." She smiled and nodded with an unusual bit of pride, perhaps for her friend Peter.

"I especially enjoyed the game drives at dawn and at dusk. God, Morgan, the South African sunsets are breathtaking. I forgot to mention the Limpopo River. They do fabulous outings along the river amongst the elephants. It excites me to think about it. Actually the Petica Lodge is situated just south of the river. It's a fabulous location, near the borders of Botswana, Zimbabwe, and Mozambique. You know what they say: location, location, location."

"Clare, you're talking fast and kind of jumping around. Relax and slow down."

"Okay, I'm sorry. I get excited about Africa. Anyway, with professional guides, of course, you can explore the bush with bicycles, walking, and by horseback."

"Horseback?"

"Yeah, the horseback safaris are in Limpopo, previously the Northern Province of South Africa. That's the best, most beautiful area. It's pretty exciting, and you can get really close to the animals: elephant, rhino, buffalo, and the plains game. There are also leopards. I became quite comfortable on the back of a horse. Naturally, you're snapping pictures like crazy, but you've got to have a telephoto lens if you want to get great shots in Africa.

"And you're not back at the lodge every night. You're sleeping out in the bush much of the time. There's one thing that really surprised me about Africa. It's noisy; the animals are always talking to you, night and day."

"Clare, are the animals just running around the entire ranch? I mean, are you right there among them?"

"Well, I never really explained that. The game are in a separate, fenced part of the ranch. Okay, I mentioned the walking tours and the horses. They also have specially built vehicles for game drives."

"You didn't explain much about accommodations at the lodge."

"I guess I didn't. It very nice; its air-conditioned, and they have a terrific swimming pool. You can imagine how wonderful that feels after a day in the sun and the bush. And some of the sleeping accommodations are outside. They have these neat, round houses with thatched roofs. They're fun."

"Are they native huts?"

"Oh, no, they're built for the tourists. They're very nice."

"I'm trying to recall everything. Basing out of the Petica Ranch, they can take you to *Kruger National Park*, which has an abundance of game, and you travel through some spectacular scenic areas going and coming."

"Petica?" questioned Morgan. "That's an interesting name. What's the origin?"

"You know, I asked the same thing. It's the first three letters of Peter and the last three letters of Africa."

"Well, it works for me," said Morgan.

"And they use that with everything; Petica Safaris, Petica Lodge, etc."

"You haven't mentioned the hunting."

"Most people don't realize that hunting is not like it used to be. It is very restricted now, and most of the professionals are African."

"So, the days of the handsome romantic white hunter of the Hemingway novels are becoming a thing of the past, "Morgan reasoned.

"Most definitely. Peter is fortunate to still be able to do it. A lot of it is probably due to the fact that his family has lived in the country so long, own property, and have built and maintained a good reputation not only as game professionals but as good citizens. Anyway, Petica offers rifle and bow hunting as well as bird hunting. The rifle hunting is in Mozambique. Specifically, its in an area bordering *Go Na Re Zhou National Park* in Zimbabwe on the Mozambique side, and next to *Zinave Reserve* in Mozambique on the Sava River."

"How does it work? I mean, is it so much money for your safari, or is by the animal, or what?"

"I don't remember the prices, but its so much a day per hunter and professional and then each animal has a separate cost. I do remember that a lion was $3,000 and a water buffalo was $1,500. My ex-husband got an Eland, a Waterbuck and a Bushbuck."

"Uh, what kind of animals are those?"

"All those animals are from the antelope family."

"Incidentally, I've got some great pictures—lions, hippos, rhinos, zebras, crocodiles, giraffes."

"And Marshall," Morgan inquired.

"I need to show you my pictures. And you can see Marshall if you like."

"I'd be very interested in seeing the pictures. Out of curiosity, what kind of home did Peter have?"

"It was very nice, and he had servants that took care of cleaning and cooking. Did you see the movie, *Out of Africa?*"

"I sure did."

"Well, his house was pretty much like the one she owned. And Peter's servants are very much like the ones in the movie. It's interesting, isn't it?"

"Yes, indeed it is."

"Anyway, Marshall and I became good friends with Peter. And we spent time with him socially as well as when Marshall was hunting."

Clare thought for a moment and then added, "Peter's family moved there right after the turn of the 20th century: 1903, I believe he told me. Their roots are deep in South Africa."

Clare paused again before continuing. "You know, Africa has a lot to offer. And it's not all just roughing it. You can book beach holidays, golf tours, dive tours, white-water rafting, balloon rides—things like that. And there are first-class accommodations. You can get about anything you want. One of the most luxurious hotels and casinos in the world is near Johannesburg."

"Do you fly into Johannesburg when you book with Peter's company?"

"Yes, that's right. And they pick you up at the airport and take you to the lodge."

Clare tapped on her chin, deep in thought, "Peter has a tremendous operation, but there is definitely room for expansion. There is much more he could be offering."

"Lord, Clare, the South African Chamber of Commerce needs to hire you. You really loved South Africa didn't you?"

"Well, as I described earlier, there are positives and negatives, but the place really gets under your skin. I think I will always be drawn to Africa."

"Maybe Peter needs to hire you."

She scrunched up her face but didn't answer him directly.

"Okay, you and Marshall lived in Johannesburg, right?"

"That's right."

"So tell me about Johannesburg."

"Sure, I'll tell you about Joburg. That's what the locals call it. Well, first of all it's a large city of some 2.4 million people."

"That big?"

"Yes, the largest in South Africa. It's a sprawling and vibrant city with wealthy suburbs and massive townships. It has a healthy and expanding multi-racial music and theatre scene. I loved that but Marshall didn't care for it so much. It has excellent shopping, and it's a stopping-off point for world-class sites such as the *Kruger National Park*. There are art galleries, museums, a stock exchange, botanic gardens, philharmonic orchestra, a university, and an international airport. And I almost forgot. It has a world-class medical oncology centre."

"What are the religious leanings of South Africa?"

"They are mainly Christian with some Hindu, Jewish, and Muslim minorities."

"What about Catholic churches? Did you and Marshall have a place to go?"

"The Catholic Church is not prominent in South Africa, but yeah, we had Catholic churches to attend. What about you, Morgan, didn't your folks take you to church?"

"No, we didn't go. And you know, that's as much a part of one's upbringing as anything else. I'm not an agnostic—I'm just sort of ambivalent about the whole thing. I do believe in a supreme being. I suppose I could call him, or her, God. I think there has to be something greater than us—a greater force at work, than just man."

"Well, I was born into the Catholic faith, and it's really important to me. I mean, I wouldn't know how to raise my children."

"Morgan, would you be upset or offended if I talked to you about this? You know, about faith, religion, about the Catholic church."

"No. I suppose not. I'm not closed-minded about it. And I respect you and your convictions. You can talk to me about it."

Clare was pleased at his willingness to discuss matters of religion.

Chapter 14

"TELL ME MORE about your family, Morgan. Do you mind?"

"Oh, no, not at all. My father was a Marine in World War II. I think I already told you that. Anyway, he fought the Japanese in the Pacific. He was on Guadalcanal, the first major United States offensive of the war. He later fought on Saipan and Tarawa, where he won the Congressional Metal of Honor." Morgan's voice broke. "I am very proud of my father. In fact, my first book was a non-fiction account of the major battles of World War I, World War II, Korea, and Vietnam. I didn't even have an agent. I sent the manuscript to about thirty agents, and I had a contract within thirty days. The book came out a year and a half later and sold like crazy."

"How crazy?"

"Over a million copies, crazy."

"No kidding?"

"No kidding. That book launched my career, and I dedicated it to my father."

Morgan paused a moment. "Am I off the subject? I guess not completely. You wanted to know about my family and the book thing kind of got caught up in there. Anyway, after the war Dad came home to Austin and married Mom."

"You didn't tell me their names."

"I didn't? Okay, it's Eugene and Irene. Kind of has a ring to it. As I told you before, Mom got a degree in music and taught mixed choir in high school. Some of Dad's Marine Corps buddies joined the Austin Police Department and persuaded him to join as well. So he did." Morgan's demeanor turned somber when he disclosed, "About five years ago he was killed by a drunk driver."

"Oh no, Morgan, I'm very sorry."

"Well…uh, he was working a wreck at night on the upper deck of I H-35, and this drunk ran through a barricade and killed him. It was very sad and hard to deal with."

"Yes, I can imagine."

"It just about did in my mom. After about eight months she sold her house and moved to Colorado Springs to live with her sister. Her husband, my uncle, was also a cop and died in the line of duty. I think they kind of consoled each other."

"That's terrible." It was getting a little depressing, and Clare wanted to change the subject, but there was more.

"Mom died last October of a massive heart attack. She didn't have high blood pressure or any symptoms or warning."

"Oh, Morgan, I am so very sorry. That's so sad."

He sighed. "Well, what was really sad was that she never got over the loss of my father. She missed him so much that her will to live was impaired. I think that kind of hastens death. I like to think that she's with him in heaven—if there is such a place."

"There's a heaven, Morgan! And your parents are there," Clare assured him.

"Well, it's a nice thought, anyway."

Clare glanced at her watch. It was eleven fifty. "Morgan, it's almost midnight. I can't believe it. Where did the evening go?"

"You know the old saying, 'Time flies when you're having fun.'"

"Well, you're right about that. I've had great fun. It has been a terrific evening; the wonderful food, the mood music, the laughter, and great conversation. Please believe me when I tell you that time stands still when I'm with you. I never tire of our conversation. Where is Bogart? I want to tell him goodnight."

"He's gone to bed. No, come here, and I'll show you."

They peeked into the wash room where Bogart's bed was, and sure enough, he was curled up fast asleep. She put her arm around Morgan's waist as they proceeded to the front door. Pausing, he held her close and looked into her compelling green eyes. His warm breath greeted her as his eager mouth covered hers. They kissed for a long time. "Clare, there is real electricity in our relationship. I feel it now; I felt it immediately. When we kissed on that first date, I knew that we would have difficulty going slow. But I think we could have something very special, and I trust I'm not being presumptuous."

"Oh no," said Clare, smiling broadly, "I feel the same. I totally agree."

"Well, let's just let the game come to us, as they say in sports. If this relationship is what I think it's going to be, then things will happen as a matter of course."

She smiled up at him and nodded in agreement.

He walked her to the car and they kissed for a long time before she climbed in. *She has the softest lips*, he thought.

"Thank you again for a perfect evening. And thank you also for my lovely rose."

Chapter 15

Tuesday, June 13, 2000

AS MORGAN APPROACHED his northwest Austin townhouse, he saw Clare's car parked out front. She had called during the day to ask if she could come by and pick up her sunglasses that she left on the dinning room table. He promised to leave a key under the front door mat. He pulled around back and the sound of the garage door opening and closing alerted the household that the master of the manor had arrived. The key turning in the back door lock sent Bogart bounding down the hall to meet him. The playful little pup was jumping up and down and twirling around. He could hardly contain himself and was blocking Morgan's entrance to the house. As he reached down to pick him up, Clare stepped into the hallway from the kitchen.

"Bogart's glad to see his daddy."

"Yeah, it appears he is. How about you? Are you glad to see Bogart's daddy?"

She wiped her hands on a kitchen towel, and grinned broadly. "I'm very glad to see Bogart's daddy." She tried to give Morgan a kiss, but Bogart wanted to lick both of them, and he was squirming like crazy so Morgan put him down.

"Let's try that again. But you may want to reconsider. I'm pretty nasty from my workout."

Clare gave him a kiss but declined to hug Morgan's sweaty body.

"I'm surprised you're still here, Clare. What's going on?"

"Dinner—that's what's going on."

"Well, okay, sounds good."

"Listen, baby, why don't you take a quick shower. It's not quite ready. When you reappear, I'll serve you a nice glass of Merlot and a better welcome."

"Okay, I think I'll do that." He hesitated before going upstairs and inquired, "What's for dinner anyway?"

"Well, I want you to know that I fired up the 'barbie' and have a fine New York steak grilling outside. I am mixing up some arugula, pitted calamata olives, crumbled blue cheese, steamed fresh green beans, and cherry tomatoes. Then I'll toss all that with my own mixture of balsamic and olive oil. Then I'll divide all that evenly between us on some of your good china. Now, when that steak is finished, I'm going to slice it thin and lay half of it on yours and the rest on mine. I'll pour you another Merlot, and then, my sweet man, you're on your own."

"Wow. I'll contemplate all that while I'm cleaning up and see you in a jiffy."

Clare heard him singing upstairs. *He sings a lot—he's a very happy man. Morgan is not moody, and he's even tempered. I like most everything about him.* She heard the water come on, and he continued to sing until the shower drowned him out. *I'll bet he's still going at it. I just can't hear it anymore.* She picked up Bogart, scratched him under the chin. *I hope he likes dinner, Bogart. We've been dating for two months, and I'm finally cooking for him, and in his own home.*

When the shower stopped, she heard Morgan singing again. She looked down at Bogart, who was following her around the kitchen. "Your daddy is just like the energizer bunny. Nothing shuts him up." Morgan, dressed in faded blue jeans and a white T-shirt, finally descended the stairs.

"Feel better?"

"Oh, yeah, I feel like a new man."

As Morgan made his way to the sound system, located in the left corner of the living room by a window and a large green plant, Clare had straightened pillows on the couch and he noticed a bottle of Windex and a paper towel on the coffee table. A bit irritated he inquired, "Clare, what are you doing?"

"Well, dinner is done, and I thought I'd do some straightening and cleaning."

Perhaps it is not such a big thing, but it is symptomatic of how anal Clare is about cleaning and straightening her own house, he thought. *She overdoes it, and I don't want her to get started doing it here.* "Don't straighten, and don't clean. You're not the maid. She comes on Thursday."

Clare was taken aback by Morgan. "I'm sorry, baby, I didn't mean anything by it. I was just trying to help."

"I know you didn't. Listen, I'm looking forward to the evening. You are going to stay a while?"

"I'd planned on it unless you kick me out."

"Fat chance." He smiled, opened the CD compartment, and loaded three disks. "That should take us through dinner, coffee, and some pleasant conversation." He punched the play button and headed for the kitchen.

"The system has a beautiful tone. Who is that singing?"

"That's Jack Jones, one of my all-time favorite boy singers. Then we'll hear from Barbara Streisand and Frank Sinatra: great music for just about any occasion."

Clare had managed the meal beautifully so that everything would be ready to serve when Morgan came down. The food had been plated when Morgan stepped into the kitchen. "This is such a wonderful surprise. And I know that you are ready to serve. But we have unfinished business." He moved in close, and gently but firmly put his arm around her waist and pulled her up tightly next to him. Without a word he tenderly kissed Clare for a long time.

She sighed when the kiss was over. He released his grip in a controlled, deliberate fashion. As they separated they seemed to instinctively grasp each other's hands. They silently stared, smiling at each other, in the joy of the moment.

"Let's eat," he suggested, and reached for his plate. Clare stopped him. "Sit down," she insisted.

When Morgan was seated she put his plate in front of him. She unfolded the napkin and placed it across his lap. She lit the two candles, dimmed the lights and fetched her own food. Ever the gentleman, he started to stand as she approached but she raised a hand to signal that it was not necessary. Clare put down her plate and took her seat. She looked at him tenderly and said, "Bon Appetit."

"Sweetheart, this is wonderful food. You're terrific. What a treat in every respect. But what prompted you?"

"Do I have to have a reason?"

"Well, no, but…"

Clare interrupted, "Look, I just felt like it. I was sitting at my desk today checking contracts, a little bored with my work and thinking of you. That's when I decided that I wanted to see you. Then it hit me to fix dinner and have it ready when you came in from your workout at seven."

Morgan grinned from ear to ear. He leaned over and playfully pooched out his lips. She kissed him.

"So your day could have been better?"

"Yeah, well, you know how it is. I really love my job, but there are those days, every now and then, when you're bored, or irked at a co-worker, or the banquet people screw up your meeting set-up. You know, stuff!"

"I know," said Morgan, sympathetically.

"You're always so up beat, and you make me laugh. I needed to be here tonight."

"I'm sorry I quizzed you."

"Oh, I'm fine. As soon as I came in the back door and saw that little puppy wagging his tail I was better. And then I knew that the next male through that door would be you—and then my little tail would be wagging."

Morgan roared with laughter. "Well, you've made my day, darling girl."

"Then what else can I say? That's part of why I came. I was hoping you'd be pleased."

"I'm pleased."

"Morgan, that's great music."

"Well, I think so, and I'm glad you approve."

"Jack Jones is doing Michel Legrand. I think it's one of his better albums. It's the one playing now. The Streisand album is the thing she did after she and James Brolin married. It's called, *A Love Like Ours*, and I think it's the best stuff she's ever done. The Sinatra album is last up. It's from the Reprise Collection, *Sinatra Reprise, The Very Good Years*. You know, Frank is Frank; what else is there to say?"

"Why don't you write all that down for me. I might want to get them."

"I can do that." He pushed back his plate and sighed with satisfaction. "Outstanding groceries," he proclaimed.

"I'm glad you enjoyed it."

"I did—and you can do it again some time if you wanna."

"I wanna."

"Let's let Boggie back in while we clean up. He should have done his business by now."

"Baby, I've got a tiny bit of steak left. Shall I give it to Boggie?"

"I'd really rather you didn't. I've been warned about giving him table scraps because he might quit eating his regular food."

"Okay by me. That's a good point, but it's hard not to do it."

"Sometimes I don't think I'm a very good daddy. He is so cute it's hard for me to get on him when I should. He's just playing and trying to love you."

"Well, really Morgan, Bogart is still a puppy, a little boy. He'll probably grow out of some of the stuff that bugs you."

"That's probably true," said Morgan. "Mornings are interesting around here. Bogart is excited when I get up and insists that we play a bit. When I'm finished with my shower and am trying to dry off, he grabs the towel. Then he tries to grab my shorts when I put them on, and then he usually runs off with one or more of my socks and buries his head in my shoes when I try to put them on. But you know, I don't get mad at him. He's just playing, and it breaks me up, it really does. I love that little guy. But as you suggest, Clare, he'll probably grow out of some of it."

"Speaking of dog food," said Morgan. "I've got that *Best of Carson* video series. You know, some of Johnny's best shows. Anyway, one of them has this piece with David Letterman. He's talking about his own dog. He says, 'This dog food label says it doesn't have a scrap of cereal in it. It's all meat. My dog digs in the garbage can and drinks out of the toilet. Chances are he won't mind a little cereal.'"

"That's funny!"

They cleaned up the kitchen together and continued to chatter away. After the dishwasher loaded, Clare and Morgan stood in the kitchen and talked another half hour while he finished the remaining coffee. "Baby, I should be going on down the road. I've got a few miles to go before I get home."

"I know, and I'm sorry you have that drive. But I do appreciate your coming over."

Before he walked her to her car, he opened a tiny drawer in a small kitchen chest. He extracted a small key with a tag that read, "Mason House." He got an extra garage door opener from the wash room and handed both items to Clare.

"I want you to take these. If you want to take a break at lunch and get away from the hotel, just come on over. You can kick off your shoes and rest for a while. You're welcome to eat lunch here if you wish. I'm pretty good about keeping the place stocked. If you're uncomfortable with that then bring your own food. If you've got a meeting to go to after work, you can come by here and freshen up, even shower if you'd like. And there may be evenings when you want to let the traffic thin out a bit before you head off to Round Rock. Anyway, just use the place any way you wish. It doesn't matter if I'm here are not; just make yourself at home. Boggie will be glad to see you. I think you guys have already bonded. And if you take a notion to cook for me again—I'd love it."

She took the items and put them in her hand bag without comment.

"You okay with all this?"

"Oh sure, a bit surprised, trying to figure…"

"Don't figure."

"Okay, I won't."

He walked her out to the car as Bogart tagged along, wagging his tail in approval. Morgan opened her door, as always, and she slipped into the seat. He motioned for her to lower the window, and leaned over and gave her a long slow passionate kiss. Then he sighed, crossed his arms over his chest, as if overcome by the experience. "Darling, you have the softest lips."

"Thank you, baby."

Morgan picked up Bogart, and they stood in the street until Clare's car was out of sight.

Chapter 16

CLARE WAS TIRED when she finally reached the duplex in Round Rock. She found herself in a bit of a quandary, should she collect the mail or do it in the morning. She put her shoes back on and reluctantly dragged herself to the mail box. Thumbing through the various bills and solicitations, she spied an envelope from Peter. Pitching the others on the dinning room table, she kicked off her shoes and plopped down on the couch. She sighed as she slowly tore at the sealed flap, finally relieving it from the sticky substance that had held it captive. She sighed again as she extracted the contents. As she opened the card a picture fell out. Picking it up from her lap she smiled at the sight of Peter holding a small chimp. She loved South Africa, and the picture brought back memories of pleasant times gone by.

The front of the card was a picture of an African sunset—*beautiful*, she thought to herself. The inside was blank, save the hand-written message from her friend.

I stay busy, which helps me some. But the nights are the worst of it. I think too much—always of you—and I smoke too much. And I drink too much. But the whiskey helps dull the nagging pain of loneliness. I long to see you, to talk to you, and to look into those emerald eyes. Come to Africa.

Peter.

Clare shook her head, slowly, as tears welled up in her eyes.

Chapter 17

Wednesday, June 28, 2000

"WOULD YOU CARE for another glass of wine, baby?" Clare asked of Morgan.

"No thank you, sweetheart, but I'd love another cup of coffee with my cake. By the way, where is that painting you started when you girls went camping? You never showed it to me."

"It's not finished, baby. I'd like to wait until it's done."

"Oh, no, fetch it. I want to see."

Reluctantly, Clare got the painting and brought it to the table. She pressed it against her body, still not willing to grant him a premature showing.

"Hand it over," Morgan demanded.

Clare backed up, displayed the unfinished work, "Paintings should be seen from a distance."

Morgan laughed, which befuddled and confused the aspiring artist. "Baby, that hurts my feelings."

"I'm sorry, Clare; I'm not laughing at the caliber of your work. In fact, it's quite good. I'm laughing at the subject matter. I expected to see a scene from the highland lakes."

Clare was painting a canal in Venice, Italy. It was from a snapshot she had taken while she was there. Morgan got up and approached Clare. He took the canvass, laid it aside, and put his arms around her. Holding her tight, he kissed her on the forehead. "You are a very talented lady, and I can't wait to see the finished product."

She pulled away, grinning. "I don't know when I'll finish it. You take up all my spare time."

"Oh, sure, blame me," said Morgan, laughing.

Clare returned the canvass to its designated spot and Morgan returned to his coffee. Clare was an excellent cook and that was something else they had in common. They loved to get in the kitchen, soft music in the background, and prepare a meal together. But tonight, Clare had done the honors at her place. She was adept at everything but Italian food was her favorite and her specialty. Tonight she had prepared bruschetta with peperonata, linguine with saffron and mussels and Italian cream cake.

They were still at the dinning table, engaged in small talk, enjoying coffee and soft music when April burst through the front door.

"What's going on?" she blurted.

"Well, April, I didn't hear you knock," said Clare sarcastically. "I thought you were flying."

"I got in a few minutes ago, saw his car, and decided I would pop in and meet your boyfriend. You haven't ever introduced us."

Morgan stood, being very much himself. April approached, ignored his outstretch hand and gave him a kiss on the mouth. She made a point to brush her breasts against his chest. Laughing, she plopped down at the table and said, "Sis, give me a glass so I can sample this wine."

April was shorter than Clare, had brown eyes instead of green, but otherwise they look very much alike. April was a brunette and generously endowed like her older sister. She was barefoot, braless, wearing skin-tight jeans and a tight, white, cotton half-shirt that showed plenty of skin. Her nipples and the curvature of her breasts were plainly visible. Clare was furious.

Morgan didn't know how to react. Clare had told him about her rather impetuous sister, but this was the first time they had met. *Some first meeting,* Morgan thought.

Clare handed her a glass, sat down across the table and glared at her in silence.

April poured herself a full glass of Merlot. "So, looks like you had Italian. I'm sure it was delicious. My sister is a great cook, unlike me. Mom and Clare can both cook, but I'm not very good at it. I'm real good at eating though," said April, laughing loudly, "and drinking."

"And making an ass of yourself," said Clare, disgustedly.

April gulped down her wine, jumped up from the table and walked directly to Clare's bedroom. She hollered over her shoulder, "Can I see you in here, Clare?"

Clare reached over and gently touched Morgan's arm, "I'm so sorry, baby, I have no idea what's going on. She is…"

"It's okay. Go see what she wants."

Clare closed the bedroom door and glared at April. "What in God's name do you think you're doing?"

Laughing loudly, April said, "Give me fifty dollars, and I'll get out of here. Look, I'm sorry, sis. I don't know what came over me. I apologize for everything. But I really am short. You know how I am with money. I'll pay you back next week."

Clare anxiously fumbled in her purse and pulled out her wallet. Picking hurriedly through the bills she said, "I can let you have 40 dollars, and you're lucky to get that."

April took the money, rolled up the bills and pushed them into her tight jeans pocket. She gave Clare a hug and kissed her on the cheek. "Thanks, sis."

"I hope you're not going out like that," said Clare, disgustedly. "You look like a hooker."

April shrugged and walked out of the room. Morgan stood as she approached. This time she extended her hand, "Nice to meet you Morgan. My sister is a first class gal; you're lucky to have her. I hope to see you again, and next time I'll be on better behavior."

Morgan looked shocked, "Uh…yeah…nice to meet you, too, April." He shook his head and said to her, "Stay out of trouble." April shut the door quietly behind her and returned to her side of the duplex. Clare stood in the bedroom doorway, a perturbed look on her face. Morgan took her in his arms and gave her a hug, stroking her hair. "Forget it, Clare, it's not important. Please don't let this ruin our evening."

She sighed, "Okay, baby."

She hurried to the front door and turned the lock. Then she closed the blinds and turned down the lights. She motioned for Morgan to join her on the couch. She put her arms seductively around his neck, looked longingly into his expressive blue eyes, "Where were we?"

Chapter 18

Friday, August 4, 2000

BOGART'S EARS PERKED up at the sound of the key turning in the lock. True to his breed, the little guy had uncanny hearing. As the front door opened he bolted down the stairs, two steps at a time, barking at the top of his lungs. At the bottom of the stairs the bark turned into a whimper as he recognized that this was no intruder, but a friend. His tail began to wag as he stood on his hind legs with his paws in the air. He loved Clare and wanted her to pick him up. She cuddled him lovingly as Morgan appeared at the balcony.

"Hi, baby," said Clare, "You're not supposed to be working. I thought you usually knocked off at about five."

"I usually do but this is one of those days when I can't seem to quit."

"You didn't go to the gym?"

"No, I didn't go."

"I hope you don't mind my stopping by?"

"Of course not. What a lovely surprise. Bogart knew you were coming before I did. When I'm writing dialog I'm impervious to distractions. I'm kind of in another zone. Are you just getting off work or what?" He impulsively glanced his thin gold Lucien Piceard. It was nine-fifteen.

"I just got off. We had a big wedding reception tonight, and they wore me out. I needed to see my boys—and I could use some major league TLC."

Morgan descended the stairs and wrapped his arms around Clare, holding her close and rocking her from side to side. "Poor baby, is that better?"

"That's much, much, better."

He kissed her forehead and worked his way down. Then tenderly kissed her soft lips and continued to hold her. "Sweetheart, did you have dinner?"

"Dinner, I didn't even have lunch!"

"Well, let daddy feed the baby."

Morgan went upstairs and came back with one of his big denim shirts. "Here, put this on. Then kick off your shoes, and take a seat at the table." Morgan poured her a glass of Merlot. "You work on that while I see what I can do."

"Baby, I love your shorts. I haven't seen them before." She laughed.

"What's so funny?"

"Well, really, shorts that look like the map of Texas kind of amuse me. But I must admit that large white star on you butt is awfully cute."

"Look here little lady, you can laugh at Morgan Mason all you want. But when you make sport on the flag of our beloved state, well, ma'am, that's another matter indeed."

They laughed.

Morgan had fixed a giant shrimp and baby spinach salad for his own dinner and there was plenty left. He tossed some of it for Clare and heated some ciabatta bread. He had also made some squash soup with a little curry in it to give it a bite. "Here you are, my love."

Morgan poured a glass of wine and sat down beside his girl. She tried the soup and then clapped her hands in approval. "You are really too good to be true."

"I bet you tell all your men the same thing," he suggested playfully.

"Shut up," she responded, with a smile.

"No kidding, baby, this is wonderful. Where did the soup come from?"

"I just dreamed it up today."

"You did not!"

"Yes, I did."

"I can't tell exactly what it is. I can't quite figure…"

"It's summer squash with yellow onion, bacon, salt, pepper and half and half."

"The half and half makes it creamy."

"Right. And I added a little sugar."

"There's still something else."

Morgan smiled. "It's curry power."

"Morgan, the curry power sets it off. Very nice. You are a wonder. And this shrimp salad is equally terrific."

"Just glad the kitchen was still open, and the chef was in a good mood."

She laughed.

"Clare, do you need to talk about today? Would that help? I'm all ears if you do."

"Oh, God, baby, I have lived through a day in hell! I had this group in for an all-day seminar, and I needed to get on property early to make sure everything was set. I was running a little late. Guess what. I had a flat. By the time I got it fixed I was really late. Well, when I got to the hotel my client was snorting fire because the room was set incorrectly. We got it fixed before his first session started, but he was still miffed, and he let me know about it. Then the first coffee break was late."

"What do you mean late."

Clare took a bite of food and a sip of wine. "Baby, this is sooooo good. Thank you."

"My pleasure."

"To answer your question, we didn't get the Danish and fresh coffee to the room by the time the break was scheduled on the program. My client stormed into the sales office and caused a scene, and I wanted to crawl under my desk. The other sales manager, my director of sales, and my general manager, Tom, were all in there and heard the whole thing. After I got over the shock and embarrassment I really wanted to kill him!"

"Smooth sailing after that?" questioned Morgan.

"Not exactly. We served the wrong meal at lunch. Well, actually, we served the meal he ordered, but he claimed that he changed his mind after he returned the conformation. He swears he called catering and made the change, but nobody in catering could confirm it. At that point, I didn't know what the truth really was. But he made another scene. We did get through the rest of his meeting without any more trouble."

"And then the wedding reception was pretty trying. Baby, do you mind if I don't talk about my day anymore? I'd much rather just enjoy my evening. By the way, where is puppy?"

"Look under the table."

Bogart was lying across Morgan's bare feet, eyes closed, with his little head resting between his outstretched paws. "God bless his sweet heart. He is so precious."

"He is that. This morning I was reading the newspaper in the back room. Bogart started barking at me."

"Why would he do that?"

"Most of the time it means he wants to potty. Some times it means he wants to play. I told him I was reading the paper, and we would play later. He grabbed the ball in his mouth, jumped up on the couch and squirmed underneath the paper. Then he stepped up on my chest and just stood there looking at me," said Morgan, grinning and shaking his head.

"So what did you do?"

"I got down on the floor and played ball with him."

She smiled and shook her head from side to side. Morgan and Clare continued to talk. She wanted to know how the book was going and he loved to tell her. She got tickled at how energized he became about the characters and the various situations. Sometimes he let her read various chapters as the work progressed. She enjoyed previewing it and it made her feel like she was a part of his work. Morgan found her to be an honest reviewer and valued Clare's opinion. She was a good sounding board.

"Sweetheart, did you get enough? Is there anything else I can get you?"

" No, thank you, I'm full." Clare pushed back her empty plate and took a sip of wine. "Baby, do you believe in providence?"

"I'm probably the wrong person for that question. Why do you ask?"

"Well, I do believe in providence. I was thinking that if I hadn't taken the job at the White House, I would never have met you.. Well, there was the airport, but you know what I mean. Anyway, we connected; that's all that matters."

She followed him into the kitchen. He began to sing along with Sinatra, on a CD that was playing in the living room. Clare said, "Baby, you have a really good baritone voice. You should do something with it."

"You know of a record company who might be interested?"

"No!" she laughed. "But I do know of a singing group that needs a baritone."

"What are you talking about?"

"I'm talking about my group, the River City Singers. We're really short on baritones, and besides that, it would make me very happy. I mean, music is important to me, and you know how much I enjoy singing. And it would be another thing we could do together. We just practice one a week. And the concerts are really fun. The audiences really enjoy us and think we're pretty good."

"Take a breath, Clare. Okay, I'll do it."

"You'll do it?"

"Yeah."

"Just like that?"

"Clare, is this a female thing? I said yes! You know, you're in sales, but you don't know the golden rule of salesmanship."

"Uh, well, maybe I don't. What is it?"

"When the customer is ready to deal, you shut your mouth and show them where to sign." They stared at each other and then began to laugh.

As he washed her plate she put her arms around his waist and laid her head on his bare back. He turned around and picked her up. She gently put her arms around his neck and her head on his shoulder. He carried her in the living room and laid her gently on the couch.

"Baby, I don't relax when I'm at home. I see a jillion things to do. I don't know how many times I've rented a movie on the way home. I plan to pile up on the couch and watch it, but the next thing I know, it's eleven o'clock. But over here, I can really unwind."

"Well, I'm pleased to hear that."

He turned out the kitchen light and dimmed the track lights in the living room. He leaned over the back of the couch and carefully looked through the stack of compact discs until he found the sound track from *Somewhere in Time.* It was perfect, just what Clare needed.

Morgan pulled Clare up against him, her back against his chest and put his arms tenderly around her neck. Soon she was resting peacefully. There was no need for words. It was time for the music do the talking—for a man and a woman simply sharing a quiet moment at the end of the day. Clare thought to herself, *It is so wonderful to have a man who truly understands a woman's needs, a man who knows when to be tender, to be understanding—a man who knows the power of just holding a woman—a man who truly understands intimacy.*

THE HOUR WAS late and Morgan tenderly awakened Clare. "Sweetheart, it's midnight. Don't you need to be going?"

She sat up, shook her head to clear it, and said nothing for a brief moment. "Don't go away," said Clare, as she walked slowly toward the downstairs bathroom. Morgan was standing when she came back. Smiling coyly she ran her arms up slowly, exploring the black hair that covered the definition of his hard bronze chest. She continued until her arms around his neck and softly, breathlessly, whispered at his pulsating temples. "Baby, I'm not going home tonight."

Chapter 19

Monday, August 7, 2000

CLARE STARED AT the computer screen but saw nothing. She was motionless except for the incessant tapping of her number two pencil on a small open spot on her cluttered desk. She couldn't get the weekend out of her mind. Morgan had prophetically remarked that when it happened they would both know it was right. It was right—and it was the most exhilarating experience of her life. As a woman, she had never experienced such utter fulfillment. Morgan was a beautiful lover; strong but tender. He had taken her places, sexually, where she had never been. He was also correct that sex can cloud the mind, interfere with reality. But reality, by now, was Morgan Mason. She loved him with unimaginable passion and yet he was also her friend. She liked him as well as loved him. She knew the importance of it, she knew the difference. Physically, she was at the White House, but emotionally and mentally, she was a million miles away.

"Clare!" shouted Jan. "Your telephone is ringing. Pick it up, will you. What's with you today?"

Oh, yeah, the phone. "Clare Casey, may I help you?"

∘ ∘ ∘ ∘ ∘

"ANGIE AND I are going for Mexican food after work and then to a movie," said Cindy. "Come with us Clare."

"I appreciate the offer, but I've got a client coming in at five-thirty, and then I need to check on Bogart. Morgan's gone to Tyler and won't be back until about nine tonight. He'll be tired and hungry, and I thought I'd go by Suzi's and pick up some Chinese food and have it there when he comes in."

"What on earth is he doing in Tyler?" Angie asked.

"This man is so generous with himself, I can't believe it sometimes," Clare lamented. "Here's the story. The mayor is a guy Morgan played football with at Texas A & I. His wife is president of a large book club. It's a classic case of asking an old friend for a favor, but it's turned into a pretty big deal. Morgan gets the keys to the city and has a street named after him for the day. Then he does a Junior League luncheon because the mayor's wife is the president of that as well. Then in the late afternoon he does a lecture on romance writing to the book club, a book reading, and a book signing after that."

"Wow, they do have him busy. Does he get paid for that?" Angie asked.

"They pay his expenses, but that's it."

"Really, that's all?" questioned Angie.

"But you know, Angie, he loves to do it, and he gets energized by the people. I mean, he's like a politician on the campaign trail, except that he's not full of himself. In spite of his enormous success, he is very down to earth, and I suspect he is very much like he was before he hit it big. Anyway, thanks for thinking of me; maybe another time."

Chapter 20

BOGART WAS EXCITED as Clare opened the door from the garage. Morgan had left the little fellow outside and his bowl was empty. He jumped up on her legs and barked, wanting to play. "Hi there, darling; how is our little man today? I'll bet you are hungry and thirsty."

Clare took the Chinese food inside and stored it in the refrigerator. Then she collected Bogart's green plastic food container from outside and gave him fresh water and food. He jumped around as she put it down in the wash room where the little guy's bed and extra toys were kept. He lapped up the food and most of the water. "You were hungry, weren't you?"

Morgan always took Bogart outside after he ate. She took Bogart, and the ball as well. "Potty, Bogart, you need to potty." The little fellow sniffed the grass, circling again and again, over here and then over there, in the next-door neighbor's yard, and then close to the steps. He finally got the smell he was looking for. After finishing, he wanted his treat and ran immediately to the front door, because his goodies were kept in the wash room inside. But Clare had thoughtfully brought one of the little flavored bone shaped treats with her so they could stay outside and play. "Good boy, Bogart. Here's your treat."

Clare loved the little dog almost as much as Morgan did. She pitched the ball, and he retrieved it. They played until it was dark. She took Bogart inside and put on some music, *Toscana* by Andrea Bocelli, a favorite of hers and Morgan's. She poured herself a glass of Merlot, took a sip, and lay down on the couch in the living room. She was awakened by the sound of thunder and lightening. *Were we supposed to have weather today?* she asked herself. She rubbed her eyes and looked at her watch. It was ten o'clock and Morgan should have landed in Austin at about nine. *Give him thirty minutes maximum to drive it, and he should have been home by nine-thirty,* she thought. She turned on the television and clicked on the weather station. There was a squall line that would have crossed Morgan's flight path. Alarmed, she wrung her hands and paced, not knowing exactly what to do. She called Round Rock but there were no messages from Morgan on her recorder.

Morgan had been delayed. It was ten o'clock before he reached the private airfield to board his charter flight. The plane was loaded and the twin engines were toped off with fuel for the flight back to Austin. The pilot had checked the weather, which is customary before departure, and approached Morgan with the report. "Mr. Mason, we may get into some weather. It's not bad right now and won't be for a while, but I am concerned that we may not be able to make it all the way back to Austin."

"Bob, I'm just the poor old passenger. This is what I've got you for. If you don't think we should go then we won't go. I don't have anything so pressing that I have to get back to Austin tonight. We can stay here tonight and see what the weather is like in the morning."

Bob returned to the pilot's lounge for one more weather check. "Mr. Mason, I think we'll be fine."

With assurance from his pilot, Morgan climbed aboard and crawled into the back seat. He loosened his tie and collar and took off his jacket as Bob asked for clearance. "Tyler tower, this is Cessna 520, ready for takeoff."

"Cessna 520, you are clear to go."

"Thank you, sir, Cessna 520 rolling and out."

The twin engines hummed as they gained ground speed. The feeling of power always gave Morgan a sense of exhilaration. They lifted off and circled as they climbed out. Morgan glanced downward, the lights of the city looked like a field of diamonds. *Beautiful, simply beautiful*, he thought to himself. The Cessna reached cruising altitude and leveled off. It was a clear night, full of stars. *Weather? What weather?*

Chapter 21

MORGAN MASON HAD made numerous flights in small charters and the thing that always struck him about flying at night was that you could almost always see lights on the ground. It was if you were never really alone; you were always in touch. It had been a very long and active day. He leaned back and drifted into a sound asleep.

Sometime later Morgan was awakened by severe turbulence. The Cessna was bouncing around all over the place. Bob had his head phones on and was talking on the radio. When there was a break in the conversation Morgan leaned forward and got his attention.

"Sorry for the bumpy ride, Mr. Mason."

"Do we have a problem, Bob?"

"Well, we're in a storm, but I think we can handle it. I'm in constant touch with the ground."

CLARE WAS BESIDE herself, in a state of near panic. It was eleven-thirty and still no Morgan. *I've got to do something!* She was anxious as the telephone rang, "Tyler Aerial Service, this is Randy."

"Randy, this is Clare Casey calling from Austin. I'm trying to get some information on a friend of mine who flew in there this morning. His name is Morgan Mason, and he was flying in a Cessna charter, but I'm sorry, I don't know the call numbers are anything else. It was my understanding that they were to leave there at approximately seven-thirty this evening. I believe he told me that would put them at Browning Aerial here in Austin at nine o'clock. It's eleven-thirty, and I'm worried to death. I saw the squall line on the weather channel. What can you tell me?"

"Oh, yes ma'am, we know who Mr. Mason is. They were here all right. But they were late leaving."

"How late, Randy?"

"It was ten-twenty ma'am."

"Ten-twenty!" Clare exclaimed. "I wonder why so late?"

"I wouldn't know that, ma'am."

"What about the weather, Randy?"

"Bob, the pilot, he checked on it, and I saw him talking to Mr. Mason. I assume he was explaining the situation. Then a little later Bob went back into the pilot's lounge, I'm assuming, to check the weather again. He came out and they talked again. Soon after that they climbed aboard and took off."

"What do you make of that, Randy?"

"Well, ma'am, it looked to me like Bob must have been satisfied with the weather situation, or they wouldn't have gone. He's an experienced pilot. I don't think he would have taken any chances."

She paused for a moment, putting what she knew together, trying to figure it all out. "The fact that they were two and one half hours late leaving helps a little, although I still don't understand what the delay was about. They should be touching down in Austin about now."

"Ma'am, with this front like it is, they won't be able to make very good time. They're sure to be delayed, but I can't tell you how long."

"Well, thank you very much, Randy. This has been somewhat helpful. I'm not quite as worried as I was before."

"You're welcome, ma'am. But let me just say this. Bob is a very experienced pilot, and they are in a very good airplane. I'm sure they're okay. You should have nothing to worry about."

Clare picked up Bogart and cuddled him. "I want your daddy home."

She paced and then put on a pot of coffee. Clare had trouble relaxing anyway, especially if she saw things that needed to be done. It just her nature and besides, tidying up Morgan's place decreased her anxiety level and took her mind of the situation. She unloaded the dish washer, then rinsed and loaded the dishes and glasses that had been left in the sink. There were two empty bottles of Benadryl on the floor. Morgan used a lot of the syrup due to frequent allergic reactions. His doctor thought it was food related but couldn't seem to pin it down. There was also an empty bottle of vitamin E. Bogart's unusual assortment of toys consisted mostly of plastic medicine bottles, although he got very frustrated at his inability to pick them up when they were on the slick tile kitchen floor. There were also two tennis balls and a rope chew toy. She left the rope and put the other toys on top of the clothes dryer and then vacuumed the living room and the carpet in the back bathroom and study. She made the bed upstairs and picked up more of Bogart's toys. Back downstairs, she poured a cup of coffee and paced. Nothing really tempered her distress.

"Operator, give me the number for Browning Aerial Service."

The recorded message explained that the hours of operation were six-thirty to twelve-midnight. She glanced at her watch which displayed twelve-ten. She sighed and impatiently slammed down the phone. Bogart barked. He sensed that she was upset. He knew something was wrong. She had no way to communicate with anyone. The weather channel didn't indicate any break in the weather. She prayed for Morgan's safety. She didn't know what else to do. She could only wait and hope for the best.

Chapter 22

MORGAN MASON WAS never one to worry about much of anything, including his safety. He'd been in tight spots before but refused to accept that anything bad would ever happen to him. Weather, bumps or no bumps, he went back to sleep. Morgan could sleep regardless of circumstances.

He stirred when the Cessna touched down. It came to a stop as he gathered himself. Bob cut the engines and took off his headphones. Still a bit fuzzy headed, Morgan inquired, "Are we home?"

"No, sir. Not unless you live in Waco."

"Waco! What are we doing in Waco?"

"We were forced down. We can't continue until it clears."

It was coming down hard, beating an uneasy crescendo on the fuselage of the ship. "You want to go in with me?" Bob inquired.

"I'm not getting out in that stuff. I'm going back to sleep."

Bob laughed and said, "I can't say that I blame you. I'll be back when we're clear to leave."

THE NEXT THING Morgan remembered was the sound of Bob in the cockpit. He was seated and putting on his headphones. Be buckled himself in and asked, "Mr. Mason, you awake?"

"I'm awake."

"We can leave now."

"What time is it?"

"2:30 a.m."

It was wet and misty as they took off but the bad part was over. They cruised into Austin and landed safely at Browning Aerial Service.

BOGART HEARD IT first and began to bark as he dashed to the back door. Clare followed and opened the door as Morgan appeared from the garage. He was drenched and his jacket sleeve was torn. He looked terrible but at the same time wonderful. Before he could explain, Clare threw her arms around his neck and began to cry uncontrollably.

"I'm here, sweetheart, and I'm okay."

"Oh, baby, I thought you were dead. I could just picture the crash. When you were late, and it hit here, I checked the weather channel and saw the squall line. I was terrified. I called the airport in Tyler and…"

"I'm so sorry, sweetheart. But what were you doing here in the first place? You shouldn't have even known about this."

Clare explained about checking on Bogart, and the Chinese food, and being there when he came home.

"Oh, Clare."

"Baby, this made me realize something I guess I already knew. I love you more that you can imagine, and I thought I'd lost you. The thought of it was unbearable. It made me sick to my stomach. It made my heart hurt. I was in total despair. I have never experienced anything like it."

Morgan's eyes teared up. He held her close and stroked her long, black hair. "Clare, I'm truly sorry you had to suffer through this."

Bogart was watching, head cocked in one direction and then another. They saw him and laughed. Clare gathered herself and asked, "Baby, what on earth has happened to you? Honestly, you look like road kill."

Morgan dropped his wet jacket in the wash room, along with his shirt and grabbed a towel to dry his wet head. He poured himself a glass of straight scotch whisky, sat down on the kitchen floor, leaned up against the cabinets and explained the entire evening.

"God, Morgan, that's unbelievable. But why are you so messed up and your jacket is even torn. And you're limping, what on earth…"

"Well, I'm not finished with my story. When my charter dropped me off here in Austin it was still raining. It wasn't hard, but it was steady, and I didn't have an umbrella." Morgan had a confused look on his face when he explained, "Clare, Browning Aerial Service was closed. I don't just mean the office and terminal; I mean the entire complex, including the gates from the tarmac to the parking lot. I was locked in. I'm standing there in the rain, after all I've been through, and I can't even get off the stinking airstrip."

Morgan sighed and continued, "I finally spotted a couple of large crates. I dragged them over by the fence and stacked them on top of each other, which was no small order in itself. Anyway, that was high enough for me to put my foot on top of the wire. Fortunately, the barbed wire on top of the chain length fence was pointed out and not in. I threw my brief case over the fence and climbed up on top of the wire. I tried to jump clear but I hooked my left arm on the barbed wire and tore my jacket. I'm probably lucky that it didn't tear my arm open. I landed in a large puddle of water, turned my ankle, and fell to the ground. That got me further soaked and dirty. And my ankle hurts like hell. I was really mad when I got in my car, but as I drove home I decided I was just happy to be on the ground in Austin. In a strange sort of way it was kind of funny. And how could you make up a story like that. Anyway, I'm home and safe. I can get my jacket fixed, and my ankle will heal. I've had more ankle sprains than I can count."

"You're right; no one could make up a story like that." Clare sat down beside him and patted his cheeks. She leaned over and gave him a kiss, then held him around his waist with her head on his chest. After a few moments she raised her head, as tears welled up in her eyes. "Oh, baby," she said softly, shaking her head back and forth. He smiled and they kissed.

Chapter 23

Wednesday, August 23, 2000

"MR. MASON, WE at Barnes & Noble are very pleased with the arrangements for the September event. Your willingness to do the lecture, the reading, and the book signing is most generous."

"No, Alan, you are the generous ones. I'm still humbled by the tremendous acceptance of my work. I still get a kick out of this sort of thing and genuinely enjoy meeting the people and answering their questions."

"Well, it shows. And Mr. Mason, you are one of the few best-selling authors who will actually take the time to get the person's name and write a message. Most of them just sign their name and that's it. I can't tell you how much the people appreciate the attention that you give them."

"Well, you're most kind to say that. I'm just grateful to be a part of the literary business. Frankly, I think you've got to be a bit lucky."

"No, no," said Alan, "it's not luck when one writes as well, as you."

The two men shook hands and Morgan headed for the Boxter. The White House, a short drive from Barnes & Noble, was the centerpiece of the 95-acre arboretum complex, which featured an upscale selection of boutiques, restaurants and other retail establishments. Morgan knew that he should be on his way to Dallas, but his thoughts were of Clare. He was overwhelmed with the most unexplainable urge to see her before he left town. A guest pulled out and Morgan was able to take what appeared to be the only vacant spot in the entire parking lot.

Morgan, as always, was struck by the grandeur and opulence of the hotel. The stark white marble exterior was impressive but no less magnificent than the interior. He entered the foyer with its marble columns and mahogany paneling, which were a prelude to the nine-story atrium, the focal point of the hotel. The open space was complimented by huge pots and marble boxes of assorted greenery along with contemporary sculptures. Bars, restaurants, public space and offices surrounded the perimeter. His heart was racing as he entered the executive offices. The sales co-coordinator, Angie Adams, greeted him. "May I help you, sir?"

Morgan was a gregarious man, a cut-up and flirt. But this morning he was strangely out of character. He couldn't explain his own mood. He did not speak but simply pointed to Clare who was on the telephone with her back to him. When the call was over, Angie said, "Clare, this gentleman is here to see you."

He had never come to her office during business hours; she was struck by his serious demeanor. "Morgan! What is it? Has something happened?"

Morgan turned and walked out of the office. Clare followed. She was more distressed than ever. Outside the door he explained, with a sigh, "Clare, I apologize for coming to your office, but I just had to see you — to touch you — to smell you."

Clare was overwhelmed! She gathered herself and said, "Oh, Morgan, the things you say, they just..."

"Clare, those weren't the words of a writer." He choked up for a moment and then finished his thought, "They were just the words of a boy — very much in love with a girl."

He wanted to take her in his arms, but the double doors to a nearby meeting room were suddenly thrust open and hundreds of conventioneers came flooding out for their morning break. There were people everywhere and Morgan did not wish to embarrass Clare.

Tears were welling up in her eyes. He took her hand and whispered something in her ear. She squeezed his hand, so overcome with emotion that her nails dug into his palms. With tears in his eyes, he gently touched her face. "I must go, sweetheart. I must get on the road."

"I know," said Clare with a sigh.

Clare stood alone until Morgan disappeared around the corner. She tried to collect herself and then returned to her desk. She was crying softly. Cindy, the other sales manager, rushed to her side, "What is it, Clare? Bad news? Please..."

Clare, head down, motioned with her left arm. They had seen the gesture before. It meant, "Not now. Don't talk to me."

Angie, Cindy, and Jan Jenkins, the Director of Sales, took Clare to lunch. She explained, "Morgan Mason told me he loved me. He had never done that before. The way he did it—so intense—so emotional. I had never seen him like that. I was breathless, totally overwhelmed!"

"But happy?" Cindy questioned.

"Happy—more like delirious."

They talked non-stop until it was time to go back to work. Clare explained that it was also Morgan's birthday and she hated not being with him. They would celebrate on Saturday night. Her co-workers were curious about Morgan Mason. Clare loved to talk about Morgan but was careful not to get too personal, not to divulge things that were just for them to know. The girls in the White House sales department were a close-knit group, really good friends, and quality people. They stood by each other. They had been worried for their friend Clare. But what had seemed so alarming earlier had turned out to be something wonderful. They were thrilled for her.

"DELIVERY FOR A Clare Casey," blurted out the boy from Mesa Flowers.

"That would be me."

She put the roses on her desk and hurriedly opened the card. It read, *See you for dinner Saturday night. Love you. Morgan.*

Roses were always appropriate for most women. A dozen red roses was standard, but these were an exquisite peach color. Most men would have sent a dozen, but Morgan sent two dozen. Morgan Mason wasn't like other men.

"From Morgan?" asked Jan.

"Of course," responded Clare.

"What's the occasion?" questioned Cindy.

"You see," said Clare with a sigh, "that's the wonderful thing about Morgan Mason. There doesn't have to be an occasion!"

Chapter 24

Friday, August 25, 2000

"HEY, APRIL, ARE you flying today?" Clare asked.

"Yes, I am, but I'll be home by six. Did you need something or were you just being nosey?" asked April, with a laugh.

"I thought we could just hang out. And I'm hungry for Italian, and I'll cook."

"What about wine?" April wanted to know.

"If red will do then we're set. If you want something else, then you can bring it."

"Red will do nicely." April thought a minute and asked. "This is Friday. Why aren't you with Morgan?"

"He's in Dallas and won't get in until tomorrow morning. I'll see him tomorrow night for his birthday."

"Well, Clare, we haven't done this in awhile. It should be fun. And I'll expect to be brought completely up to date on you and your writer."

"We'll see."

o o o o o

"AND JUST WHO is this little sweetheart?" questioned April as she picked up the little dog.

"That's Bogart, Morgan's little dog," said Clare.

Bogart licked April's neck and then her ear. She couldn't help but giggle. "Bogart, you little darling, I love it, but that tickles. What is he, Clare?"

"He's a Shih Tzu. Morgan loves that dog, and you should see them together. They are some pair. Anyway, I baby-sit when he's out of town. You should be honored, April; Bogart doesn't take to very many people. And when he licks your ear, well, that's the ultimate in affection."

She put her hands under his front legs and held him up, putting her nose against his. "You're a precious, handsome little man. Do you know that?"

Bogart barked. "I think he agrees with you, April."

"CLARE, THIS FOOD is terrific. I don't know why I couldn't have gotten a little of that talent for cooking. You and Mom got it all," April lamented.

"April, it doesn't have anything to do with talent. It's all about practice, practice, practice. But, I did inherit the creativity from Mom. And it shows up in my painting and my cooking."

"You're very creative. I guess that's what I meant."

"I know you want to hear about Morgan, but what about you and Ken? Have you guys set a date?"

Smiling broadly, April announced, "The wedding will be November 9, 2001. Even though we both have some seniority, we're afraid if we wait until later we'll get caught by the heavy holiday travel season, and the company won't let us off."

"That's probably smart," said Clare. "Do you think Southwest will let you guys have the same flight schedule? If not, you'll never be together."

"We've already talked to them about it, and they've agreed."

"That's good news," said Clare. "Is Mom going to help you with arrangements?"

"Yes, she is. And she's real excited about it."

"I don't know if you and Ken have made a decision about the reception, but I could talk to Morgan about having it at the Headliner's Club if you're interested."

"Well, thanks, sis. Let me talk with Ken. I'd like to do it, but let me see what he says. So what about Morgan?" April asked.

"Well, we've picked up the pace considerably, and we're seeing a lot of each other. I'm nuts about him." Clare sighed, sipped her wine and said, "You've read his books, right?"

"I've read the romance novels."

"April, honest to God, Morgan Mason is every bit as romantic as the characters he writes about—and he's my man. What's the chance of meeting a guy like that?"

"I couldn't do the math," said April. "Incidentally, how is he in the sack?"

"April! That's none of your business," said Clare. Then a coy smile broke out on her face. "He's unbelievable. As you know, I was a virgin when I married Marshall. He was the only man I ever slept with until Morgan." *I am never going to discuss the other with anyone,* she said to herself. "But I can tell you this, I had no earthly idea what real sex was like. I hate to admit it, but after two years of marriage to Marshall, I never had an orgasm."

April shook her head. Smiling, she inquired, "And all that's changed?"

"April, I have multiple organisms. Morgan Mason has taken me on a sexual rocket to the moon. That's enough, right? You get the picture. Someone once said a woman shouldn't advertise her man."

"I'm your sister, for God's sake."

"I know, but I'm still uncomfortable talking about it."

"I wonder how many women he's had?" April speculated. "Have you asked him?"

"No, I haven't asked him." She grimaced. "I wouldn't ask him. What would be the point?"

"Well, I asked Ken. And he wanted to know from me as well."

Clare stared at April, a bit perturbed at her sister's ridiculous notion. "Would a certain number be a deal breaker? What's the point of it? Frankly, I don't want to know. And besides, how would you ever know if you got the truth?" Eager to change the subject, Clare said, "Anyway, Morgan knows I love him. I already told him. But he's never said he loved me; until he left on Wednesday."

Clare explained to April what had happened at the White House, the scene outside her office, the roses, all of it. She was crying by the time she had finished. April was crying too. They hugged each other. "Oh, God, Clare, that's just beautiful. I am so happy for you."

"April, the guy just blows me away! And I'm sure he has no equal when it comes to intimacy."

"You said this subject made you uncomfortable," April reminded her.

"My dear sister, there is a great deal more to intimacy than just sex."

"Okay, okay, you're right. Well, you're one lucky girl, big sister. I love Ken, and you know, he's a good man. I think were a good match, and I think we'll have a good marriage. But I doubt he's any Morgan Mason. Clare, you caught lightning in a bottle. Hold on tight."

"Yeah, I will." She picked up little Bogart, hugged him tightly, and scratched his tummy. "But, he worries me."

"Really? What' are you concerned about?"

"For one thing, religion. And that's big with me. He told me he has an open mind about it, and he said he doesn't mind my talking to him about it."

"We'll, that's good. What's the problem? I'm confused."

Clare explained that Morgan had gone to mass with her on numerous occasions but didn't particularly like it. He didn't mind her going but didn't have much of an interest in attending himself.

"Well, of course, I don't have that problem. Ken was raised a Catholic."

"April, I just don't know what to do about this. He is such a tremendous man in so many ways, and I love him so. But I just can't seem to get past this."

"Well, look, what if he agreed to marry in the Catholic Church and for you to raise your children Catholic? I mean, that's a pretty big concession, isn't it?"

"Yes, it is, but you know, couples ought to be a team. That would be one area where he wouldn't be a participant. And I have to wonder if at sometime in the future he might get hostile about the Catholic Church. What if he decided later that he didn't want me to take the children? And then there's Catholic school. He could object to that. It just ties me in knots, April. I just can't seem to get any peace of mind about it."

"We'll, sis, you're the only one who can make that decision. I'm as Catholic as you, but it would seem like a shame to lose him over this. Surely you guys can find a way to settle it."

"Well, it wouldn't be an issue if we were just dating. But we both love each other, and there is no real reason why we shouldn't get married. So we have to settle it."

"Have you spoken with Father Quigley about it?"

"Not really."

"Well, I think you need to do that, and soon. I mean, get his thinking on it. And maybe you guys could both talk to him. I don't know, sis; it's something to consider. What's the other thing?"

"The other concern is that he's been single for sixteen years. I don't quite know how to assess that. I could easily rationalize that he simply hasn't found anyone he truly loved."

"Yeah, right, uh—was he burned real bad his first time out? Do you think he's gun shy or something like that?"

"He wasn't burned. It's nothing like that. They were very young and just grew in different directions. He told me all about it."

"You'd have to think that a man like Morgan has had a lot of opportunities in sixteen years. Have you asked him, Clare?"

"He just says he's never found the right girl. And he said he's a man who doesn't have to have a woman."

"Clare, you need to take him at his word."

"Well, we can't go on dating forever with no closure. I mean, we could, but I wouldn't want to do that. I want a family."

"Clare, I think it will work itself out in due time. I wouldn't push it or give him an ultimatum or anything like that."

"Yeah, you're probably right. I don't think I need to be overly concerned about that, at least not yet."

"Clare, what is your idea of the perfect man?"

"You know, Morgan is witty, clever, and has a great sense of humor. As I grow older I'm coming to understand how important this is in a relationship. We laugh and cut up all the time. To answer your question, he has everything I'd ever want in a man except for one thing."

"He's not a Catholic."

"That's right."

"Sis, you can't lose this guy. You've just got to deal with the religion thing. I really think you should talk with Father Quigley. Look, Clare, there are a lot of relationships that drag on, and you never know where you are. He's everything you want except for one thing, and you know he loves you. It will all work out. I'm sure of it."

"April, I'm glad we talked about this. I feel better. Hey, did I tell you Morgan joined my musical group, the River City singers?"

" No, you didn't. That's neat."

"Yeah, we're having fun."

"Fill my glass, sis; this is excellent Merlot."

Chapter 25

Wednesday, September 13, 2000

"CLARE, I HAVE access to a place at Horseshoe Bay, and I thought we might spend the weekend up there. You could bring a canvass and your paints. I'll do some writing, and we'll just hang out and relax."

"I'm kind of stressed out, and that sounds simply wonderful. Oh, and Morgan, I get off at noon on Friday so that would be perfect."

"That's great. I would like you to meet my cousin and his wife in Marble Falls for dinner. He's an urologist, and she's a school counselor. They live in Baytown but they have a place at Blue Lake Estates on Lake LBJ. It's been in the family for 40 years, and we've all enjoyed it. They are meeting with a contractor on Saturday about some improvements to their place. They want to meet you, and this seemed like a good time to do it. And we can do some shopping beforehand. Marble Falls has really developed some neat shops. It should be fun. After dinner, we'll buy our groceries and head for Horseshoe Bay. It's close by. Does that sound like a plan?"

"It most certainly does. You always have a plan, don't you?"

"Yeah, I guess I do. Important stuff should not be left to chance."

○ ○ ○ ○ ○

"LET'S PARK HERE on Main Street. The Wild Stallion Grill is across the street there on the corner, and there are shops on both sides of the street. I think this is perfect," concluded Morgan.

"Wow, they have really made this area nice. I haven't been up this way in years. And the Wild Stallion, how long has it been there?" asked Clare.

"A couple of years I believe, but wait until you see the menu. There's nothing in Austin any better."

"Really! I can remember when they only had that one place. It was up there on main street, on your right, as you came into town."

Morgan laughed, "You're exactly right. Well, anyway, this isn't your father's Marble Falls. They are getting it together."

They shopped both sides of the street. "Okay, we've got forty-five minutes left. Let's go into Jessie's Fine Jewelry," said Morgan. The establishment was owned by a man and his wife, and their only daughter also helped out some after school and on Saturdays.

"Good afternoon, Mr. Mason. Is there anything special you all are looking for?" said Jessie.

"Looking, is the key word, Jessie," said Morgan. "I'd like you to meet Clare Casey. Clare, Jessie owns the place."

They exchanged pleasantries. "Now let me know if I can help you," said Jessie.

They didn't get any farther than a case full of rings with a wide assortment of round stones. The idea was that you could interchange the various stones to give the ring a different look depending on the occasion and attire. Clare was fascinated. She found an unusual gold mounting and began to play with the various stones, holding the ring out so she could get a better look. "Oh, Morgan, I'm having so much fun."

"I can tell."

Jessie walked by the glass case and offered a word. She wasn't pushy, but she was an experienced saleswoman. "Three stones come with the ring. You can pick any that you like. And, you can purchase any of the others. They're all for sale."

"Listen, Clare, we have to meet Herb and Anna in ten minutes. You're going to have to make a decision."

"A decision? I'm just playing!"

"Well, I'm not. I'm going to buy you the ring so pick out the stones you want, and let's pay out!"

"Oh, Morgan, are you sure?"

"I'm sure."

"Okay, then."

"Thanks, Jessie. We'll see you next time," said Morgan.

"Sure enough, Mr. Mason, come in every chance you get. It's nice to meet you, Clare."

"Same here , Jessie."

Clare admired her ring as she and Morgan crossed the street. As they entered The Wild Stallion, Herb and Anna were waiting, smiling broadly. "Dr. Hampton, I'd like you to meet Clare Casey."

"Clare, it's my pleasure."

"And this lovely lady is Anna, his long-suffering wife."

"Oh, Morgan!" said Anna, and gave Clare a hug.

"I am very glad to meet you. Morgan has been telling us about you."

"Dr. Hampton, party of four," announced the attractive hostess.

"We're all here," said Herb.

"Right this way, folks."

During dinner Herb told Clare about the family. Their grandmother, on their mother's side, had six girls and five boys. They remained close through the years. Strangely enough, most all the siblings and their children and grandchildren lived in Austin. The Hamptons were the only ones from out of town. Herb's father built the first hospital in Baytown and with his partner, established a renowned surgical practice. He explained that he and Morgan were the last children born in the family. They were just two years apart, more like brothers than cousins. Anna asked Clare about her family. She explained her work at the White House. There was talk of Morgan's books and Herb explained some of the most recent methods of treating prostate cancer.

"Herb," said Anna, "I don't think Clare is really interested in this subject. And besides, we're having dinner." And there was talk of politics, one of Herb and Morgan's favorite topics.

It was pleasant outside the restaurant. A nice cool breeze had sprung up while they were having dinner. "This has been great, you guys," offered Herb. "Let's do it again really soon."

"It has been nice," said Morgan.

"Yes, it has, and I'm so pleased to meet Morgan's favorite cousins," said Clare. There were hugs, and both couples went their separate ways.

Back in the Boxter, Clare commented, "They are really nice, Morgan, a lovely couple. And they are the first of your family that I have met."

"You know, that's true." He cranked up the engine, "We need to go grocery shopping."

Chapter 26

THEY TURNED ONTO the circular drive of an impressive Southwestern style house. Clare thought to herself, *Some little weekend getaway!* Morgan pulled the car under the impressive portico. On the front of it, hanging by two rings was a hand-carved sign that red, "Taos."

"Taos, like the town in New Mexico?" asked Clare.

"That's right. The owner built a house similar to what you'd see in that area and thought it was appropriate."

Clare noticed that a string of Sago palms lined each side of the entrance, with large pots full of flowers by the massive, hand-carved double doors. Clare thought they looked like they had once belonged to a fine Spanish hacienda. It made a spectacular first impression. "Baby, these doors…" She was noticeably impressed and wondered about them.

"There is this place in Taos, Doors Architectural Antiques. The office is in back, but this entire yard is full of these type doors and frames, every kind you can imagine. He found these and had them shipped." Morgan turned the key and extended his hand. Clare stepped inside. "Let me show you around, and then we'll unload the car."

It's huge, she thought, wide-eyed. There was an enormous fireplace across the room on the right with a massive coffee table in front. The fireplace was designed like a Kiva oven, with an extension that wrapped around it. There were built in benches on each side of it with colorful comfortable cushions and pillows to match. The walls around it were a mosaic on insets and irregular surfaces which the owner had decorated with pots, ceramics, nick-knacks and small paintings. It was surrounded by a large sofa on each side. It made for a most comfortable setting. There were windows, from floor to ceiling, all across the back of the living room which opened onto a deck.

On the left side of the room, opposite the fireplace, was a large almost commercial style kitchen. Every convenience was there as well as all the latest in design features. The bar featured six high-backed director's chairs. In front of the kitchen, toward the deck was a formal dinning table with a smoky glass top, set for ten with high back cane chairs. A massive, but creatively attractive, artificial flower arrangement was positioned in the center of an equally attractive table runner. To the left of the kitchen was a study but the doors were closed and they didn't go in. "Let's go down stairs," suggested Morgan. Clare was speechless over the magnificent accommodations.

In the downstairs lower level was an entertainment center with a large built in screen. A half-dozen square tan leather chairs were side by side in front of the screen. Behind the chairs was a custom made credenza with a slate top and doors on the opposite side. The owner could play DVDs and Morgan explained that the arrangement had a sound system, for radio and compact disks that could carry music to every room in the house, as well as the outside deck or to specific rooms or areas individually. There was also a game table and the room was attractively decorated, repeating the Southwestern motif. There were two bedrooms with their own baths and each bedroom opened onto the lower part of the deck by the boat stalls.

"Wow," declared Clare, "this is unbelievable!"

"Let's go upstairs," suggested Morgan.

At the top of the stairs was a Chase lounge under a skylight for reading. To the left was a library with a polished hard wood floor. Book shelves ran the length of the room on both sides. At the very back of the room was a comfortable looking rawhide-colored couch with track lights above for reading. An attractive coffee table was in front. There were two bedrooms, with their own separate bathrooms. By the lounge was a spiral staircase. Morgan looked at Clare with a broad grin on his face and suggested, "Let's go up another level."

At the very top was a circular room with a counter top work space, a computer with monitor and printer, a small refrigerator and coffee pot. A door led outside, guarded by a circular metal railing. It looked like a light house. "Nice view, don't you think?" said Morgan.

"Unbelievable, simply unbelievable!" said Clare.

"Let's go back down to the first floor. You haven't seen the master suite." As they entered, Clare could see how the two-way fireplace served both the bedroom and the living room. And it was the exact same look. Two large chaise lounge chairs sat invitingly in front with a table and lamp in between. The bed was king sized. Morgan led Clare into the area were there was a huge walk-in closet, a tub, shower, commode, bidet and lighted dressing area. Back in the bed room Clare was struck by a feature that she had never seen before; hand carved Southwestern style doors on the inside of the room to the right of the bed. This allowed clothes to be accessed from both sides of the closet. It was ascetically pleasing to the eye and functional. She loved the design.

"That's about it except for the study," said Morgan.

"I thought maybe it was locked," suggested Clare.

The entire house was attractively decorated, consistent with the overall Southwest theme. But one feature was particularly interesting, an almost excessive use of boxes. There were leather boxes, wooden boxes, metal boxes, plain boxes, carved boxes and painted boxes. Each arrangement had three to four of the same boxes in different sizes. They were attractive, but so many. "Your friend, the owner of this place, must have a fetish for boxes," Clare remarked.

"You think so?"

"Well, yeah."

The study was dark and Morgan turned on a single light that illuminated a picture behind the massive desk. It was an Indian warrior with a bronze colored chest. He had long black hair and beautiful features. He was very handsome. The figure, which was twice life size, depicted the man from just below his waist to above the head. It was mesmerizing.

"My God, Morgan, I have never seen anything like it. And the way it's hung and lighted, Well, it's just spectacular!"

"Yes, isn't it?"

"Where did it come from?"

"It was painted by an artist named Rory Wagner, a native of Taos, New Mexico. His work is on exhibit at the Wilder Nightingale Gallery in Taos."

"And it's huge!"

"Yes, it's actually 72 x 60 in size. It was purchased for this very spot and shipped here from Taos. It's the most magnificent painting I have ever seen. Clare, don't you get the feeling he is going to speak?"

"Of yes, yes I do, and those eyes. He looks like he's tearing up."

"Who is he, baby?"

"He is a Nez Perce man. They were a tribe indigenous to Washington, Idaho, and Oregon."

"Baby, this painting, it must have cost your friend a pretty penny?"

"Ah—walking around money."

"How much was it, do you know?" Clare pressed.

"Twenty-eight thousand."

"Oh, my God!" she exclaimed, shaking her head and then putting her face in her hands.

"It's only money," said Morgan, matter-of-factly.

She shook her head in disbelief.

Morgan turned on the other lights in the study. There was a matching credenza, more bookcases and more books. And more western art, really nice pieces. There were four polished wood pedestals, two on each side of the room. Standing prominently on top of the stands was a bronze longhorn steer, an Indian warrior on horseback with lance, a cowboy on horseback and a buffalo.

"Where did all this come from?" Clare inquired.

" Taos, Durango, Santa Fe, and Sedona, Arizona."

"Well, it's all magnificent."

As Clare examined the rest of the room she suddenly noticed pictures of Morgan: with celebrities, at book signings and the like. "Morgan! Morgan Mason! My God, this is your house!"

He paused momentarily before coming clean. "Yes, it's my place. I built it about three years ago. I kept my townhouse, though, because it's in a great location. It's in town, and it's the house I lived in when I hit it big in writing. I always want to remember where I came from, so to speak. But this is my pride and joy."

"Baby, I don't know whether to be mad at you or not."

"Look at it this way. A good writer will develop his characters, and his story, a bit at time. So why don't you just look at this little revelation in the same way?. I always want to have a few surprises for you so you'll stay interested. I don't want to get boring."

"Yeah, right!" said Clare.

She eased up close to him, touching her body to his. She ran her fingers through his hair and kissed him tenderly. "You do keep things interesting."

He smiled down at her, "I try to. Hey, you haven't seen the deck. Let's take a look before it gets dark."

The deck wrapped around the back of the house, at two levels, next to the water. A gazebo housed a bar and cooking area. It was well equipped for cooking, serving drinks and entertaining. The deck also had comfortable lounge chairs and a dinning area. There was a huge Kiva oven built against the house. It was used for cooking but was also a great spot for guests to sit around while having hot beverages in the fall and winter. "It's like the Navajo Indians used," Clair observed.

"Yeah, but a great deal better that theirs were."

"Well, sure," she acknowledged.

Flower pots ringed the outside of the deck, and large Plexiglas panels secured the perimeter without obscuring the view. A sail boat, an inboard ski boat, and two jet skis were housed at the lower level.

"Let's unload the car, and then we can play."

Chapter 27

ALTHOUGH NO ALARM was set, Morgan woke at seven o'clock, his usual time. He shaved showered and donned shorts, Mexican sandals and a tank top baring the name, Maui Surf Club. He went down to the media area and started several Sinatra CDs which he piped to the deck. Then he made coffee and a bowl of chopped cantaloupe and strawberries. He took them out to the deck along with a new book by Jack Higgins. He was sipping coffee and staring out at the lake when Clare appeared, rubbing the sleep out of her eyes.

"What time is it, baby?"

"Uh—eight thirty. Did you get your nap out?"

"Yes, I did, but why didn't you wake me?"

"Clare, that's silly. We don't watch the clock up here. I wanted you to sleep until you were ready to get up. You can't do that during the week. You have to be at work by eight o'clock, and you have that drive in from Round Rock."

"That's true," she confessed, stretching both arms above her head.

"Coffee?"

"Oh, but yes."

"Clare, do you like anklets?"

"I don't know, I never thought much about them. What on earth prompted you to ask?"

"Well, you don't see them very much, and I was struck by the fact that both the young hostesses at the restaurant last night were wearing them."

"Do you like them?" she questioned.

He perked up at the question. "Yes, as a matter of fact I do. I find them very sexy."

"Well, I guess that means I'll have to get one."

They laughed.

"Tell me, what else do you find sexy?"

Oh, Lord, what have I started? he thought to himself. "Clare, that's one of those loaded questions a man can't possibly win. But this time, I actually think I'm on firm footing. First off, French-braided black hair drives me wild. Then there's women with wet hair—in black evening wear—in dark baseball caps and tight, starched jeans. Oh, and I like brunette women in men's dress shirts, and nothing else."

Clare beamed. "For real, baby, you're not playing with my mind, are you?"

"Absolutely not. If I couldn't tell the truth, I'd have ducked the question...or just lied."

She approached him and pulled his head up against her body. She ran her fingers through his black curly mane. Then she bent down and kissed him passionately.

"So you find me sexy, do you?"

"You know I do."

"Clare, I've just picked at the fruit, really haven't eaten anything. We could have that or, how about me fixing us a big breakfast?"

"You know, I don't eat much breakfast at all during the week. I sleep until the last minute and really don't have time to fix it. A big breakfast would be a real treat."

Morgan proceeded to the gazebo and motioned for Clare to take a seat on one of the bar stools. Before he removed the cover from the cooking surface he fetched fresh squeezed orange juice and champagne from the fridge and fixed two mimosas. They talked and laughed while he fried eggs and sausage and did toast right on the hot griddle. There was also hot black coffee.

"Baby, this food is wonderful."

"Well, thank you. And it always tastes better when you're outdoors like this. Hey, want some picante sauce? And don't forget the fruit."

"I won't."

"Clare," Morgan inquired, "what did Marshall look like?"

"Why, you want to see how you compare?"

"Not really. You don't have to tell me. I was just curious."

"He was about your height but overweight and not athletic, and was beginning to get a belly. He had dark brown hair that was thinning on top. I suspect he will be bald some day. He was pretty nondescript, actually."

Morgan did not comment. Clair took a sip from her second mimosa, a big bite of sausage and completely changed the subject. "Baby, I was watching the travel channel the other night, and they had this show that featured the ten best beaches in Mexico. They looked great."

"They are great. Remember, I told you before that I've traveled extensively in Mexico. Was anything in Puerto Vallarta mentioned? Do you remember?"

"Yeah, they did. I don't remember the name of the beach, though."

"It's a great place; great hotels, great food, great shopping, great fishing, and great scuba diving. As a matter of fact, that's where I had my first dive, before I was certified. I got hooked. I dived for a few more years until I was in Hawaii one time and they told me that I couldn't do a deep-water boat dive unless I was certified. That really made me mad. I took the course as soon as I got back to Austin. Funny thing though, when I found out what I didn't know it kind of alarmed me."

"Why was that?"

"Because I did some risky things through ignorance, and I didn't know how to evaluate equipment or the dive shops, both of which are important."

"I like to dive, but I haven't been in a while. I'd love to go with you sometime; out of the States, of course."

"That can probably be arranged."

She smiled with satisfaction.

"The summer before we divorced, my wife, her brother, his wife, and I went to Puerto Vallarta. I always got a jeep for us the knock around in. We went to this place called Chino's Paradise, up in the mountains. I don't think we could have gotten there without the jeep. This place is built by a waterfall. The water comes down out of the mountains really fast, hits the rocks and levels off, then drops down into a pool and then runs off and on down the mountain."

"You mean, the water had two levels where it kind of pooled?"

"That's right. Anyway, they built tables, by a rail, alongside the waters edge all the way to the top. You kept climbing up these rock stairs until you reached the main seating area and a neat bar underneath a thatched roof. You got the picture?"

"Yeah."

"Anyway, they have great grilled seafood which they serve on large wooden plates. One of the really fun things to do was to get a cold cerveza and sit in the water at the upper level. You braced yourself against a rock to resist the current. The swirling water was cold and wonderful, and you just took in the warm sunshine and sipped your beer. Well, my idiot brother-in-law wanted to go up a ways and let the current carry him down to where it pooled at the top, where we were. I told him it was too dangerous. I was a considerably better swimmer than he was, and I wouldn't do it. But he was hard headed."

"What happened?"

"He went up there, and did it anyway. That current got him, and he couldn't do anything about it. It pulled him under and slammed him up against a big rock. He came up out of the water right in front of me. His face was red, and it looked like he was going to explode. He was obviously in pain, bad pain. I grabbed him under the arms and pulled him to me to keep him from going over the falls. He was gasping for breath, coughing and spitting water. After only a very few minutes I could tell he was in bad shape. He was in so much pain that I decided we needed to take him to a doctor. The bumpy ride down the mountain, over that rocky road, was pure hell for him. Every time I hit a bump he would scream. We finally got down into town and just started looking for a doctor's shingle. We found one, but the doctor wasn't there, and they suggested we go to a clinic which was on the other end of town, past the luxury hotels, on the way to the airport. Well, we eventually got there, but the only doctor on duty was busy. He finally got to see Clyde and decided he needed an x-ray. It took forever for them to come out and give us the results. Anyway, it showed he had broken ribs. He was really in pain.

"The doctor wrote out a prescription for pain medicine and taped up his side. We debated about what to do, but we finally decided to just stay there in Vallarta. You can't do more for broken ribs than they had done. We figured as long as he was going to convalesce, a resort on the Pacific was a pretty good place to do it. And my wife and I could go on and enjoy ourselves. We thought he could sit by the pool and drink tequila. Well, he finally got comfortable after he took the medicine. We didn't do much more that day. They went to bed early, and my wife and I had a nice dinner. The next morning we found out that he had had a very bad night. He finally had to get out of bed and sit in a chair and place his arms and head on a table in front of him. That was the only position that gave him any relief."

"This is beginning to sound like the vacation from hell," Clare suggested.

"You haven't heard the worst of it. Okay, I decided that we needed to take him back out to the clinic for more x-rays to see what was going on. He shouldn't have been in that much pain. Well, it was an ordeal getting him downstairs and into the jeep. Poor guy was in such pain—groaning all the time. The new x-rays showed that some of the rib slivers had punctured his lung. That's why he was in so much pain."

"The doctor said, 'We can't help him here. You need to fly him to St. Luke's in Houston.' They felt it was imperative that we get Clyde to Houston pronto. 'We'll call and alert them that you're coming.' We made all the arrangements, and Clyde and I boarded the flight. It had an intermediate stop in Guadalajara and then it was non-stop to Houston. The girls were to get our stuff together, turn in the jeep, check out, and follow as soon as they could. Now picture this, Clare; we are in shorts, T-shirts, and flip-flops. I was carrying Clyde's x-rays. When the plane descended for the landing in Guadalajara, the change in altitude gave him fits. It was very painful, and they had to hook him up to pure oxygen to get him any relief. The head stewardess explained the situation to the captain when we landed. The pilot said Clyde couldn't handle the altitude changes to Houston, and he wasn't going to be responsible for him."

Morgan had a strange expression on his face. "Clare, they kicked us off that airplane."

"No."

"Yes."

"And what was really bad was that the airline took no responsibility for helping us in Guadalajara. After much frustration, I finally found a nice lady who spoke English, and she told me of a Mexican-American Hospital. She said they had English-speaking doctors, were very well equipped, and that we should go there. I got Clyde in a cab and off we went. When we got to admitting they wanted a thousand dollars up front. He didn't have it, and neither did I."

"What did you do?"

"I assured them that I could get the money and finally talked them into admitting him to a room so he could get in bed."

"I bet he was exhausted?"

"Wiped out."

"What did you do then? What about the thousand dollars?"

"I had left most of my money with my wife. I thought I was going to be in Houston, not Guadalajara. So I got a cab and drove to the American Express office. Thank the Lord I was able to get the money with my credit card. That was a godsend. So I went back to the hospital and put down the deposit. I went to Clyde's room and found out he hadn't even seen the doctor. But he was resting pretty well, and, surprisingly, not in too much pain. I guess they had him pretty well medicated."

"Are you sure it wasn't tequila?"

Morgan laughed, "Well, I guess it could have been. Clyde was a pretty reluctant patient, but if they offered him Tequila, he would have taken it."

"By the time I finally got to call Puerto Vallarta, they had left for Houston. I called St. Luke's and left word. Then Clyde's wife had to get back on a plane and fly back to Guadalajara. My wife just came with her. We had to find a place to live that was cheap because they were going to be there a while. I worked that out, and we got settled. Clyde's doctor spoke very good English, and he seemed competent. He operated in a couple of days and took a pint of clotted blood out of the rib cage area. He had an awful incision. After the procedure, my wife and I flew back to Austin. We had to get back to work. Clyde's mother flew down to be with his wife. He was there awhile, about ten days I believe, before he could come back. They apparently cut some nerves during the procedure and the last I heard, he was still having discomfort. All of that pain, the operation, and the money—for one moment of poor judgment." Morgan shook his head.

"Well, enough of the Mexico adventure. Look, I'll clean all this. Why don't so do some painting?"

"Are you sure?"

"Yes, I am. Do you want me to set up your canvass out here on the deck? I think there are several interesting views, or I can drive you around and let you look from something you like better."

"No, no," said Clare, "I want to stay right here. I like this setting."

"I've decided not to write this weekend. I've got a new book to read, and I'm going to be right out here with my girl."

"Oh, baby, that's so sweet of you." She thought for a moment and then commented. "So writers read as well."

"Of course we do. We learn from each other. And I appreciate the art and skill of writing much more now. Before, I just took it all for granted."

"Baby, that room upstairs, I mean the tower?" Clare asked.

"Yeah, what about it?"

"You write up there don't you?"

Morgan smiled broadly, "Yes, yes I do."

The morning was bright and sunny and a gentle breeze took the edge off the sun. It was delightful. Clare fixed a light lunch of curried chicken salad. They ate and took a nap. Clare continued to paint and Morgan read. When it got cooler, they took the sail boat out. Clare had never sailed and she was giddy at the experience. He needed her to help and she was excited at every maneuver. Morgan grilled tilapia for dinner and Clare prepared a wonderful salad. The chilled champagne went well with the meal. It had been a lovely day.

As they finished cleaning up after dinner, Clare mentioned something to Morgan. "Baby, I don't have a picture of you. It just hit me."

"Well, we can remedy that. Come in the study." Morgan opened a desk drawer and pitched a large brown envelope on the desk. "There are lots of pictures in there. A lot of them were taken for book covers and various promotions and press releases. Help yourself. But I'll expect the same from you."

Clare smiled. "I'll take care of it when we get back to town."

Both Clare and Morgan liked table games and both were excellent players. As they were arranging the chess men in the proper position, Clare had an idea. "Baby, could we have some friends up for a weekend. God knows, we have the room."

"Sure thing; I love to entertain."

"Well, I was thinking about Angie and Frank, Cindy and Andy, and Jan and Mel. You haven't met the fellows yet, but Morgan, they are all really fine men. I know you would like them. Maybe you could arrange a golf game. You'd have a foursome."

"Let's look at our calendars when we get home and see if we can find a date," said Morgan.

"Oh, baby, this is exciting to me. I really appreciate it. I know we'll have a blast."

Morgan poured Clare a fresh glass of champagne and one for himself. "Let the games begin," declared Morgan.

Clare was wearing one of Morgan's long sleeved shirts with the sleeves rolled up. Her long raven black hair was in a pony tail. He thought to himself, *This young woman is a living doll.*

They played for two hours, without talking much. Chess was, after all, a serious game. Clare had made a move that had Morgan stymied. He squirmed, looked at the board and then at her. Her green eyes were dazzling. She smiled mischievously and reached over with her bare foot and began running it up and down his leg. He tried to concentrate on his next move, studied the board and then looked at Clare. She was slowly licking her lips. His eyes struggled downward. He messaged his eye brows and studied the position of all the chess men. He couldn't keep his eyes off of Clare. She was slowly running her index finger in and out of her mouth. He cleared his throat, studied the board and tried desperately to concentrate. He looked again at the exceptional young woman sitting across from him. She was running her index finger up and down slowly between her cleavage. Morgan pushed back his chair and slowly stood to his feet. He looked at Clare for a brief moment and then approached her. Leaning down, he gave her a long slow kiss, tasting her full luscious lips.

"Let's play something else!"

Chapter 28

Monday, September 25, 2000

CLARE USUALLY WENT to the mailbox shortly after arriving at home each evening. She began sorting through the envelopes, *Telephone bill, utility bill, MasterCard, junk, junk, junk.* Then there was another envelope; not a bill and definitely not junk mail. She opened it and observed the scene on the outside of the card; a man and a woman walking on the beach at dusk. She smiled and read what was printed inside.

> *Sometimes life hands you something so perfect it's hard to believe it could really be true. That's how I feel about us. That's how I feel about you.*

It was signed, *All my love. Morgan.*

"MESA FLOWERS, I'VE got a delivery for Clare Casey," the delivery boy announced. He knew Clare, since he had made a number of trips to her White House office. "Here are two vases. I've got to go back to my truck; there's more." He didn't know exactly what was going on with this delivery, but he suspected it was something special and he enjoyed it.

Clare put one vase of nine exquisite yellow roses on her desk and looked around for a suitable spot to put the other vase of nine elegant white ones. On the card he had written:

I just wanted to get your special day off to a good start. Happy birthday, darling. I'm looking forward to tonight. Love, Morgan.

The boy delivered the final vase of nine red roses.

The sales staff was buzzing and, curious. Cindy chimed in, "They're from Morgan, no doubt."

"Who else?" replied Clare, excitedly.

"There are twenty-seven roses. I counted. Does this have a special meaning?" asked Angie.

Jan made her own observation, "And the three different colors. Tell us what it means."

Clare grinned broadly, her arms outstretched with palms up. "Beats me, but I love it."

Curious about the commotion, his giggling sales staff and the three vases of roses, the White House general manager came out of his office, "Clare, what in the world is going on?"

"Billy, today is my birthday, and my boy friend sent me flowers. But if you want to know anything else, I'm afraid I won't be able to help you. I don't know myself what this is all about."

"It may be confusing but it's kind of wonderful. I wish Stan would confuse me like this. The big lug thinks flowers are a waste of good money," said Jan.

Clare sat down and held the last vase of nine roses in her lap; beamed and gazed at each emerging bud, then drew in their aroma. It was as if these were the first roses she'd ever received. She sighed, "This is so typical of Morgan. I never know what he's going to do. But of course, what he does is always wonderful." She paused a moment, smelled the roses again, and said, "I guess I'll find out tonight."

"Hey, I've got it, and this is so cool," said Cindy. "It's a rose for every year of your life."

"But there are only twenty-seven," said Angie." I counted them twice. Clare's twenty-eight today."

"I'm sure that's it, though. He's just miscounted. But it's so cool!" concluded Cindy.

Clare, still seated, smelled her roses and glanced, from time to time, at the other vases, "Morgan doesn't miscount. He intended to send twenty-seven. I'll tell you the answer tomorrow," she said.

The sales staff took Clare to lunch at the Macaroni Grill. They had all purchased small gifts and funny cards. There was an abundance of giggles and laughter, talk of men, and romance and expectations. She enjoyed the occasion and tried to be attentive to her thoughtful friends. She would celebrate with her family on Sunday but tonight it was all about Morgan. Her thoughts were of him and other surprises that might be awaiting her. He always made things interesting.

Chapter 29

THE BOXTER STOPPED at the light at the corner of Steck and the Frontage Road along side Mopac expressway. A young man, who looked to be in his middle twenties, was working the cars. He had on a stocking cap, and sported a full mustache and beard. His ill fitting sweater was tattered and stained. His baggy pants were torn and dirty, and dragged along the ground as he walked. He wore high topped black tennis shoes without socks. He was repulsively filthy and looked like he hadn't washed in weeks. He was holding a sign which read, "Homeless-hungry-please help! God bless."

"Oh Morgan," said Clare compassionately, "I want to give him something."

"I'll take care of it," said Morgan. When the man noticed Morgan's power window coming down he approached the car in anticipation.

"Why don't you get a job, you big ,fat, tub of guts? Better yet, join the army!" screamed Morgan, angrily.

The startled man stopped dead in his tracks.

"Morgan, I can't believe you. I am shocked at your lack of sensitivity to the needs of others less fortunate."

Ignoring Clare's caustic admonition, he continued to jaw at the man. "The Army will tighten up that lard ass of yours, and you'll get a roof over your head and three square meals a day. Then you won't be homeless or hungry."

The young man turned red; he was fuming. He started to say something, but Morgan instantly reacted and opened his door as if he was going after him. The man quickly retreated to the grassy area next to the road as the light turned green and the Boxter sped away.

"Baby, I can't believe you did that. Would you have hit that poor man?"

"Nah, I just wanted to mess with him. But I meant everything I said, and it's people like you who encourage these bums to continue begging and shaking down the public instead of getting real work. Understand — this is a racket. They coordinate their activities; alternate the corners they work at. I'll bet they pick up a nice piece of change by the end of the day. And I'll bet they all live in a nice apartment in the area."

"Oh, Morgan, that's crazy. You're just prejudiced. I feel sorry for them."

"Did you get a good look at that character? I'll bet he weighed 260 pounds. I mean, really, Clare, does he look like he's been going without food? And if you notice, they always have a big dog and plenty of cigarettes. They seem to always have money for that. And I'll tell you another thing; this community is as giving as any place I know of. We have a huge social-services network. There is no reason for this kind of thing. But here's the thing that really pushes my button. I just don't buy that they are needy. They choose to live that way, and I'm not going to help them."

Clare crossed her arms, slumped in her seat, and stared straight ahead in silence. Morgan soon tired of her little pout and said, "Clare, this is a special evening. It would be a real shame to let something like this ruin it."

Chapter 30

THE ELEVATOR OPENED at the 21st floor of the Bank One building. A left turn and a few steps placed them in the foyer of the Headliner's Club. The maitre d', Fernando Casanova, was beaming. "Mr. Mason, it is so nice to have you and the lovely lady with us this evening. And we're honored that you've chosen our club for such an important occasion." He kissed Clare's hand.

"Would you care for a cocktail before dinner?" asked Fernando.

Morgan glanced at Clare, and she nodded her approval. "Yes, we would, Fernando."

They were seated in the lounge and the waiter took their order. Clare was still upset over the incident with the homeless man, but as Morgan suggested, it would be a shame to let that spoil the evening. She was determined to put the whole thing behind her, for the time being, time to enjoy the evening with her guy. She recounted her day, especially the roses.

"Baby, I'm curious as to the number and color of the flowers. In fact, Mason, you've got the entire sales staff whacked out."

"In due time, my darling, all in due time."

"Morgan," she lamented, "you're always doing this to me."

"You want me to stop?"

"Oh, no." Clare assured him. "My girl friends are so envious of me. They're all married, but I can tell that their husbands are not very thoughtful or creative—or romantic. Sometimes I think they are living vicariously through me."

Morgan shrugged. "That's a shame. Women should be tended to like a fine English garden. I rather enjoy the work."

Clare leaned over toward Morgan and motioned him forward. She gave him a little kiss. "Baby, I appreciate you so much. I hope I have always shown my appreciation."

"You have," Morgan assured her. "But remember what I told you a long time ago. I expect nothing from you. I do what I do and get pleasure from it."

"You're something," she said, and patted his hand.

Fernando asked, "Will you have another, or shall I show you to your table?"

Morgan looked to Clare.

"I'm hungry, baby."

"Fernando, the lady has spoken."

As they approached their table for two by the windows, Clare spotted a long stem red rose lying across her plate. A card rested under it. She smiled broadly as Fernando seated her. She immediately opened the card and read what Morgan had written:

This single red rose is meant as a tribute to your extraordinary beauty. The red signifies my heart, which belongs to you. And this rose is number twenty-eight, one for each year of your precious life. Happy birthday, my darling, Clare.
Morgan.

Clare clutched the card and crumpled it slightly as her emotions ran the gamut. She reached across the table and squeezed his hand. "I am speechless so much of the time when I'm with you. The things you do and say—I don't..."

Morgan smiled warmly and interrupted, "I love you very much."

Clare began to cry.

"You can't cry, it's against the house rules."

Clare finally got control. "You know, Cindy figured it out, sort of. But it was only twenty-seven, and that threw her off. Then someone thought you just miscounted. I assured them that you had done no such thing. It was fun; I loved it, but what about the different colors?"

"Well, there were so many beautiful colors it just seemed like a shame to pick only one. So I sent three."

Clare just shook her head and smiled broadly.

Their waiter appeared and took their dinner order, refilled their glasses with the essence of a fine Merlot, and said, "I'll have your soup out right away."

Smiling broadly, Morgan extracted a small, neatly wrapped box from his coat pocket and placed it in front of Clare. "This is also for you."

Clare looked surprised, stared at the box and back at Morgan as if she wasn't sure what to do. "You can open it, Clare. It really is for you."

She quickly tore off the shiny silver wrapping paper and opened it. Delicately nestled in white cotton, like a babe in a crib, was a beautifully crafted gold cross on a delicate gold chain. "Oh, baby, how exquisite, I'm very moved." She just stared at it for a moment and then said, "Morgan Mason, you make me very happy. And I want to wear it now. Would you help me with it please?"

Morgan obliged. "Clare, it looks great on you. I just thought my good Catholic girl should have a really nice cross to wear."

She felt of it and sighed, "I will cherish it always."

Three men with violins, who approached at Morgan's cue, played *Our Love Is Hear to Stay,* to Clare's delight. When the music finally ended, they continued their ever engaging conversation. They felt more and more a part of each other's lives. There was nothing off limits in their conversation, everything was on the table and nothing was uncomfortable. However, Clare still struggled with one subject, religion, and Morgan's relationship with the Catholic Church in particular.

Their waiter was reluctant to interrupt, but Fernando gave him the go-ahead. "Are you folks ready for dessert?"

Clare clasped her hands, "Oh, yes, may we see the dessert menu?"

The waiter looked at Morgan. He needed some direction. "Clare, I have already taken care of that."

She grinned, laid down the menu and leaned back in her chair, "Well, bring it on."

In no time at all a line of waiters in black ties, white jackets and white gloves moved toward their table. The man in the lead held up a beautiful cake. It had a few candles to signify the occasion. Clare clapped her hands in delight as they sat it down in front of her. *Happy Birthday Clair,* was artfully inscribed in an eatable substance across the top.

Clare had not seen Fernando approach but noticed when he began to sing Happy Birthday in his deep base, Argentine voice. It was wonderful and Clare continued to clap with delight. She happily blew out the candles and Fernando personally cut and served the Italian Cream cake, her favorite. Clare and Morgan had coffee and later, an after dinner drink. They thanked Fernando and the staff for a wonderful evening and left for dancing at the Hilton on Town Lake.

As the Boxter headed north toward Clare's place, she thought to herself, *What a wonderful day it had been. My first birthday with Morgan.* She quietly hoped that by this time next year, she would be Mrs. Morgan Mason. The thought of it gave her great joy and it showed on her face. But she would not mention it tonight. But sooner or later, she concluded, they must discuss it—seriously. And they need to deal with the religious issue as well.

Chapter 31

THE FOLLOWING SATURDAY night, Clare and Morgan attended the Texas vs. Texas Tech football game in Austin at Darrell K. Royal Texas Memorial Stadium. The Longhorns looked formidable in a 42-7 pasting of the Red Raiders. They had met friends for barbeque at a Longhorn Foundation pre-game event and had gone to an after game party at the home of Jan and Stan Jenkins. It had been another nice day. Morgan pulled up in front of Clare's Round Rock duplex at fifteen before midnight.

"Baby, will you go to church with me in the morning?" Clare asked.

"Oh, I don't think so, Clare. Why don't you call me when it's over, and I'll take you out for brunch."

"I'd really like you to go," insisted Clare.

"You're wearing me out with this Catholic thing, do you know that? I mean, you can be a real pain in the ass sometimes. Really, Clare, do we have to have this conversation every time we're together?"

"No, we don't," Clare said curtly. Her face was red, and she was hyperventilating. She was mad, really angered. He had never seen her like this. Morgan had really set her off.

"In fact, we don't ever have to have this conversation again! You don't seem to understand how important my church is to me. Or maybe you do, and you just don't care. If you don't want to be a part of everything in my life, then maybe you shouldn't be a part of any of it." With that declaration, Clare opened the door and got out. She slammed the door with all her might.

Morgan was taken aback. He sat there stunned. Clare stormed off and never looked back. She disappeared inside her duplex. A light went on and then quickly off. Morgan thought it was symbolic of something larger. It was — and Clare meant it to be.

Chapter 32

Saturday, October 28, 2000

EACH MEMBER OF the White House sales staff worked one weekend each month as the manager on duty. On Saturday Clare closed the office for the day and proceeded to the front desk. She asked the clerk for a favor. "Call this number. If a man answers, just say you have the wrong number."

"I'm sorry, I must have dialed the wrong number." Clare smiled and thanked the clerk. She hurried to her car and was soon underway. *When you're in a hurry, you invariably hit every light, and traffic seems to be at a standstill,* she thought to herself. *This is one of those occasions.* Her heart was beating faster as she turned onto the street, and a little faster as she turned into the drive that would take her to the rear of Morgan Mason's townhouse. As the garage door opened, she pulled in beside the Boxter. She checked her lipstick, and her teeth, in the rear view mirror. She thought it a bit strange that Morgan had never asked her to return the key and garage door opener.

As she turned the key in the back door, she could hear Bogart barking. As the door opened she saw Morgan sitting on the floor. He and Bogart were playing ball. She had seen it so many times. Morgan would throw the red and green ball to the front of the house. Bogart would chase it and skid as he hit the tile by the front entrance. He would bounce off the wall, grab the ball in his mouth, and scurry back to Morgan. But he wouldn't give up the ball. Morgan would tug at it and Bogart would growl. Then Morgan would ignore him and he would drop the ball and paw at his master. It was all part of the game. Then it was time to do it all over again.

When Bogart saw Clare he dropped the ball and made a beeline to greet her. He began to jump up on her legs, eager to be picked up. She cuddled the little man as he gently licked her ear. "Well, at least one of the boys around here is glad to see me."

Morgan leaned against the refrigerator, and smiled broadly. *This was a good sign,* she thought to herself. Frankly, she wasn't sure what the reception would be. They hadn't seen or talked to each other in over a month. *Pride, stupid pride,* she thought to herself.

"Well, what brings you to our humble cottage this fine evening?" asked Morgan. "Aren't you that girl Clare, the one from the hotel?"

Grinning, Clare put Bogart down and approached Morgan. She playfully pushed him down on the carpet and sat on his stomach. He grunted as if he was in great pain. "Oh, that didn't hurt you, you big sissy." They laughed. Clare placed her fingers between his and pinned him against the floor. Then she bent down and kissed him tenderly, as her body tingled with anticipation. He pulled her down and kissed her passionately, skillfully using his tongue, as he had done so many wonderful times before.

Clare stared at Morgan. Her face suddenly portrayed the sadness that she felt inside. "I don't know how many times I picked up the telephone. I can't sleep, I can't work, and I'm a wreck!"

"I drove over to your hotel on several occasions but never got out of the car. I can't write; I lost my appetite. I don't sing anymore!" Morgan responded.

They kissed for a long time. Bogart's tail was wagging his approval, his little head in one position and then another, drinking it all in. Finally, he started barking and they began to laugh. Bogart jumped in and started licking Clare and Morgan on the face. They both rolled over on their backs and began to laugh. Finally Morgan rose to one elbow and looked longingly into the eyes of this exceptionally beautiful woman. He reached for her hand and asked, "What time is mass?"

Chapter 33

November 2, 2000

"DO YOU REMEMBER when we were driving to the Headliners' Club for your birthday, and we saw that fat boy begging at the corner on the frontage road?" asked Morgan.

"Yes, I remember that situation quite clearly," said Clare, sternly.

"Well, you remember my theory that they are organized?"

"Yes, I remember!"

"Well, today I stopped at that light and saw a well-dressed man talking to that fat boy under a tree. He seemed to be giving the kid instructions, and the boy was all ears. Then I saw the fellow leave, cross the street and disappear into Luby's Cafeteria parking lot. I guarantee you that man is controlling those beggars. I'll bet you anything he puts them up and gets a percentage of what they get from sympathetic citizens like you."

"Morgan, are you trying to pick a fight?" asked Clare, squirming in her chair.

"Oh, not really, I just wanted to share my evidence about these poverty pimps."

"Give it a rest, will you, please?" she snapped. She was in no mood for his devilish banter.

"Incidentally, Morgan, I'm going to start volunteering occasionally at the River City Homeless Shelter. I've talked with the project manager about it," said Clare, making sure she got in the last word.

○ ○ ○ ○ ○

"CLARE, I'D LIKE to run out to Las Vegas. I've got this itch, you know, and it needs to be scratched."

"Yeah, you and you're itches. Well, were you planning on taking me or one of the boys?"

"I was actually thinking of you, my darling."

"I must say, I'm relieved, but remember, baby, there's April's wedding."

"April's wedding. When is that exactly?" Morgan asked playfully.

"It's November 10."

"Darling, I'm aware of April's wedding. How could I forget? That's all you and your mother are talking about these days."

"That's not nice," she lamented, smiling.

"Just kidding. I was thinking maybe the weekend after the wedding. That would be November 17, a Friday, if you can get away. What it would be is a Friday through Sunday. We'd fly out of Austin on a Friday morning and come back on Sunday afternoon. Do you think you could squeeze out a Friday?"

"Actually, I have some time coming, and I like to take a day here and there. I could swing it. I'll put in for the 17th right away. Jan likes to know a little ahead of time. Would you believe I've never been to Las Vegas?"

"Really? Well, I've been going for twenty years. I know my way around pretty well. I'm pretty confident I could show you a good time."

"Good. I'll expect your very best effort."

o o o o o

THE GROOMSMEN WERE laughing and cutting up while the nervous groom was pacing and ringing his hands. He had been to the bathroom a couple of times. "Ken, are you sure you're up to this?" asked Morgan playfully.

"You did this one time, didn't you Morgan?" Ken asked.

"Yeah, in another life."

"Weren't you nervous?"

"I was a little nervous, as I remember. But you're beyond nervous. You may need to be medicated." The others laughed.

"Gentlemen, it's time to go in," advised Father Quigley. "Ken, are you ready for the old ball and chain?"

"Well, Father, I guess I'm as ready as I'll ever be," he replied, looking pale. Father Quigley led the fellows in and took his place.

Ken doesn't look so good, Marge Brown thought to herself. *He looks pale. Oh well.*

The bridesmaids, in pale lavender dresses and hats, made their way down the center aisle and took their places. As maid of honor, Clare was the last to enter. Morgan winked at her as she reached the front of the church and she smiled warmly after reading his lips, *You look fantastic.*

April, with Burt on one side and Arch on the other, appeared at the rear of St. Jude's Catholic Church and Father Quigley signaled the guests to stand as the Wedding March began.

For some reason, when the arrangements were being made, Ken didn't want Arch Casey to help give April away. It didn't make a lot of sense and Ken couldn't come up with a good reason. It wouldn't have mattered anyway. April told him, "It's my family; I love them both and both of them are giving me away. That's it, Ken; end of discussion."

"Who gives this woman?" asked Father Quigley.

"We do," answered Burt. "And her mother," Arch replied.

Each man gave April a kiss on the cheek and then joined her hand with Ken's. Clare was impervious to the words of the ceremony. She could only think of when Burt and Arch would be giving her to Morgan Mason and how wonderful that moment would be. It was not until Father Quigley announced, "May I present Mr. and Mrs. Kenneth J. Collins," that Clare regained her composure and concentration.

WHITE-GLOVED WAITERS served champagne from shiny silver trays to the 200 guests who crowded into the main dinning room area on the 21st floor of the Headliners' Club. Morgan had offered the club for the reception and Ken and April had eagerly accepted. Morgan paid for the reception as a wedding present. The room's L-shaped configuration was decorated beautifully and included an installed portable dance floor by the windows in the corner of the two adjoining rooms. Food stations were appropriately placed around the area.

Morgan and Clare were sipping champagne and standing near the bandstand. "April looks beautiful, don't you think?" Clare observed.

"Yes, she certainly does, but she's not in your class."

"Oh, come on, Morgan; April had to beat the boys off with a stick. She's actually rather gorgeous." Clare paused for his reaction but got nothing. She pressed the point. "So, you really think I'm more beautiful than my sister? You really think so?"

"Most definitely."

Clare squeezed his hand, gave him a kiss on the cheek and said, "Well, you're a keen judge of women."

Arch Casey walked up and said, "Morgan, this is a wonderful place, your club, and I want you to know how very appreciative we all are for your generosity."

"Col. Casey, I'm happy to be able to do it. And I'm pleased that this occasion has finally given me the opportunity to meet you."

"Please, call me Arch."

"Okay, but you've gone through a lot to get those birds on your shoulder, and it's important that you're given the respect you deserve."

"Well, you're nice to say that, but I'd still like you to call me Arch."

"Very well, Arch, if you say so."

"Arch, I want to thank you for your part in raising this girl. She tells me that she and April were never involved in a tug-of-war between parents. She says she always felt loved by each of you. That's not always the case, and it can really mess up young children and can carry over to adulthood and cause real problems."

"Well, thank you, Morgan. We always put the girls first, and were always civil to each other. Actually, it wasn't an acrimonious divorce. Marge grew weary of military life, always on the move—new housing, new friends, new schools. I could understand that."

"Well, anyway, you guys did well by your girls."

"Waiter," Morgan called, holding up his empty glass. "We need a refill all around."

"Burt and Marge are enjoying this," Arch remarked. "Just look at them."

"Yeah, it's almost like they're the ones who got married."

After Burt, Arch and Ken's father offered toasts to the bride and groom, the combo began to play soft dance music. Burt led off by dancing with April and Arch was next. Everyone clapped. Later on, April and Ken cut the cake and there were lots of pictures. The reception was coming to and end and when April tossed her bouquet, she made sure Clare would catch it. Everyone cheered. Many at the reception knew that Clare and Morgan were a serious couple but no one put them on the spot by asking when they would tie the knot.

"They'll love San Juan," said Morgan. "Puerto Rico is terrific spot for a honeymoon. It's got everything."

"A nice honeymoon is important. It's a special time," said Clare.

"I agree." Morgan thought for a moment. "I hope this takes. The divorce rate is awfully high. You and I can attest to that."

Clare didn't respond but the remark set off a hailstorm of negative thoughts and emotions. She and Morgan had not discussed marriage and she knew they must, but not today. There would be a time, perhaps very soon.

Chapter 34

Thursday, November16, 2000

"SWEETHEART, WOULD YOU fill my coffee cup and then come over here? I want to give you a blackjack lesson," said Morgan, repeatedly shuffling the cards.

"Okay, I'm ready for my lesson, professor."

"Let me start by giving you some fundamental knowledge of the game, its important principles to remember. As we play, I will point these out again so you'll understand what I mean. Generally speaking, the odds are with the house; meaning they win, and the players lose."

"Then why do people play?" Clare inquired.

Morgan laughed. "It's exciting to try and beat the odds. And then there's the stupidity factor. I only play blackjack because I think the odds are pretty good for the player, provided you play smart and with discipline. I'll explain as we play. Another name for the games is 21. That's because a perfect hand equals 21 points. But your goal is not to make 21, and you'll want to remember that. Your goal is to beat the house, beat the dealer's hand. Let me show you."

It all became clearer as they played hand after hand. "Clare smiled and clasped her hands. "I like this."

"Now, here's a house rule that is very beneficial to the players. The dealer must stand on 17 and hit on 16."

Clare pondered the dynamic of that. After a few minutes he explained.

Morgan continued to deal the cards, and they discussed each combination, what it meant, and what should be done in each situation. He also explained how to double-down, about splitting cards, and other ways to enhance the bet when the odds are in favor of the player. They continued for a couple of hours, and then Morgan suggested, "Why don't we knock it off for tonight? But we'll practice more before we leave. I think you're beginning to get it. You're a pretty quick study."

"Well, really, who wants to be just another pretty face?"

○ ○ ○ ○ ○

AT THE END of the Jet-way, a half-dozen men were holding signs. They were dispatched by fine hotels to collect high rollers who, for the amenities, were expected to gamble large sums of money at their casinos. Morgan was one of them.

Clare and Morgan approached a shaggy haired blond kid hoping his client was on time and that he'd find him without difficulty. "I'm Mason."

Showing his relief at the successful connection, he smiled and shook hands with Morgan. "Welcome to Las Vegas, Mr. Mason. I'm Leo from the Mirage, and I'll be taking you to the hotel."

"Leo, this beautiful lady is Clare Casey."

Obviously impressed, his demeanor gave him away, he shook her hand, "Very nice to meet you…ugh…Miss."

Easing his mind she graciously replied, "You can call me Clare."

"Thank you, Clare. If you guys will just follow me we'll collect your bags and get you to the hotel. May I have you claim tickets, Mr. Mason?"

As Leo started to walk away, Morgan hollered, "It's Southwest flight 234 from Austin."

"Oh yeah, right; meet you at the baggage-claim area."

"BABY, THE STRIP is very impressive."

"Just wait until you see it at night. There isn't more glitz or neon anywhere in the world."

As they approached the Mirage, Clare inquired, "What's that in front of the hotel?"

"Oh, that's the volcano. It erupts every thirty minutes in the evening. I think I'm right about that. We'll ask at the front desk. Anyway, it's quite spectacular."

Leo opened the limousine door and told Morgan, "You guys go on in and claim your rooms. Ask for the front desk manager. They are expecting you. Your bags will be right in. Oh, and Mr. Mason, when you want me just call the bell desk. It would be helpful, though, if you could give us some lead time."

"We can do that. Thank you, Leo," Morgan handed him a twenty-dollar tip.

They paused once they had passes the double doors. Morgan wanted Clare to get a good look at the impressive front entrance; an extraordinary lush rainforest housed under a 100-foot-high dome with a variety of trees, some reaching 60 feet tall. A cascading waterfall meandered through the forest which also included tropical flowers. Guests gained access to the main hotel and casino over an arched wooden bridge.

"What do you think?" asked Morgan, solicitously.

"Wow, that's really something."

"It requires six full-time gardeners over 240 hours a week to keep this area like you see it now." They continued to admire the indoor tropical creation until Morgan said, "Come over here. I want you to see the registration area."

"Oh, my soul!" exclaimed Clare. Set into the wall was an enormous aquarium that ran the full length of the service area; 50-60 feet. Infinite varieties of fish swam nonchalantly as if they were in the ocean.

"Sharks," exclaimed Clare, "there are sharks in there, and some of them are pretty large."

"It's quite spectacular, isn't it?"

"Oh, yeah."

"Mr. Mason," shouted the front desk manager, "Did you just arrive?"

"Yes, we did, Conrad; we've been here five or ten minutes."

"Your suite is ready. Why don't you go on up, and I'll have your bags delivered right away."

"Fine, we'll do that. Conrad, this is Clare Casey."

"It's very nice to meet you. I trust your stay will be satisfactory. As Mr. Mason can attest, we try very hard to meet the unusually high expectations of our preferred clientele. But Mr. Mason is one of our favorites. He is gracious and never complains about anything."

Clare looked at Morgan and smiled, "Yep, that's my Morgan. He's a good citizen."

Conrad handed Morgan two plastic key-cards to his suite.

"Conrad, were on our way."

"Let me know if I can do anything at all."

"I'm not bashful," Morgan replied.

A special elevator key was required for guests that were accommodated in the exclusive Mirage tower. Security guards checked all persons who entered the tower elevator area. As they stepped into the marble entry, Clare was immediately struck by the opulence of the penthouse suite—handcrafted furnishings, imported silks, exotic carpets, and polished marble. Morgan allowed her to explore on her own. He enjoyed just watching her. Every now and then she would audibly exhibit her excitement.

Morgan opened the door to frenzied Mirage employees, scurrying in with fresh flowers, fruit and cheese baskets, fresh strawberries and champagne.

On her tour of the suite Clare discovered two king-sized bedrooms, a separate living area, separate dinning area, wet bar, an elegant parlor, two bathrooms and a spectacular view of the city.

"Clare," summoned Morgan. "Come in here, darling."

"He handed her a glass of sparkling champagne and pointed out the strawberries, which also came with a choice of chocolate or powered sugar for dipping. She took a sip of the bubbly. "I appreciate all this, baby, but it must be costing you a small fortune. You don't have to do all this. As long as I'm with you, that's all that matters."

Morgan gave Clare a hug and explained, "It's all on the house, my darling. It doesn't cost me anything."

Clare was speechless. She didn't understand.

"Clare, I have a $100,000 line of credit here at the Mirage. That means I don't even use my own money when I play. They have checked with my bank and know that they will cover my losses, if necessary, up to that amount. When I check in they give me a special identity card. A lot of the dealers and pit bosses know me. But it's business, so I give the card to the dealer and he gives it to the pit boss. So they know my credit limit. I ask for so much money in chips, and they give it to me. Then they create a marker for me which shows how much money they have extended me. We settle up at the end of my stay, or they draft on my bank, whatever I want."

Clare listened intently to the explanation.

"It's not particularly how much I lose but how much I play for. Anyway, for people like me, everything is free. They pay for the plane fare, the limo, this suite, and all the food and drinks I consume at the Mirage."

"Wow, that's pretty neat. But if we go to another casino and have drinks and dinner, you would be responsible for that."

"That's right."

"I like it," Morgan admitted with a grin, "but that's not all. We also get priority seating at the shows, and that's also complementary. You see, it's all about gambling. That's where they make their money. It's worth it to them to provide all this to get people like me to the tables. And I'm small potatoes. Some players wager in the millions—and lose in the millions. Most of the big money is wagered at the crap tables or at Baccarat. I'll show you tonight."

"Do you lose a lot of money?"

"I only play blackjack, as you know, and I'm very good at it. Of course I lose on occasions. Everyone does. But I can honestly say that in some twenty years of gambling in this town, I'm at least even. And it's great entertainment.

"I didn't book a show for tonight. I want to have a nice dinner, show you the strip, and play blackjack! Let's go down to the lobby and check out the dinning opportunities. The restaurants are all spectacular, but the look of them is equally impressive and oftentimes influences the decision."

"Okay!" Clare exclaimed. She jumped to her feet and took Morgan's hand. "I'm very excited."

"I know, and so am I."

In the casino area Morgan and Clare began the restaurant tour. "Okay, this first little gem is Moongate. Don't you like the look of it?"

"Absolutely, I love it."

"Clare, I've eaten at every place in the hotel. They are all wonderful. It's sort of about what you're hungry for at the moment. Moongate serves the classic Szechwan and Cantonese dishes of China. One of their specialties is a platter of deep-fried prawns, egg roll, barbecued pork ribs, and crab Rangoon.

"Here is Onda, which features Italian and American cuisine in an elegant contemporary setting.

"Okay, this next place is Samba, a Brazilian steakhouse. They feature Brazilian-style barbecue, marinated meats, poultry, and seafood."

"Oh, Lord, it does become a bit overwhelming, doesn't it?"

"Yes, it really does, and there are so many."

"This one is Mikado. It was designed to suggest the quiet elegance of a fine Japanese home. They have a sushi bar, and they serve traditional dishes."

"Well, I guess the good news is that you can't go wrong with any of them."

"This is true. Okay, that brings us to Kokomo's. I love the setting here because it's reminds me of Hawaii, and you get the feeling you are dinning outside in a tropical rainforest. They have steaks, chops, fresh seafood, and lobster from Maine, Australia and South Africa."

"And last, but certainly not least, is the fabulous Renoir. It's French and it's elegant—decorated with original works of art. They have an award-winning chef and do contemporary cuisine. It's class, personified."

"So what do you think?" Morgan asked.

"Like you said, you probably couldn't go wrong with any of them. But I think I'd like Kokomo's tonight. The atmosphere and food sound perfect."

Morgan grinned. That would have been his choice, but he wanted her to decide. "Okay, what time do you prefer?

"Well, we had that snack in the suite. We could skip lunch, unless you are hungry, and eat an early dinner, say six o'clock."

"Clare, my love, I couldn't agree with you more. Let's walk back over there and give them our names."

○ ○ ○ ○ ○

"BABY, THAT WAS a fabulous dinner, and I loved the atmosphere."

"Well, I'm pleased. Leo, I want you to take us from one end on the strip to the other and start out in the direction of the Tropicana, whatever direction that is. We want to actually go in the Tropicana, Luxar, and the MGM Grand. Then drive the outskirts of the area and then take us down town. I want Clare to get a feel for Las Vegas and to enjoy the neon."

"Yes, sir, I can do that."

"Baby, I see what you mean. These properties have spent millions on their signs and everything. It's like each hotel is trying to outdo the other."

"And you're going to find that the inside of these properties is equally spectacular. I've never seen anything like it."

"THAT WAS A great tour, Leo."

"It really was," Clare concurred. "I have a pretty good perspective on everything now."

"Now drop us at the Bellagio," said Morgan. "Pick us up about ten."

"I'll be here," said Leo.

Morgan and Clare headed for Olives, a restaurant which featured an outdoor area for dinning and drinks and a first hand view of the huge manmade lake and its dancing fountains. Morgan smiled at the hostess and slipped her a fifty dollar bill, "Two please, and do you have any open tables outside?"

"Let me check."

Quickly returning with good news, she led Clare and Morgan to a nice table for two. They ordered champagne cocktails, and chocolate soufflés to be followed by piping-hot black coffee. "I expect our desserts to be really first class," said Morgan. "Bellagio has a French pastry chef — one of the best in the world. I am told he produces over 20,000 desserts every day."

"No kidding," said Clare.

"Yeah, that's one of the great things about Vegas. They spare no expense to attract and please the people who come here."

"But it's still about the gambling, right?"

"That's right." Another culinary moment hit Morgan. "Clare, there is a restaurant here at Bellagio called Circo. They feature Tuscan cuisine. I thought that might interest you."

"Are you kidding?" said Clare.

"Look, Clare, they're starting up the fountains. I'm told that some of the water will shoot to a height of 60 feet."

"Well, I've seen it all now," declared Clare, "water dancing to a ballad by Frank Sinatra."

"Watch out, we're getting some of it over here," cautioned Morgan.

○ ○ ○ ○ ○

"SLOW DOWN, LEO, I want Clare to see the sea battle."

"What is it, baby?"

"Up ahead is one of the main attractions on the strip. It's part of the Treasure Island Resort Hotel and Casino. In front of the hotel is this manmade body of water they call Buccaneer Bay. The pirates are in port. Then an English naval vessel approaches, and a battle breaks out. The pirates sink her, right before your very eyes. Look, Clare, it's started."

AS THEY ARRIVED at the Mirage, the volcano began to erupt. "We'll jump out here, Leo. Thanks a million, and we'll see you tomorrow."

"Oh, my God, baby, that is really something!" Clare was beside herself. "There is really nothing like this place, is there?"

"Well, it's pretty special."

They entered the Mirage, and Clare followed Morgan as he searched for an open blackjack table. The casino was crowded so they stood behind the players until two of them left. Morgan and Clare quickly took the two empty chairs. The dealer was a man named Mickey from Sedona, Arizona. He and Morgan knew each other.

"Nice to have you back in town, Mr. Mason."

"Nice to be back, Mickey. Say hello to my lady, Clare."

"Hey, Clare, welcome as well."

"Thank you."

"How much, Mr. Mason?"

"Oh, give me two thousand, Mickey."

The dealer turned toward the pit and announced, "Marker here."

The pit boss approached. "Oh, hello, Mr. Mason, it's nice to see you again, and good luck."

"Thank you, Angelo."

Mickey signed the marker and Angelo initialed the form. All was in order.

"How do you want it, Mr. Mason?"

"Oh, mix it up, Mickey, and give my lady a stack for $500."

Before the deal, Mickey checked the table to see that all players had placed their bets.

"How much should I bet, baby?"

"The money is yours. You know how to play. Don't ask me what to do. The best way to learn is by doing it. So just play."

Reluctantly, Clare slowly slid a stack of chips worth twenty-five dollars into the circle in front of her, her first ever hand of blackjack.

Morgan bet $100.

Mickey began to deal, one card at a time, from right to left. Clare's card was a jack of diamonds. Morgan drew a six, a bad card, but he didn't react. Mickey's up card was a ten of spades. Mickey dealt the second round of cards and Clare got an ace of diamonds, Morgan a four.

Morgan whispered to Clare. "Now, my two cards equal 10. With a little luck this could have possibilities."

"Why don't you double down?" Clare inquired.

"Remember what you've learned. You double down when the odds are in your favor."

"Okay, okay, I see. You'd double down if Mickey had a six or under."

"Exactly," confirmed Morgan, "But not with him showing a 10."

Mickey's second card went face down under the ten so the players didn't know what he had.

Clare suddenly realized she had a blackjack. "Oh, baby, look what I did, and on my first hand at that!" She couldn't conceal her excitement. As is customary, the dealer paid all blackjacks immediately. Mickey slid over her winnings.

Each player in turn, which began at the dealer's right, indicated whether they wanted more cards or would stand pat with the cards they had. Under the Mason rule, he assumed the dealer had a ten count in the hole. He assumed his hand must beat 20. Calmly, Morgan motioned with his index finger that he wanted another card. It was an ace of clubs.

"What do you have, baby?" Clare asked anxiously. Aces are confusing because they can be counted as either one or eleven.

"Twenty-one," said Morgan calmly, inserting his cards under his chips.

"No kidding."

When all players had taken their cards, Mickey turned over his hole card. It was a ten as Morgan had played it. Mickey had twenty, and Morgan had twenty-one.

"Baby, you just won a $100."

The players were friendly, and there was lively conversation between each of them and the dealer. Morgan enjoyed the socializing almost as much as the gambling. Three hours passed by rapidly. Clare whispered to Morgan, "Baby, I'm about ready to turn in. Do you mind?"

"No, darling. In fact, I'll come with you."

Morgan pitched Mickey a 100-dollar chip. He tapped it one the table to indicate to the pit that he has received at tip. Then he dropped it in his shirt pocket. "Thank you very much, Mr. Mason."

"Thank you, Mickey."

Morgan and Clare approached the cashier's cage. She shoved her chips toward the clerk who quickly calculated her winnings. "Six hundred twenty-five dollars," she announced as she quickly counted out the cash. Clare was gleeful. "Hey, baby, I did pretty good. You're a good teacher." She offered the wad of bills to Morgan.

"No, it's yours. Next time we play it's with their money."

"You're right," she said, giggling.

Morgan turned in his chips. The clerk counted out fourteen hundred and thirty-five dollars. "Well, we didn't break the casino, but we had a nice bit of luck, and it's just our first day," reasoned Morgan.

As they walked toward the elevators, Clare took Morgan's hand. She looked joyously into the eyes of her handsome escort and declared, "I'm having a wonderful time. Thanks for asking me."

"Thanks for coming."

Chapter 35

"GET UP, SLEEPY head; you want to sleep your life away?" Morgan was used to rising at seven in the morning, regardless of when he went to sleep and regardless of where he was. He had shaved, showered, and dressed; ordered coffee and a paper, and finished both.

"What time is it anyway?" Clare asked as she sat up in bed, rubbed her eyes, and stretched.

"It's 10:15 a.m. Grab a shower and get dressed. I'm hungry, and we have things to do."

Cheerful, even when she woke up, Clare responded, "Right away, sir."

She gave Morgan a kiss and he gently smacks her on the bottom as she headed for the shower.

○ ○ ○ ○ ○

"WHAT'S THIS FOR?" Clare asked.

"It's where they keep the white tigers when they are on the premises."

"What are you talking about?" asked a confused Clare.

The exit toward Caesars Palace took Clare and Morgan right by the White Tiger habitat, an environment which featured a swimming pool and simulated mountain terrain. Everything was clearly visible to the spectator behind the thick, clear, protective-glass panels. Soon enough, a large male entered the area and strolled nonchalantly as if he were in the wild. Soon two large females joined him.

"Oh, my God, Morgan; they are huge."

"Yes, aren't they? White lions have long been a featured attraction at the Siegfried and Roy show here at the Mirage."

"I saw the marquee out front when we arrived. What exactly is the show?"

Hesitating a moment to decide how to describe it, Morgan said, "Well, it's a combination of Broadway, the circus, and magic. There is nothing quite like it. When Siegfried and Roy first started working in Vegas, they were a filler act while the stage was being reset. Now they are perhaps the most renowned headliner on the strip. We're gonna see them Saturday night."

"Fantastic!" Clare responded, excitedly.

"Anyway, they use the great white tigers in their show. These guys have dedicated their lives to protecting and preserving these rare animals. The purest of the breed are snow white and have no stripes. And they all have the ice blue eyes."

Clare sighed, "They are quite magnificent."

"When we come back you might be interested in seeing the other wild animals here at the *Mirage*. They have a kind of sanctuary out back that is open to the public."

"Yes, I would like to see that."

As they exited the Mirage, the sun was shining brightly. I can already feel the Nevada heat," Morgan said. "It hot, but it's a dry heat. I actually find the absence of humidity invigorating."

"It's not bad, but I'm not sure I want to spend all day outside."

"We're going to Caesars for breakfast. We can go in right here. They have a Stage Delicatessen, and the food is every bit as good as New York."

"Okay," said Clare, "I'm game."

MORGAN LEFT NOTHING on his plate, which had been heaped with corn beef hash, eggs, and hash brown potatoes. Clare could not finish her pastrami on rye.

"Did you enjoy that?" Morgan asked.

"Oh, I enjoyed it very much, but it's too much food."

"Yeah, they do give you a lot, but that's the way it's done at the Stage Delicatessen."

"Okay, since we're here, I might as well take you on a tour. Caesars Palace has been here a long time but they've done a great job of keeping up the place and expanding. It's still one of the best in town."

"Have you stayed here?"

"Yes, yes I have."

They begin by touring the Forum Shops. "Clare, this is a truly amazing collection of stores, restaurants, and entertainment set in an ancient Roman marketplace. And Clare, for clothes and jewelry, Las Vegas in general, and Caesars in particular, has the world's finest. I have shopped all over, and this is the best."

"BABY, I'M WORN out. Can we have a light lunch and a break?"

"Sure, let's eat here at Bertolini's."

They sat at a table for two on the perimeter. "This is great," said Clare. "We can enjoy the fountain and the *people watching* is priceless."

Morgan chuckled, "Yep, better than the airport."

"Baby, it's getting dark," Clare observed. "What's going on?"

"Well, if you sit here long enough the weather will change many times. It's programmed by a computer and it changes continuously. I think it's fun."

"Well, yeah, but at first it takes you by surprise."

"You've been to Rome," said Morgan, "don't these fountains kind of remind you of the Fountain of Trivi?"

"You know, they do. No wonder I'm enjoying this so much."

"After we eat, I want to show you the pool complex."

"You folks need anything?" the waiter asked.

"Yes, two more glasses of wine. May I ask? Do you happen to know the size of the pool area? I was trying to describe it."

"It's a 4 ½ acre complex, sir. And we're mighty proud of our fitness area as well. Sir, you look like a lifter or something. You should check it out. It's 23,000 square feet with a spa. It's world class."

"Just what one would expect at Caesars."

"You're absolutely right, sir."

As they left the restaurant, Morgan took Clare's hand, and they ducked into a small jewelry store. "I love to look at jewelry," Morgan confessed.

"Wow, baby, you were right about Vegas. Some of this stuff is incredible!"

Morgan noticed a unique white diamond and sapphire ring in an unusual mounting. "That one right there," he said to the clerk, pointing to the precise location, "Let's see that baby up close."

"Here, Clare, let's see how it looks on you.

Clare held out her hand, spread her fingers, and admired the unusual creation. "I like it. How much is it?" she asked, positioning the small tag so she could see the number.

"Twenty-six thousand, five-hundred! Am I reading that correctly?"

The clerk quickly verified the price. "It's 26,500, my dear, a very good buy, and may I say, it looks lovely on you."

Clare quickly removed it and handed it back to the clerk. "It should be at that price."

"Thank you for your help," said Morgan graciously, as they left the store.

"Like I told you, Clare, Vegas has the best…and the most unique."

"You'll get no arguments from me."

After they left Caesars, they toured The Venetian, Paris, and New York, New York. "Vegas is constantly changing," said Morgan, "But I would have to say for the better. Most of the hotels we've seen, aside from the Tropicana, Caesars, and the Mirage, weren't even here a few years ago."

"They are really interesting and opulent," Clare concluded.

"Okay, tonight I'm taking you to see the Follies Bergere at the Tropicana. This has been their signature show for as long as I can remember. One of the reasons I want you to see it is because it represents old Las Vegas, the kind of show that made this place famous and where a lot of other acts got started. And it's a fast-moving, fabulous show—spectacular costumes, musical productions with really great choreography. In some ways it's reminiscent of the old MGM musicals of the 40s, the lavish Busby Berkley productions. There's one huge difference, though; old Busby didn't have any topless women in his productions."

"Topless women, is it?"

"Beautiful, shapely, topless women."

"So that's the real reason you want to go," Clare suggested with a laugh.

"My darling, Clare, I already have the best of the best."

"Well, aren't you sweet?"

"Truthful, my dear, just being truthful." They laughed.

"Seriously, it's a truly spectacular show. And with respect to the nudes, after a few minutes you don't pay that much attention to them because it's just a small part of the overall show and tastefully done."

Clare grinned, "It's okay, baby; it's not a problem." They laughed.

"If you don't mind, I want to go back to the *Mirage* and do some gambling. And you need to tell me what you're hungry for so I can make our dinner reservation."

○ ○ ○ ○ ○

SOUTHWEST FLIGHT 1320 had leveled off at its cruising altitude. "Baby, this was a fabulous trip. I mean, the food, the entertainment, the suite, the neon—it was every bit as you advertised. And didn't I do good at the tables?"

"I'll say you did. Gambling is gambling, and the odds are against you, but don't you agree that blackjack is a great game if you play it correctly?"

"Yes, I do. Oh, I need to give you back this money."

"Give me $500; the rest of it is yours. You won it."

Beaming, she said, "I approve of your logic. Baby, how much did you wind up winning?"

"Enough to buy you this."

Quickly discarding the white ribbon, Clare hurriedly tore into the silver paper covering the small attractively wrapped box. "Sweet Jesus, Mary, and Joseph!" exclaimed Clare. It was the diamond and sapphire ring she had tried on at Caesars Palace.

Chapter 36

"RAMSEY HOUSE, MAY I help you?" said the operator.

"Let me speak to Betty Ann; Morgan Mason calling." Morgan decided to let his New York publisher help him with the arrangements. Betty Ann was his agent's secretary. She could handle this.

"Mr. Mason, how are you?"

"I'm fine, Betty Ann. Listen; I'm coming to the city December 27, and I'll leave on January 2. Get your pencil. I have a few things I need you to do for me. But before I tell you, let me explain. I'm bringing my girlfriend. This is strictly pleasure. I don't want Ramsey House doing anything for me. I don't expect them to pay for anything, and no publicity or events. This is a pleasure trip, and I don't want anyone to know I'm even in town. Got it?"

"Yes, sir. I've got it."

"Okay, here we go. Get me a suite at the Plaza with a view of Central Park. I want dinner reservations at the Russian Tea Room the first night, and I'd like tickets to *The Producers.* After the show get me reservations at the Stage Delicatessen. For the second night get me tickets to *Les Miserables* and dinner before at Mary Lou's in the village. On the 29th, get us tickets to the *Phantom of the Opera,* and I want dinner before the show at

Spark's Steak House. Get me tickets to the Radio City Music Hall *Christmas Show* for Saturday night. After the show get us reservations at The Supper Club.

"A late supper and some dancing?" she concluded with a giggle. You are so romantic, Mr. Mason."

"I like women, good food, and dancing." They laughed.

"Let's see," said Morgan, carefully thinking through his plans.

"I want to take her to Tavern on the Green for lunch on Sunday. I think that's it."

"Okay, I think I've got it. When I get everything set I'll fax you the confirmation." She paused for a moment and then quizzed Morgan, "Mr. Mason, you didn't mention New Year's Eve. It's New York City and…"

He laughed, "Good thinking, Betty Ann, but I've got it covered."

"Oh, okay. I just didn't want…"

"I know. You're a sweetheart, and you're very efficient, Betty Ann. Look, when you fax me the confirmation, could you include the cost of the pre-paid stuff so I can send you a check?"

"Sure thing."

"Good."

"It's none of my business, but this lady, she's new?"

"Not real new, we've been dating about nine months."

"Serious?" Betty Ann asked.

"We'll, the preacher's on hold but maybe. She's a terrific girl."

"She's a brunette, right?"

"You know me pretty well, don't you?"

"Good looking?"

"Drop-dead, gorgeous! But she's a quality woman, Betty Ann. After all these years, I'm lucky I found her. Yeah, this could be it."

"I'll expect you to keep me posted."

"I can do that."

A FAX ARRIVED from Ramsey House.

Mr. Mason:

All the arrangements you requested have been made. I will fax you the confirmations and the pre-paid expense. Ramsey House will honor your request but with one exception. They are providing a limousine for you and your lady while you're here. They won't take no for an answer. Lets me know your carrier, your flight number and your arrival, and I'll have them waiting.

Betty Ann

Chapter 37

November 23, 2000

BURT BROWN LEANED back in his chair and patted his stomach gently, indicating his satisfaction. "Marge, that was a tremendous meal; you outdid yourself. I love Thanksgiving. I always have. I can't wait until Christmas so we can do it all again."

"Wait just a minute there, Mr. Brown," said Marge. "We may need to negotiate that."

"What do you mean, we may…"

Morgan interrupted Burt before he could finish. Clare had been telling Morgan how hard her mother worked in the kitchen during the holidays. And even though she enjoyed it, she was often worn out to the point where she couldn't appreciate the celebration herself. "I would like to issue an invitation to all of you to come to Taos for Christmas."

"That's very sweet of you, Morgan, but we've always spent the holidays here in Austin. There are the church services and just everything; its tradition," said Marge.

"He doesn't mean New Mexico, Mom, he means his place at Horseshoe Bay," said Clare. There was laughter.

"Marge, I'd like to do the cooking for Christmas; well, Clare and I. That way you can enjoy this special time without any responsibility. My place is about 4,000 square feet and has five bedrooms and plenty of bathrooms. Depending on the weather, we can play some golf, tennis, do some boating, hiking. If it's cold or messy, we can just relax; read, listen to music, play games, or sleep. Anyway, I think we can handle everyone. You mentioned church. There's a Christmas Eve mass, right?"

"That's correct," said Marge.

"What time do they have it?" asked Morgan.

"Seven o'clock."

"Fine, we'll all go to mass, and then we'll head for the lake. Bring the presents, and we'll open them whenever, Christmas Eve or Christmas morning. And with your approval, we'll depart from tradition a bit."

Burt looked suspicious. "I do the best shrimp gumbo you ever put in your mouth. I'd like to serve that Christmas Eve with some garlic bread, a Greek salad, and a nice vintage red wine."

"Don't sweat it, Burt," Clare chimed in, "Morgan Mason can cook almost as well as he can write. Keep an open mind. He won't disappoint you. And who knows, we may start a new tradition."

Burt Brown began to grin, "Okay, fine; you sold me."

"Morgan, you are a sweetheart. I can't tell you how much I appreciate this," said Marge.

Morgan put his arm around Marge and gave her a kiss on the cheek. She giggled and blushed. I hope you don't mess this up, Clare. This man is too good to be true."

"Oh, Mom — quit it."

"Okay, for Christmas day we'll probably do beef tenderloin, garlic mashers, and all the trimmings. And I'll do something special for dessert, perhaps something that you've never had before — but fabulous. Clare and I will collaborate on it. She's very good in the kitchen as well. I presume you guys know that? Anyway, we won't disappoint you."

"Oh, I just remembered something. Dad will be here for Christmas. Mom, I want him to come up and stay, like everyone else. Is this going to be a problem for you or Burt?"

Marge looked at Burt then said, "No problem at all."

"Nope, no problem," agreed Burt, matter of factly.

"Good," said Clare, "I am very pleased with this. I'll call him and tell him our plans."

The women were clearing the table while the men had retired to the living room to watch football. April and Marge were alone in the kitchen.

"Morgan's quite a catch and quite a hunk, isn't he, Mom? Clare has won the dating lottery."

"He's something special, all right," said Marge. She had given birth to Clare when she was 22 years old, and April came along two years later. She was a very youthful and still quite a beautiful 50-year-old woman, who didn't look a day over 40. She was a runner and had always kept herself fit; neither of her girls was prone to exercise. One could easily see where Clare and April got their looks and figures.

"You know something crazy, April," said Marge with a gleam in her eye. "Under different circumstances, I could actually be dating Morgan Mason."

"Mom, you devil," said April, "are you fantasying about Morgan?"

Marge answered coyly, "He's 40 or 41 right? If I couldn't attract a man his age, I'd be very disappointed in myself."

"Mother!" exclaimed April, with frightened shock, "I've never heard you talk like this."

"It's just talk, April, my love, just talk."

No sooner were the words out of her mouth, than Clare walked through the kitchen door. "I think this is the last of everything from the table, Mom."

"Thank you, sweetheart, and thank you, too, April."

Chapter 38

December 24, 2000

MORGAN AND CLARE were in his Boxter, with a certain shaggy little fellow resting comfortably on Morgan's left thigh. His front paws were spread with his head in between. He traveled well. April, Burt, Marge and Arch were in Burt's Chevrolet Suburban. "Did you get Bogart something for Christmas?" asked Clare.

"I certainly did," said Morgan, "what kind of a father do you think I am?"

She laughed and soon they all arrived at Taos, pulled up in the circular driveway and under the portico and got out. "Wow, this looks very nice," remarked Marge.

"Give me a minute. I want to show you something," said Morgan. To the right of the house was a circular brick wall with an irregular surface. He turned on the gas and lit the four evenly spaced lights that were attached across the front of the structure. That illuminated the main attraction, which was a large life-sized Indian warrior in bronze, adorned in full headdress with both arms outstretched toward the sky.

"Oh, my soul," exclaimed Marge, "that is truly spectacular!"

Everyone voiced their own comments, and they were all suitably impressed.

"Let's go in, and I'll give you a tour. Then I'll tell you where everyone is sleeping, and we can come back for the bags."

"That sounds like a plan," said Arch.

Bogart jumped up and down, barking anxiously.

They looked over the spacious and attractively decorated downstairs and then went out on the deck. "Show them your study," Clare insisted, excitedly. She knew what an impact it would have, and she was correct. Then Morgan showed them the master bedroom.

April whispered in Clare's ear, "What a sexy setting for a tumble. How is it, sis?"

Blushing, and laughing, she tried to shush her playful little sister, "Quit it, April."

Then they proceeded upstairs, toured the loft, a couple at a time, and then the library and bedrooms. "April, you and Ken can bunk up here. And Marge, you and Burt will be up here as well. You guys can fight over which bedroom you want."

They went downstairs, to the lower level, and Morgan showed them the entertainment room and the other two bedrooms. "Arch, you and Clare can sleep down here."

"Morgan," said Marge, "this house is fabulous. I have never seen anything like it." The others joined in with a variety of observations and compliments. "And your Christmas decorations: the house is just beautiful."

"Thank you, Marge," said Morgan, "Clare and I did it last weekend."

There was garland around the front door with twinkle lights and attractive large red bows at the corners. A large wreath hung perfectly in the center. On the inside, there were wreath-cradled red and green candles. They were placed in every bathroom and around the house at well-selected locations. There was garland down the stairway and over the fireplace. Once again, large attractive red bows had been used at just the right spots. The eight-foot-tall tree was between the fireplace and the door leading to the outside deck. Wide red and gold ribbon and multiple strands of tiny white lights were wrapped around the entire outer perimeter. Every size and type of Christmas ornament, which Morgan had collected from childhood and trips out of the country, adorned the tree from top to bottom. An angel, with outstretched arms, stood atop the spectacular Yule tide symbol.

As they started for the cars to unload the bags, April pulled Clare to the side. "Why aren't you sleeping with Morgan? This crap is not necessary. For God's sake, Clare, you're an adult, once married, and a divorced woman; you can damn well do what you please. And if someone doesn't like it they can kiss your ass. Or they can kiss my ass."

"How do you really feel about this situation, April?"

They laughed.

Clare sighed. "I know, April; Morgan and I talked about it. But I felt like it might be uncomfortable for Mom. I doubt that anyone else would care, but I didn't want to throw it in her face."

"Fine," said April, disgustedly, "but if Morgan Mason was my man, he wouldn't ever sleep alone."

o o o o o

"ANYONE NEED MORE gumbo?" Morgan asked.

"Whew, not me," said Arch, "but I wouldn't want to speak for anyone else."

"My family always had shrimp gumbo on Christmas Eve," said Morgan. "This was my mom's recipe."

"Morgan, will you please see that I get the recipe?" said Marge. "Now I'm going to clean up."

Morgan put his big arm around her shoulders, kissed her on the cheek and said, "No, you're not. Now if you'll remember, part of the reason we're up here is so you don't have to work every holiday."

She smiled at Morgan, "Okay, but you're the sweetest man."

He had completely won her over. Marge thought Morgan Mason could do no wrong. She was constantly nagging Clare about holding on to him.

"Arch, you and Burt go outside if you're going to smoke. Don't you dare light up in Morgan's beautiful house!" Marge instructed.

"Baby, I'll clean up. Why don't you go with the boys?" Clare, put her arm around Morgan's waist, walked him to the doors leading out to the deck. She gave him a kiss on the cheek and said, "I love you for doing this for my family."

"Not a problem," Morgan responded. "When is Ken due to arrive?"

"April said he was to land in Austin at 8 o'clock in the morning."

"Okay," said Morgan, "then he should be here by 10 o'clock, easy. That will work out just fine."

"Can I get you anything, baby?"

"Yeah, bring me another glass of Merlot."

Burt overheard Morgan's request and asked for another glass himself.

"Sure Burt, I'll bring you one as well."

"Baby," Clare suggested, "why don't you light up the Kiva oven? When we get done here in the kitchen we can all sit by the fire and chat."

"Okay, that's a good idea."

"Mom, Burt's really throwing down the wine."

"Yeah, I've noticed."

"Arch," said Morgan, "may I ask about your prospects for a star?"

"Interesting you should mention that," he responded. "I'm to be promoted to brigadier general next February."

"Arch, that's wonderful. I'm very proud for you. I guess you were in Viet Nam?"

"Yeah, three tours. We were flying the F-4 Phantom and the F-105 Thunderchief. Service in Nam, for an officer with a command, gave almost everybody a boost up the career ladder in any branch of the military."

"Do you know what your assignment will be after your promotion?"

"As a matter of fact I do. I'm going to command the American fighter contingent patrolling the no-fly zone over Iraq."

"Hey, fellows, come here. I want you guys to hear about Arch."

○ ○ ○ ○ ○

MORGAN, I REALLY appreciate you helping me get Burt to bed like this. He may not wake up until tomorrow afternoon. He can't drink, but would deny it, of course."

"It's okay," said Morgan, "but does he do this often?"

"Actually he doesn't. But when you can't handle alcohol it doesn't take much to overstep. And you know, with the holidays and all. You're in a festive mood."

Morgan nodded. He understood.

"Anyway, I apologize for this."

"It's not necessary, Marge."

"At least he doesn't get mean, or loud, or throw-up like some people do when they have too much to drink."

"I said it's okay, Marge, really. I'm glad he enjoyed himself."

Marge put her hand on the back of his neck and rubbed it gently. Then she kissed him on the lips. "Thanks for everything."

Morgan was taken aback. He didn't quite know what to say so he kept it simple. "Goodnight Marge. See you in the morning."

Marge grinned and nodded. Morgan retreated down the stairs.

Chapter 39

THE HOUSE WAS buttoned down for the evening, and everyone had gone to bed. Morgan, who never retired early, was listening to soft music in the master suite, staring at the lake through the large picture window. He had succumbed to the serenity of the moment and did not hear the bedroom door open ever so quietly. She stepped inside and was instantly mesmerized by the erotic sight of Morgan in the nude, visible only by the glow from the flames, slow dancing in the fireplace. His muscular body had a bronze cast, like the Nez Perce warrior in the painting. She hurriedly but silently squirmed out of her form fitting pale blue silk gown, stepping out of it as it fell at her feet. She was tantalized as she walked stealthily across the room toward him on the thick plush carpet until she was standing immediately behind his magnificent straight sculptured frame. He was not startled but sensed her presence and slowly turned to face her. She slipped her arms around his neck.

Chapter 40

Christmas Day, 2000

"I WANTED TO tell everyone how much I enjoyed the Christmas Eve mass. That was a first for me, and it was special. Marge, I can see why you were so passionate about it."

"Oh, Morgan, I'm so pleased you enjoyed it," said Marge. April glanced at Clare and smiled.

"We've got coffee, juice, and strawberries," announced Morgan, to each guest, as they intermittently wandered into the kitchen. A gracious host, Morgan inquired as to whether everyone had slept well. All the guests had finally gathered and consumed at least one cup of coffee, when the front door opened, and Ken stepped in.

"Merry Christmas," he shouted.

"Merry Christmas right back at you," hollered Burt.

April greeted him, nonchalantly, at the door and walked him into the kitchen where everyone said hello.

"It's about time you were getting here," said Marge.

"Ken, you missed some great gumbo last night," said Arch.

"Yeah, thanks for reminding me. I had airplane food." Everyone laughed.

"Here, have a cup of coffee," offered Morgan, who had a suggestion.

"Why don't we open our presents, and when were finished, Clare wants us to take a boat ride. It will be a little cool, but you can bundle up, and that will make you enjoy the hot cider even more when we return. After we get back you guys can relax while Clare and I put the finishing touches on our lunch. How does that sound to you, Marge?"

Morgan paid a lot of attention to Clare's mom, which pleased Clare and endeared him to Marge.

"That's a fine idea, Morgan. Burt, why don't you play Santa?"

"Before we get into the presents, I'd like to thank all of you for being here. You see, I'm an only child and my parents are both dead. I have no immediate family to enjoy during the holidays. And there's no other time during the year when one's thoughts so dramatically turn to family. You guys are as much like family as I have. So thank you for helping to make this time so special for me and Bogart."

"Oh, darling, thank you for having us and taking care of the food and everything. It is greatly appreciated," said Marge.

"Yeah, Morgan, thank you for opening up your fantastic home to our family," echoed April.

"And the gumbo was out of this world," blurted Burt.

"I have welcomed the opportunity to get to know you better. You're a class act, Morgan," said Arch.

"Quit it, you guys; you're going to break me up," said Morgan. "It's not nice to make a grown man cry."

Clare had taken a seat in one of the tall director's chairs next to Morgan at the kitchen bar. She ran her fingers through his hair, massaged his neck lovingly, and said, "It's a wonderful thing you've done for mom, and all of us. Thank you, baby." She gave him a quick, but tender kiss on the lips.

"Enough, enough already," pleaded Morgan. "Let's open some presents." There were cheers, clapping and laughter.

Burt passed out one present at a time so everyone could enjoy what the others received. There were sweaters and pipes…jewelry and books…luggage and slippers. Wrapping paper, boxes, bows, and ribbons covered the floor. Bogart jumped on the crinkly paper and wrestled with pieces of ribbon. The only thing left under the tree was a pale lavender envelope. "Burt, can you hand me that envelope?"

"I sure can."

Morgan examined it for a moment and then handed it to Clare. "This is yours. Open it up."

Anxiously, she tore at the flap. She nervously dropped it and then picked it up. Finally extracting the contents, she quietly mumbled the message scribbled on plain white paper inside. *Go look in my bedroom closet. There's something there just for you. Merry Christmas, Love Morgan.*

Clare squealed, dropped the envelope, and ran into Morgan's bedroom.

"She appears to be excited," said Morgan with a chuckle. There was laughter.

Her heart was racing as she opened the closet. The sight of it stopped her in her tracks. She screamed at the top of her lungs.

"Sounds like she found it," said Morgan. The others were looking at each other in anticipation. Clare modeled the coat in front of a full-length mirror on Morgan's closet door. She turned to get different looks as she stroked the soft fur. "Bring it in here so everyone can see it," shouted Morgan.

Clare appeared in the bedroom doorway, pulling it tight around her neck with both hands. "Nice, don't you think?" she inquired of the group.

"Oh, my soul, Clare, it's beautiful," said Marge.

April jumped up and ran over to Clare. She stroked the fur and admired the coat. Looking back over her shoulder at her husband, Ken, she asked, "Well, when am I going to get mine?"

Embarrassed, red face and all, he said, "We'll see; maybe next year. I don't want you to get spoiled."

"Yeah, right," quipped April.

Clare walked up to everyone individually so they could touch it and feel it. She was very excited. After the floor show she approached Morgan and plopped down in his lap. "Will you guys excuse us a minute?" She put her arms around Morgan's neck and gave him long slow kiss. Everyone yelled and clapped as Bogart barked. The little fellow knew something special had happened.

"So, you like it?" Morgan inquired, coyly.

"Like it—I love it!"

"Well, good. I didn't want you to get cold when we're in New York."

"New York!" questioned April. "When are you going to New York?"

"We're leaving on December 27 and coming back on January 2. When that ball drops at Times Square on New Year's Eve, look for us. We'll be there."

"There's something else in one of your pockets," Morgan remembered. Surprised, but very curious, she retrieved a small white box, opened it to find a beautiful gold anklet nestled in cloudlike white cotton. She smiled with delight as she carefully lifted it free from its tiny manger. Like a puppet master, she worked it in and out of her delicate fingers, admiring its design and workmanship.

Giggling like a schoolgirl, she hugged Morgan tightly around the neck. "Thank you, baby; thank you for everything."

Chapter 41

Wednesday, December 27, 2000

CLARE SQUEEZED MORGAN'S hand as the limousine moved closer to Manhattan. This was Clare's first trip to the Big Apple and she was excited.

"Baby, the plans you made are so exciting, but you didn't mention New Year's Eve."

"You know, New Year's Eve can be such a hassle," reasoned Morgan. "I though it might be fun to dress and have dinner in our suite. The hotel can serve us a fabulous dinner, and I thought I'd arrange for some chamber music."

"Baby, that's a great idea, it really is."

"Well, I thought it had possibilities. And whenever we feel like it, we can wander down to Times Square. Just so we're there before midnight for the dropping of the ball. And Clare, I've never done that."

"Really?" exclaimed Clare.

"Really. Besides, your family will be looking for us."

She could hardly contain herself as they arrived at the *Plaza*, the grand hotel she had seen in news clips and in the movies. She was wearing her fur coat, and the snow was falling lightly as they prepared to go inside.

"Here's my card, Mr. Mason. Call me when you need me," said the limo driver.

"Thanks, Tony. We have six o'clock dinner reservations at the Russian Tea Room and then the theatre at eight."

"I'll be waiting out front at a quarter to six."

"Morgan Mason, checking in."

The manager, Andre, was talking with a staffer when he heard Morgan's name. He turned and greeted his distinguished guest. "Mr. Mason, we are always honored to have you stay with us. You're in, let me see, 2101 and I'll have your bags taken right up. Don't worry about a thing."

"Thank you, Andre. You are always so accommodating, and the house is so wonderful. I'd like you to meet Clare Casey."

"Clare, I'm charmed. Really, such an honor to have Mr. Mason and his lady." As he kissed her hand, she looked at Morgan for approval. He grinned and shrugged.

Morgan gave Clare a quick tour of the elegant lobby area, the shops and the Palm Court. The Plaza had long been a landmark in New York City and so many movies had used the Plaza as a backdrop or for selected scenes. Morgan had always enjoyed staying there and he was pleased to have Clare along to share the experience.

"Baby, I'm hungry for something, something sweet. Can we go to the Palm Court and get a dessert?" She was excited as a kid in a candy store, and Morgan was tickled. "Sure we can. Wait here. They'll have to seat us."

The wait for service was lengthy. The waitress was rude and inattentive, uncharacteristic of the Plaza. Morgan was angry. Clare ordered New York-style cheesecake, which was good even if the service was not. Morgan couldn't get his coffee refilled. He finally signed a ticket and they left. "I'm sorry, Clare. That was not up to Plaza standards."

"It's okay, baby, forget it."

The Plaza had a practice of showing their dessert selections to entice their guests. Trays of the delicacies were nestled attractively on dark green cloth with impressive flower arrangements around the cordoned off perimeter. As Clare and Morgan walked by he ran his index finger through the icing of several exquisitely decorated cakes. He smiled sheepishly as he downed in one bite, the blob of mixed toppings which had collected on his finger.

"Morgan Mason! I can't believe what I just saw you do!" exclaimed Clare.

Morgan laughed, "That will teach them to mess with Morgan Mason and his lady."

Clare laughed and shook her head.

"Let's go check out our digs," suggests Morgan.

"Good idea," said Clare, "I think we need to get far away from the Palm Court."

"This is fabulous," said Clare, "and look at that view of Central Park."

"It's not too shabby, is it? But you need to put your coat back on; we're going out."

"We are? Where?"

"I thought it would be fun to walk down to Rockefeller Center. They'll be ice skating over there, and we'll get a coffee. And the weather is fabulous—with the light snow falling. And the sights you see on the streets of this city. It's worth the price of a ticket. I love it, Clare. There's no place like New York city in the winter time."

○ ○ ○ ○ ○

"BABY, THIS HAS been one great day. New York is exciting. Now I know why everyone raves about it."

Grinning and nodding his approval. Morgan leaned forward and told their driver, "Stage Deli, Tony."

"Here we are folks," Tony said, leaping out to open the back door for Clare and Morgan.

Morgan held up two fingers as they entered the popular after theatre establishment. "Right this way, folks."

On the way to their table Morgan caught the eye of Regis Phillips, the host of a syndicated morning television show. He was seated on the right with his wife Joan. He smiled and stood. "Morgan, what are you doing in town? I guess it's some big literary event?"

"Nothing like that, Regis. Clare and I are just here to see some shows and enjoy the city. In fact, I told my publisher, 'No commitments, no publicity.'"

"Clare, meet Regis Phillips."

He smiled and greeted her warmly. "Clare, I want you to meet my wife, Joan."

"Hi there, Clare. My compliments, Morgan; she's lovely."

The hostess was waiting by their table with menus. Morgan and Clare said their goodbye's and took their seats.

"How do you know Regis and Joan?" Clare inquired.

"We'll, you make the morning television circuit when you have a new book release. It's the same when an actor has a new movie coming out. And the publisher has parties and receptions and they invite celebrities to attend along with critics, writers, and book people."

"Yeah, I get the picture."

"My I take your orders?"

"Clare, what will you have?"

"I'll have the chocolate cheesecake and black coffee."

Morgan finally decided. "I'll have the plain cheesecake with strawberry topping, and black coffee."

"Will you need cream with that?"

Morgan grinned at the waitress. He tapped his chin with his index finger for a bit and then declared, "No cream."

Clare giggled when the waitress left. "They're programmed to ask, and they don't even hear you when you say black coffee."

"That's it," said Morgan.

As he glanced around the room he noticed an attractive blond woman smiling at him and nodding. He waved and smiled.

"Who are waving at?" Clare inquired, not wanting to turn and stare.

"Diane Sanders. She's with her husband, the movie director Mike Nicholson."

The ABC television Sanders?"

"That's the one," he replied.

"You're putting me on," said Clare.

"No, it's them. The Stage Delicatessen is like that. You might see anybody in here. But I don't think New Yorkers are particularly star struck. I don't think they pay a lot of attention to celebrities."

"That would be a good reason to live here," Clare deducted.

"It would."

Abruptly, Morgan stood-up, took both of Diane's hands and kissed her on the cheek.

"How are you, Morgan? And are you here for some special occasion?"

"No, we just hoped to slip into town unnoticed and enjoy the city and the season."

"Morgan, this is my husband Mike Nicholson."

"Hi, Mike. I'm very pleased to meet you. I admire your work."

"And I yours. I just finished reading *Willie John Mahoney*, and it's exceptional. I'm considering purchasing the film rights."

"No kidding?"

"No kidding."

"In fact I called your publisher to get your agent's name. If my partners and I do decide to go forward with the project, would you consider doing the screenplay?"

"Yes, I would. That would be exciting."

"Oh, Mike, Diane, may I present Clare Casey."

Mike kissed Clare's hand. She smiled.

"I too am a fan of your work," Clare confessed.

"Well, aren't you nice to say so."

Diane took a seat by Clare while Morgan and Mike continued to talk. "Hi, I'm Diane Sanders. Are you in show business? You're very beautiful, stunning in fact."

Taken aback, Clare said, "Lord, no, I'm not at all in show business. I'm a sales manager at a hotel in Austin, Texas."

"You could have fooled me."

"Diane, we must go and leave these people to themselves," said Nicholson.

"Indeed we should."

"Thanks for coming over," said Morgan.

"I hope we can work together," said Mike.

"I do too," said Morgan, "that would be fun."

Clare and Morgan took their seats and Mike and Diane took their leave.

"And how do you know Diane?"

"Same way I know Regis."

"Of course."

"Did that movie thing catch you by surprise?"

"Yes, very much."

"That's very exciting."

"Yeah, it is. I wonder if Nicholson knows that I have never done a screen play?"

Clare didn't know it either. She had never thought about it, one way or the other. "Could you do it?"

"I think so. Frankly, it should be easier that a novel."

"Really, how so?"

"Well, with a novel, the reader is deaf, dumb, and blind. We have to create everything. With a screen play, the camera is going to fill in the blanks. The main thing the writer has to do is set the scene and do the dialog."

"That's all, huh," Clare surmised, with admiration and a bit of awe.

"Well, that's what we do." Morgan thought for a moment and then added, "But a screenplay might be difficult. I could be my ego that's telling me it would be easy."

She smiled.

○ ○ ○ ○ ○

AS THEIR LIMOUSINE pulled away from the Majestic Theatre, Clare observed, "Andrew Lloyd Webber does good work."

"Yes, he does. That's for sure." Thinking back he observed, "Do you know that *The Phantom of the Opera* opened January 9, 1988. It's been packing them in here in New York and London ever since. It's quite remarkable. You never know what's going to be a hit. That's a lot of pressure on the producers—and a lot of money on the line."

Clare grinned, "It's a little like a publisher who advances an author a big chunk of money on a book they've never seen."

Morgan laughed, "You know, there is a similarity."

○ ○ ○ ○ ○

"YOU'D BETTER BRING your stocking cap," Morgan advised, "It may be cold out on that water."

"I've lost track of time," said Clare, as the limousine finally pulled to a stop. "It's Saturday, December 30," said Morgan.

As Morgan and Clare climbed out of the vehicle, she was excited. Ellis Island and the Statue of Liberty awaited her. Morgan had seen them many times but always enjoyed each and every visit. It would be particularly enjoyable with Clare. As they boarded the ferry, *Miss Liberty*, Clare was as excited as a child on Santa's knee.

Chapter 42

AS CLARE AND Morgan climbed in the back of their publisher furnished limousine, Morgan gave instructions for the next destination. "Little Italy, Tony, Mulberry Street."

Soon they were in front of Caruso's Ristorante and Pizzeria. Excitedly, Morgan opened the door for Clare and they stepped inside. Caruso's was a family eatery patronized primarily by neighborhood locals. Morgan was acquainted with the owner, his wife and several of the waiters. Carmine was behind the oyster bar when he spotted Morgan. Hurrying to great him with outstretched arms, he exclaimed, "Momma—everybody—it's Mr. Morgan. He greeted Morgan with a bear hug and kissed him on both cheeks.

"Carmine," said Morgan, "you're a sweetheart. It's my extreme pleasure to introduce you to my lady, Clare Casey." Morgan's outstretched arms protected Clare from a similar welcome. "I can't let you hug her, you might break her in two."

Carmine slapped his sides and bent over laughing. "Okay, okay, but I give her a little kiss. Okay?"

He smacked his lips on Clare's blushing cheek.

Mrs. Caruso—Rosa—appeared, smiling, and gave Clare a hug. She gave Morgan a peck on the lips and then a robust slap on the back. There was laughter throughout the restaurant.

"Mr. Morgan, here is your favorite table. 'Momma, bring a bottle of our best Chianti for our friends.'" Smiling, hands on his hips, Carmine inquired, "What brings to our city, my friend?"

"The veal. What else? You've got to try it, Clare; it's the best in town."

Rosa appeared and poured two glasses of the red wine. "Mamma," said Carmine, "they want the veal, and Momma, toss some angel hair pasta with pesto and two of our special salads. And, oh yeah, give them our deluxe antipasto to start."

Smiling broadly, she said, "Yes, Carmine, right away."

Morgan, a regular for at least the past five years, has never come to the city without enjoying a meal at Caruso's. And Carmine and Rosa were very fond of Morgan. He had had two book signings at the restaurant which had personally pleased the Caruso's and offered them publicity beyond the neighborhood.

Carmine sat down with Clare and Morgan. He chattered nonstop throughout the entire meal, which was okay with Clare. She thought he was charming, and Rosa as well. The whole experience was delightful. Finally they had finished the enjoyable meal which included ice cream and coffee.

"THIS AREA, CLARE, is the setting in my book *Willie John Mahoney*. It all took place in this neighborhood. Come let's walk."

"I couldn't help but notice the funeral home right next to the restaurant," observed Clare. "Actually, it's a bit weird. It kind of gave me the creeps."

"It didn't seem to dull your appetite," Morgan observed.

Clare laughed, "Yeah, you're right about that. I guess after a while you forget about it."

They reached the other side of the street. "This grocery store, Spiro's, is in the book. In fact, one of the principle characters works for Mr. Spiro. It was his first job in America."

"I love this, Morgan. Thank you for bringing me here."

"Let's walk this way," suggested Morgan as they moved down the narrow street away from the store. After a few blocks, Morgan stopped. He pointed to a storefront. "There, Mulberry Rod and Gun Club."

"Yeah, I see it. What about it?"

"It used to be a hangout for the Mafia in this neighborhood. They were soldiers of the Gambino crime family. It's in my book as well."

Clare and Morgan walked for blocks, talking, and enjoying the neighborhood and the local color. "You know what the locals used to say about the Mafia men who hung out around here."

"No, what did they say?"

"They're bad guys, but they're our bad guys."

○ ○ ○ ○ ○

"TONY," LET US out up there by the corner. We'll walk the rest of the way."

"Certainly, sir."

"We'll see you at about six."

As Clare and Morgan proceeded in the direction of the Plaza they saw merchants selling sweat shirts and jewelry on the sidewalk. Vendors were selling foot long Coney's and hot chestnuts. Others were playing the shell game for curious tourists and mimes were working several locations. "I wanted you to see all this, Clare. It's part of the charm of the city."

"It's something, all right," Clare admitted.

They crossed the street by St. Patrick's Cathedral and quietly went inside. Clare said a prayer and lit a candle. They returned to the hotel to rest before going out for the evening.

○ ○ ○ ○ ○

"WHAT DID YOU think of the show?" Morgan asked.

"I almost hesitate to tell you, with all the marvelous Broadway shows we have seen, but I thought this Radio City Christmas Spectacular show was the best thing of all. And the live nativity scene really moved me!"

"Yeah, I agree with you. I think it's worth coming to New York to see. And the Rockettes are pretty special. Years ago," said Morgan, "you could come to Radio City and purchase a regular movie ticket for whatever was showing. With that same ticket you got to enjoy a sing-along and a performance from the Rockettes. It was a heck of a deal. Did you see the gigantic organs on each side of the hall?"

"Yes, I did, and I was wondering about it."

"Well, there was an organist on each side that played while the audience sang. It was loads of fun."

"Well, how about some dinner and dancing?"

"Sounds fabulous."

"Tony, take us to The Supper Club. It's at 240 West 47th Street."

"I know exactly where it is."

Chapter 43

IT WAS CLEAR and cold as Morgan and Clare descended the steps in front of The Plaza. He had told Tony to take the day off. It was Sunday and the guy should be with his family. They turned left and crossed the street toward the horse drawn carriages. "Take us to the Tavern on the Green, if you please," Morgan instructed the driver.

"But we don't go the far down."

"I'll pay you whatever you want. But take us there!"

The driver looked at Morgan and sighed. "Okay, you're the boss."

He helped Clare inside the carriage and they began their slow-moving trip through historic Central Park.

"Oh, baby, this is really so special. I love it."

"Well, I rather thought you would. Just settle back, relax, and enjoy."

Clare squeezed Morgan's hand tightly, indicating the extent of her pleasure, and gave him an appreciative kiss on the lips.

"I'm sorry that the carriage ride is over. It was most enjoyable," declared Clare as they entered the Tavern on the Green. The season's decorations were spectacular: colorful wreaths, Christmas trees, reindeer, colored lights, poinsettias and ruby-red bows. Each one of the many elaborate chandeliers had its own special adornment, and fresh-cut flowers graced each colorful table. Clare reached over and put her hand on Morgan's and declared, "I'm having a wonderful time."

o o o o o

"CLARE, IF YOU don't mind, I think we should walk." This was another of those moments when she knew Morgan had a surprise for her. She had learned to recognize it and was eager to oblige. She squeezed his hand once again and they began to walk. Besides, they had enjoyed a rather hardy lunch and the walking would do them good. Central Park was crowded with all ages of people enjoying themselves. It was no longer snowing, but there was plenty still covering the ground. Soon they came upon a frozen pond covered with gleeful skaters in colorful regalia. They sat on a bench and watched.

"Oh, baby, it's wonderful. It reminds me of a Currier & Ives painting." He smiled with satisfaction.

As they came to the edge of the park they could see the Plaza, rising majestically before them, overlooking Central Park like a parent watching out over a child. "It's quite spectacular, isn't it, Clare?"

She stood in awe and concluded, "You don't realize how huge it is until you have a view like this."

"Can you find our room?" asked Morgan.

"I sure can, our little home away from home."

o o o o o

MORGAN FINISHED TYING the black tie and slipped into his tuxedo jacket. He glanced at himself in the mirror and smiled; he was satisfied. He knocked gently on the bathroom door. "One minute," said Clare.

The door bell to their suite rang. It was the musicians. They set up and immediately began to play "Fascination. Morgan felt like Gary Cooper in *Love in the Afternoon.*

Soon the bell rang again and two waiters with starched white half-cut jackets, white bow ties, black trousers and white gloves wheeled in the dinner and began setting the table with fine china and silver. Clare suddenly appeared from the other room and looked stunning in her low cut black silk dress. She had gotten her hair put up in a French braid at the Plaza Beauty Salon. Morgan poured two tall slender glasses of chilled champagne. They stood by the windows and gazed at Central Park as the waiters made their final preparation.

"May I seat the lady?" inquired the head waiter, as the other man lit the candles.

Obligingly, Clare approached the elegant table and was seated as Morgan took his place across from her. The waiters served the first course, lobster bisque, followed by a baby vegetable salad with vanilla bean-cardamom vinaigrette. The main course was truffle-dusted filets mignons with a cherry port-wine reduction. Then came the braised fingerling potatoes with pearl onions and cremini mushrooms and green beans with macadamia nuts.

The dessert was chocolate pudding cake with blackberries and a raspberry drizzle and the coffee was Maui blend. The waiters took their leave, as did the musicians, after serving the final two items.

With satisfaction written all over her lovely face, Clare concluded, "My darling man, this was so very special. We could not have topped it at the finest restaurant in town; how wonderful of you to think of it."

"It was special," Morgan agreed, "But mainly because you were here."

They went to the windows once more and gazed down at the city. Soon it would be time to change into something casual and join the masses at Times Square.

Dick Clark began the historic count down. Millions of Americans, including Clare's family, would be watching. "Ten, nine, eight, seven, six, five, four, three, two, one!" Everyone looked up and screamed as the gigantic ball fell. A deafening roar of happiness erupted from the thousands who gathered for the annual event. Morgan took Clare in his arms and kissed her tenderly. Surrounded by thousands of screaming people, they were able to shut out everything but themselves. It was magical.

"Happy New Year, darling."

"Happy New Year, baby; may it be the best one ever."

○ ○ ○ ○ ○

IN THE QUIETNESS of the moment, he couldn't help but wonder, *What will the new year bring? What shall I do with this exceptional woman?* As he glanced into the bedroom he noticed Clare, barefoot, wearing only her full length ranch mink coat, staring out the window. She was apparently mesmerized by the sight of the slow falling snow flakes; like a thousand ballet dancers dressed in white, all moving to a different tune. It was cold outside and the window was frosted.

He approached her and quietly called her name, "Clare...Clare...Clare." She ignored him—or perhaps she was so transfixed by the moment that she didn't hear him. He watched as she placed her index finger on the window pane. The chill of it tickled her and she giggled under her breath. Marking her starting point, she moved upward and in a circular motion to the left coming downward slowly and ending at a point perpendicular to the point where she started. She made the same maneuver on the right side, smiled, pleased with her artistic rendering. Then she drew an arrow through it and inserted the initials, "CC" over "MM," and grinned with pride. Morgan, intrigued by her window art, sat quietly behind her on the edge of the bed.

She turned slowly, both hands gripping the heavy coat tightly at her throat. She moved nonchalantly, but deliberately, toward him. Standing expressionless, she slowly, seductively, opened the coat as if pealing a banana. She rolled her shoulders to free herself of the heavy garment which fell to the floor behind her.

Morgan was truly in awe of her incredible beauty. He drank of her, slowly taking her in, savoring every moment like the taste of vintage wine. He gazed with appreciation, even a reverence, at her exquisite female form.

Chapter 44

Thursday, April 5, 2001

"HEY, MOM," SAID Clare, "I was wondering if we could grab a bite of lunch Saturday. I need to talk to you.

"Of course, darling. Where and when?" Marge responded.

"Well, how about La Madeline in the Arboretum area. You know, the one by my hotel."

"Yes, I know the location. If we met at eleven-thirty we might beat the crowd," Marge suggested.

"That's just great, Mom; I'll look forward to it."

o o o o o

CLARE GOT A table and was looking over a menu when Marge arrived. They hugged and exchanged kisses. Clare and Marge had always been close, even during the teen-aged years when daughters know everything and mothers are totally out of touch. Aside from sex, there was nothing they couldn't discuss and little that they hadn't. Clare had noticed, though, that as she got older her mother got wiser.

"You know, I think I'll order off the line."

"Me too, I love the petite Caesar and the tomato basil soup. You can buy it to go; did you know that?"

"Yes, I did know that."

There was a few minutes of small talk, and then Clare got right into it. "Mom, how do I get Morgan Mason to marry me?"

"What are you talking about? Do you really want a man that you have to 'get' to marry you?"

"Well, it's like I need something to push him that last little bit. We get along beautifully. And I know you won't want to hear this, but our love making is fabulous. He has shown me how to become the woman I dreamed of being. We both like music, art, cooking, and travel. And we both enjoy laughter, which is important in a relationship. We have so much in common, and money is certainly not an issue."

"Wait a minute, how do you know it's not an issue?"

"Well, he obviously makes a lot of it. I meant, there certainly wouldn't be an issue of him supporting a wife."

"Maybe he's concerned that it wouldn't last, and you'd get a healthy settlement and put a lien on future royalties."

A little confounded, Clare admitted. "Well, that's certainly possible, but I think it's unlikely."

"If he suggested a pre-nuptial agreement, how would you feel about that?"

"That would be a deal breaker for me. I mean, he would be sort of admitting that we may not make it. I would question his commitment."

"Speaking of money, Morgan Mason has spent a small fortune on you."

"You're right about that. I've been shocked and thrilled with some of the gifts. He has been very generous with his money."

"You had one failed marriage with an older man. Does Morgan's age give you pause?"

"Well, with Marshall, I think it was more about my age than his. I was pretty young and still trying to figure out who I was. I'm no longer the young and somewhat-sheltered, naive virgin." Marge did not react. Clare paused for a moment and then added, "No, I don't believe Morgan's age is a factor."

"You know," said Marge, "you always portray Morgan as this 'Mr. Wonderful,' and he sure seems like a keeper, but I'm pretty sure he's got some flaws. What is it you don't like about him?"

Clare laughed, "Well, sometimes he's not compassionate with other people, he's opinionated, and he has the worst sense of direction I've ever seen."

It was Marge's turn to laugh. "I don't hear any deal breakers on that list."

"No, but he doesn't share. That concerns me. You know, you'd like to think that the one you love would share everything with you."

"What, pray tell, does that mean?" Marge inquired.

"As best I can determine from talking to him, he's never been one to seek counsel from anyone; including his wife. When he has a problem or a concern, he just seems to work it out himself."

"Clare, is this about 'he doesn't need me?'"

"Maybe."

"Good God, Clare, that's such a girl thing. Get over it."

Clare looked away for a moment, thinking about what her mother had just said. "He's a strong man, and you should be grateful rather than hold it against him," Marge concluded.

Marge broached another, perhaps a more important subject.

"How long has he been single? Sixteen, seventeen years, something like that? He's a rich, successful, and handsome man. Now why do you think he hasn't settled down with a woman? It would be unreasonable to think he's not had his chances."

"Well, I think he just hasn't found the right girl."

"My darling daughter, that's what you want to believe. And what was that about no longer being naïve?"

Clare scrunched up her face as Marge's comments struck a chord. *She's probably right.*

"Look, just follow your heart. When you think it's time to broach the subject seriously, then go for it. You're a woman who wants to marry and have a family. You can't go on forever just being his girlfriend."

Clare starred at her. *What she says is true.*

"Let's go over there and pick out a pastry. My sweet tooth is acting up," said Marge.

Clare forced a smile as they approached the dessert counter. She didn't have sweets on her mind.

Chapter 45

IT WAS SUNDAY night, a week later, and Morgan had prepared the entire meal on the grill. He had cooked eggplant, zucchini, corn on the cob, Anaheim peppers, and jumbo shrimp. They had some good bread and a subtle red wine. Sinatra was singing in the background when Clare shattered the tranquility of the moment.

"Why aren't we married?" she inquired, bluntly.

"Because there hasn't been a ceremony."

"And why no ceremony?" Clare persisted.

"Because we haven't decided to have one."

"And why is that?" Clare continued.

"Cut the doubletalk, Clare; why are you doing this?" Morgan asked, at bit annoyed.

"I don't think anyone should consider marriage in less that a year. I think it takes at least that much time to really get to know someone. You and I have been dating 14 months. I love you, and you love me. We get along great. Frankly, I can see no legitimate reason to wait," Clare reasoned.

"We're doing so well. Why change things, Clare?"

"Because, Morgan, I want a husband, a home—children. I'm not willing to continue like this indefinitely. We're having fun, but this relationship is going nowhere."

"Well, I'm just not ready."

"Not ready!" Clare screamed. "Holy Mary, mother of God — will you ever be ready?"

"I can't answer that at this moment."

Clare began to weep. Morgan tried to console her but she would have none of it. She pushed him away. Defiantly she said, "I hate that I'm crying." Bogart began to bark; he sensed that something was wrong.

They sat there for what seemed an eternity and then Clare got up and went outside to her car. When she returned she placed the garage door opener on the corner of the dinning table and the house key on top of it. She grabbed her bag and went out the front door. She stood on the porch for a few minutes staring at the street and then stepped back inside; Morgan was sitting in the same spot with a troubled look on his face.

"Assuring me that it was coming from the heart and not just the words of a writer, you once told me you were just a boy in love with a girl. We'll it's the same with me. I don't care if you're a *New York Times* best-selling author or a waiter. I'm just a girl in love with a boy. I could almost hate you for this. I think we would have been good together. I think we could have had something special." And with that she turned on her heel and left the house. She did not come back this time.

o o o o o

"WHITE HOUSE, HOW may we serve you?"

"Marcia, this is Clare. Connect me with Jan Jennings please."

"Jan Jennings."

"Jan, this Clare. Listen, I've got a urinary tract infection, and I won't be in today. I'm sorry."

"Don't worry one bit. I've had that same thing myself, and I know what it's like. You just take care of yourself and come back in when you're okay. We'll cover for you."

"Thanks, Jan, I appreciate your understanding." Clare cried for two days. On Wednesday she went back to work. She knew she had to get control of her life and try to at least function. She had never been so low, and it was difficult to motivate herself. After a week she broke down at lunch and told the other girls what had happened with Morgan.

Chapter 46

Monday, May 7, 2001

"SALES, THIS IS Jan."

"Jan, this is Morgan Mason, is Clare around?"

"She's on her line, Morgan; do you want to wait or have her return the call?"

"I'll wait, thank you."

Jan put the call on hold and walked over to Clare's desk. "Morgan Mason's on line two. He's holding for you. I told him you were on another call. What do you want to do?" Clare had not seen or heard from Morgan since their breakup.

"It's okay, Jan; I can take it."

She took a deep breath, gathered herself, and picked up the phone, making sure to sound upbeat. "Well, Mason, what did I do to deserve a call from the great writer?" said Clare, a bit curt.

"Hi, Clare, it's nice to hear your voice."

Determined not to show the least sign of weakness, she cut to the chase. "What do you want, Morgan?"

Sensing the hostility, he wondered if he should even ask but decided to proceed anyway. "Well, I've got a romance novel being released this weekend in New York City. Ramsey House has a lot of activities planned, and I thought you might like to come with me. We'd leave Thursday night, and I'll fly you back Sunday night. The reason for that is I'm going on the road for a seven-city tour and book signing. I know you can't get away for that. Clare, there's no one on the planet I would rather have with me for this."

There was silence for a moment. Clare was trying to quickly frame a response. "Morgan, that's a lovely offer, and you know how much I like New York, but I'm going to South Africa to visit my friend Peter Wilson. I leave Friday."

Now there was silence on his side of the line. "Well, I hope you have a wonderful time. How long will you be away?"

"A month, maybe more," said Clare casually.

"That long. Well—uh, I know how you love Africa."

"Yes, yes I do."

"Well, I'll say goodbye then."

"Good luck with the book. I'm sure it will be another smash hit."

"You never really know, but I think it's pretty good."

"Well, I'd better get back to White House business."

"Oh, of course, goodbye, Clare."

Clare gently placed the phone back in its cradle. She sat quietly and stared at the wall behind her desk. In a few minutes tears began to roll down her face and then the sobbing started. Embarrassed, she ran from the sales office and headed for the ladies lounge.

Morgan sat staring into space. His eyes were red. He picked up Bogart and hugged him tight. "I miss her, Boggie, I miss her like crazy."

Chapter 47

"PETER," SAID CLARE, "everything is set. I fly out of DFW at 4:30 tomorrow afternoon. I arrive at Gatwick, at 7:35 the next morning. I've got an ugly layover so I'll probably take a cab into London."

"How ugly, love?"

"I don't leave until 7:30 that evening."

"That's pretty ugly."

"Anyway, I will arrive in Johannesburg at 7:20 the next morning. That will be Friday, May 18, 2001, so you don't get confused and stand me up."

"No chance at all of that, love. When you get to the end of the jetway, I'll be there to collect you."

"That'll be wonderful. I'm sorry it's so early."

"You forget, love, most of my days start early, much earlier than that. Oh, you'd better give me your flight number."

"Yeah, that would be a good idea. It's BA 1278."

"Got it."

"Well, I'm excited. I can't wait to see Africa again."

Baiting her, he questioned, "What about the old hunter?"

"Well, that goes without saying."

"See you, love."

"Yeah, see in Joburg, Peter."

Friday, May 11, 2001

CLARE SETTLED IN as the gigantic British Airways 747 reached cruising altitude. She had an aisle seat next to the center section. Even though the plane was almost at capacity, the seat next to her was empty, which suited her nicely. That way she didn't have to talk—or be clever, or accommodating, or anything. The wrong seat mate on a long flight can be pure agony. Strangely, her thoughts turned to Marshall. She recalled quite clearly, once they knew that the job in Johannesburg was confirmed, what he had suggested and the conversation they had.

"Clare, once I go to work, it will be like most other jobs. I'll have two weeks vacation after a year, but I suspect we will want to use that to come stateside to see our families. Since the company is paying our travel, I want to go early and see some of the country. I've been searching the net and I've found a tour that I'd really like to take. I've printed out the details."

"Well, let's have a look."

She remembered that he sat down beside her on the couch, handed her the itinerary and said, "It's with DarkCon Adventures, and it's seven weeks."

"Seven weeks!" Clare exclaimed.

"Well, yeah, I mean, if we want to see Africa, it's going to have to be something like this. I'm jazzed about it."

"Well, I'm glad to see you jazzed about something."

"I don't know how to take that."

"Ah, don't take it all. I'm just playing with your mind. Let's see. We fly into Cape Town, and the tour covers Kenya, Tanzania, Malawi, Zimbabwe, Botswana, Namibia and South Africa. This looks good, Marshall."

"Look, Clare, we also have optional visits to Victoria Falls and Zanzibar; and we have the opportunity to go white water rafting, cycling, bungee jumping, abseiling, and rappelling. And we'll be camping 80 percent of the time. You love camping."

"Marshall, it looks fantastic." She remembered how excited she had gotten. "And Marshall, we'll have to get a really good camera with a telephoto lens."

She still had fond memories of that trip. She wasn't quite sure why, but she had decided to keep a journal. The daily entries were an enlightening chronicle of the country, the people, and their fellow travelers. And in many ways it was about them, about her and Marshall. She hadn't so much as picked it up in years but had decided to bring it along and relive the initial trip. She thought it would help her to reconnect with Africa. The flight attendant had just served her a scotch and water. She took a sip and opened the diary to the first page.

Chapter 48

Cape Town, South Africa, 2:20 p.m. March 18, 1997

At last we're in an actual room, on a real bed at the Lion's Head Lodge. We arrived at 8:00 a.m. and were told that our room would not be available until 2:00 p.m. We'd been traveling since I can't remember when, and we didn't sleep well on the plane so we're rather like Zombies. Need sleep!

There is already much to write about. The first site of the city reminded me of San Francisco. It's sunny and cool, the air crisp and clean. There is little humidity, yet the ocean is in view of our hotel. Waves break endlessly on the beaches but we've yet to see a surfer. The sky is cloudless blue and although the city has several million people it is surprisingly clean, as if everyone was told that company was coming. There is no smog, little traffic, and very little of the odd tidbits of garbage you would expect to see in a city this size.

Since we had no room, at first, we decided to take a cab into the central city and check it out. It was Marshall's job to catch one of the local minivans that function as public transportation. They cost 3 Rand (30 cents) to get you wherever you want to go. Finally we walked across the street to a gas station where a half dozen uniformed Africans were talking amongst themselves. They smiled when we approached, and two of them shook Marshall's hand. Finally one of the men hailed a van for us and told the driver where we wanted to go.

Downtown, we found the city a pleasure to walk, and the people friendly. We were surprised to find the city a combination of glass skyscrapers and old Dutch-colonial-style buildings from the 1600-1700s. The streets are cobblestone in the center of town, and the whole place has a rather European feel to it. At the central market every booth seems to have the same variety of carved wooden elephants and rhinos.

Colored batik fabric is another popular item, and people dance and sing in the streets. Hawkers sometimes bothered us, although quietly because police maintain a visual presence both on foot and on horseback. Children and assorted red-eyed men engage in a variety of quick-buck schemes trying to take advantage of unsuspecting tourists.

Somewhere along the way we met Willie and Johnnie, two young teen-aged boys who assumed the role of tour guides, and we let them take us around the city. We met an old man who said he was Zulu. He wanted a handout. Willie shook his head when I gave him 20 Rand. "Look at his eyes," Willie said. "he will drink it up. Twenty is too much." Marshall also objected to me helping the man, but I felt charitable. I have a soft heart and he doesn't.

Clare laid down her diary and took a sip of her drink. She told the flight attendant to bring another. She had forgotten how furious Marshall had gotten when she gave the old man the 20 Rand. My God, it was 2 dollars American. But it wasn't the money. She had disobeyed her husband. She had seen his controlling side when they were dating, but she was young and she followed her heart far more that she trusted her brain. She had learned the hard way the gravity of that mistake. She finished off the drink and picked up her journal once more.

After the cultural museum tour, where we saw some fascinating Egyptian artifacts, we found an upscale Indian restaurant. The boys were well behaved and spoke three languages. We ordered curried ostrich, beef, chicken, and lamb. They told us that they had never been in a restaurant. Soon our waitress returned with our food. She spooned the rice into the boy's plates as if they were family. She smiled at the boys and asked where they had come from. Her family had once lived in the same poor township. She spoke to them in Afrikaans then told us, "These are brave boys. They have come in from one of the distant townships on the train. The trains can be rough. Their mother, who is a heavy drinker, sent them in to hustle money."

Marshall said to them, "She is a very nice woman, don't you think?" He told me later that Johnnie had whispered to him, "The devil came and tempted a woman. It was written long ago. From then on women could not be trusted. It is true."

Marshall told me that the boys had a general mistrust of women. During lunch the boys said they went to Catholic school. "It is for the poor because it is free," Willie said, "regular school costs a lot, maybe 360 dollars a year plus uniforms." That's a great deal of money in Africa. Marshall and I were troubled by the school situation because there doesn't seem to be a normal progression of grades but a kind of general teaching peppered with religious morality. And we're Catholics who went to Catholic school and know how excellent it is, but of course, that's in America.

During lunch the boys started working on us about needing clothes. They dreamed of Nikes and suggested that we might arrange to send them some of the shoes from America. The boys scooped up all the small packets of sugar from the table. Marshall told them to put them back. It just so happened that our waitress saw them and came over. She told them it was okay. She told us that they would put the sugar in coke cans over a fire at home to be heated up with tea. The food bill was 33 dollars American. Marshall told the boys again, "She's a nice woman, don't you think?" But they weren't sure they could trust her. They thought she might be setting them up. We paid the tab and I gave the boys 20 dollars each and the food we didn't eat to take home. They were happy. They got us a van, and we went back to the hotel.

1:30 a.m.

Darn it all. We slept too long. We had planned on getting up for dinner but didn't wake up until 10:30 p.m. and weren't hungry. We just watched a lousy movie. Marshall went back to sleep, but I'm having trouble. Jet lag really screws me up. He's snoring loudly!

March 19, 1997 7:50 a.m.

We went down to the hotel restaurant at 7:00 a.m. sharp. We both had a South African breakfast which consisted of scrambled eggs, toast, some strange crossbreed of ham and bacon, venison sausage, baked beans, sautéed mushrooms and grilled tomato. The service was poor, and our waiter spoke no English. He never understood a word we said, but seemed happy to speak his language as if repetition would somehow get through to us. We waited an eternity for our change, and Marshall seized the moment to comment on the paper money. Unlike other countries the bills have pictures of animals instead of people. The Rand 100 has a cape buffalo in blue with a herd of zebra on the *back. Other denominations had a male lion, really well done, a herd of big tusker elephants, a rhino in green with cattle and sheep on the back.*

10:00 a.m.

We met our group and our tour guides. Our guides are both female. Amanda, who goes by Mandy, is the lead guide and the other one is a six-foot-one inch Kiwi named Carol. Carol looks like she could beat the hell out of most men. Our cook is from Zimbabwe and goes by Mr. Sacko. I don't know what's up with that. We have two Scots; Will and Thomas, and a Polish couple named Dan and Elsie. We have Charlie from Australia, Maggie from New Zealand, Julie from Aspen, and Edra from Ireland. There is Brandon, a Canadian; and Tony, a very muscular, good-looking young Englishman. He is just out of graduate school.

One of the truly enjoyable things about international travel is the interesting people you meet. Thomas, the Scot, farts all the time, and he seems to be impervious to it. This should be an interesting trip. I'm looking forward to it. Anyway, after all the introductions, Mandy checked all the passports, collected our vouchers, and suggested we might make a run down to the Cape, later on, to see the sights.

In the afternoon we loaded up in our Mercedes truck for the drive out of town to the Cape of Good Hope. As we drove through the suburbs of Cape Town it occurred to me that in many ways this would be a nice place to live. Visually it is stunning, with the sweeping bays, the green hills, and the mountain rising above it all. You see tall strands of eucalyptus and large sprays of bougainvillea. Everything seems well manicured. Aside from the natural beauty, it's the houses that I really love. They are built on a rise of hills, all with ocean views. Out of town we passed through quaint seaside communities with their antique shops and cafes. We are told that the architecture is Cape Dutch, a style that seems obsessed with bleached white mortar over brick, and colored tile roofs. Most have gables, and some have thatched roofs. We were able to visit a penguin colony before arriving at the windswept Cape itself. This is one of the places we've all read about and heard about. Now we are here. Wow!

Tonight some of us went to the Victoria and Albert Waterfront. This area is similar to Fisherman's Wharf only much more upscale and immaculate. No drug addicts or panhandlers. There is a very impressive mall, and along the water are lots of restaurants and pubs. Maggie, Julie, and Edra, the three women in black, joined us for dinner. Julie is the stereotype of a dumb blond and is so gullible that it's criminal. But Julie has a major-league body. Not in my league, of course, but well endowed. Brandon can't take his eyes off of her.

Marshall and I split a "Seafood Spectacular," which came out in a large skillet the size of a pizza pan and contained a lobster, a dozen jumbo shrimp, a half-pound of calamari, a pound of fish and lots of rice. That meal was 250 Rand, which was twenty-five bucks American. We all wound up in the same pub. The beer was really good, and I'm not really a beer drinker, but I suspect I will become one by necessity. We had a time getting the Scots to leave the pub. Thomas and Will drank at the bar, and Thomas farted constantly. I think the beer made it worse.

Chapter 49

March 20, 1997, 7:30 p.m.

It was cold today, and we're all in jackets. Maggie, Julie, and Edra, who have become inseparable, are dressed in black, as usual. At eleven o'clock this morning we all went to a winery in the Stellenbach region about 40 minutes from town. Marshall and I are the token Americans on this tour, and we really enjoy playing up the fact that we are also Texans. They know about Texas all over the world. I love it.

We drove past some low-income neighborhoods and even these homes give the impression of a dignified people who do the best with what they have. Along the roads you rarely see garbage. You also never see junk cars, as we often do in the States. Another curious thing is the lack of bugs. Though we have eaten in the open-air for most of our meals we haven't seen a single fly, gnat, mosquito, ant or roach.

When we got to the wine country I got an understanding of how big the Cape region really is. Marshall was shooting photos like crazy. They are going to cost us a fortune to develop, but on the other hand it is such a photo-rich environment (listen to me) that it's hard to resist. Anyway, the valley looks like the pictures I've seen of the south of France and stretches out to distant, jagged blue mountains. We passed through huge wine estates with old Dutch homes dating to the 1700s, and miles of green farmland with wheat, and acres of wild flowers in red, purple, and yellow. I am unable to really describe the beauty of this. It must be seen first hand. We must have tasted at least 25 wines today between eleven and five. We were all in a simpatico mood.

We went for Indian food tonight. Marshall ended up seated at the head of the table. The tipsy Europeans took turns asking him about America. It bugged him after a while but one of the things I've always liked about Europeans is that they are inquisitive, well educated and usually well traveled. It gives them a broad perspective of things. All in all, for me, this has been the best day so far.

March 21, 1997

We're in the truck driving north across the Cape. Mostly rolling plains of farmland as far as the eye can see. Wheat fields dominate the landscape, as do the occasional vineyards with their perfect green rows. The three zebra in the farmer's field remind me quickly of where we are. I saw a small heard of springbok next to a vineyard. Mandy just announced our first pee stop. Just in time, I might add.

11:30 a.m.

The other members of our merry band have noticed me writing. They are curious, but I won't let they read any of it. It's driving them nuts. I'm sure they think it's all about them. We've been driving about an hour and a half and are coming to the end of a huge valley; still, lots of wheat. I saw what looked like cream-colored stones, all the same size and shape, scattered randomly in several fields. In one field there must have been over a hundred of them. The stones turned out to be ostrich eggs.

Noon

We came through the mountain pass and have emerged into a narrow river valley. On either side of us are rugged hills of gray basalt covered over with desert scrub. The valley is full of pale orange gravel and white sand. There's an abundance of orchids. The country is dry, like Northern Arizona. The group is quiet, half reading and half asleep—most of whom have their mouths wide open. Marshall is one of them. I've always been tempted to drop something in there.

1:30 p.m.

Just finished lunch; sandwiches with two versions of ham-like cold cuts, English condiments that took some investigating. There was this mustard-based gruel with pickles and other undetermined bits of something. I decided not to ask what the bits were. The English put beets on their sandwiches which turns their lips and teeth a purplish hue. The Kiwis eat marmite, which I thought was a type of rodent, and perhaps that's what's in the little brown jar. And something else called Melrose, which is a misguided version of canned squirt cheese of which tragically I had a sample of. This taught me a very important lesson. Never keep your toothbrush in your pack when it happens to be stowed away in the vehicle locker. Sadly, the world now tastes of Melrose. It has formed a waterproof layer, something akin to bathtub calking, on all the exposed surfaces of my teeth. By the evening I fear that I may need to seek the assistance of a dental professional. Marshall thought it was funny. But that's only because he declined to taste Melrose. We're on the road again. We are told that we should reach the border with Namibia by evening.

5:45 p.m.

We're driving through what appears to be the Sonoran Desert. Earlier at a pee stop we found the biggest grasshopper I've ever seen. It had bright red legs and a green back like a Christmas ornament. Hungry again, so I ate an apple. I'm still struggling with Melrose.

March 22, 1997

We have a big problem. The camera won't work. The battery light flashes even after the battery is charged. Marshall has been cursing and raving. We are both sick about the situation. It was such fun to camp last night. With everyone working together we were able to get set up in about 30 minutes, and then out came the wine. Marshall opened the Cabernet that we purchased at the Fairview winery, and immediately five people appeared with cups. We opened three more bottles and sat by the fire waiting for Mr. Sacko to finish cooking dinner.

As we laughed and talked, Thomas threw in an occasional fart. I find it gross, as do the other women, but it's also funny. But we don't dare laugh. We don't want to encourage him. It was cold after dark, and most everyone had to bundle up and put on thick socks. While we waited for the food Mandy read off the camp duties for us to volunteer for. Farting Thomas and Will were unanimously elected as bar tenders. It seems so natural to them anyway. The bar is nothing more than a large ice chest that's been stocked. The Scots returned with eight cases of beer and assorted mixers. We were rightly impressed. Marshall was assigned to the pack detail. About 7:30 each morning he has to help unload all the packs that have been stowed overnight.

As it grew colder we huddled around the fire drinking wine. We were in a circle, and Will and Thomas, who usually sit together, were on opposite sides of the fire from each other. Then they started farting, first Will and then Thomas. It reminded me of that Mel Brooks movie, Blazing Saddles. This went on until about 8:30 p.m. when dinner was finally served. We had hake fish, scalloped potatoes, peas and carrots. It was really great food and plenty of it. We are usually very hungry by the end of a day's journey. Marshall went back for seconds, as did Thomas and Will. After dinner we had hot chocolate and brandy for a nightcap.

This morning I woke up at about six and had to pee. On the way to the bathroom I heard farting from the Scots' tent. I wondered if the reverberations had wakened the girls in the next tent. As for sleeping, though, I had the best night so far. The air mattress works really well, and by the time we take turns blowing it up we are ready to crash. It was cold enough that both Marshall and I were glad to climb into our sleeping bags. He snores, but I have gotten used to it. I can usually fall asleep before him, so that helps.

With the exception of Dan, everyone in our group is personable and cooperative and really fun to be with. In spite of that, Marshall and I have not bonded with anyone. Tony, the young Englishman, flirts with me every chance he gets. He is careful not to let Marshall know about it. I am flattered but certainly do not encourage him. In fact, I just laugh at him, but he is not deterred. Throughout the day we flow in and out of activities together. We come together for a time to play cards, eat and drink, but I've noticed that all of us retreat to our own little spaces to be alone and do our own thing.

Clare remembered thinking that this was to be a test for her and Marshall. Frankly, it is not often that a husband and wife are together twenty-four hours a day, for seven straight weeks. She marveled at how some couples have a business and can work together constantly. They hadn't been married all that long, and were still getting to know each other, but Clare knew for sure that there was no possible way that she and Marshall could have been in business together.

She continued to read from the journal.

I should mention that our Mercedes truck has eight speakers in the roof, and any one can be turned on or off or adjusted if you need more quiet. There is a constant flow of good music on CDs. The word is that we'll be at the Namibian border in less than an hour. We'll cross at a place called AiAis near Fish River Canyon. There are hot springs there. The desert around us is flat as a pool table. A little low scrub here and there and along the far horizon I see rock outcroppings and small hills made of chunky marble.

Chapter 50

CLARE LAID DOWN the journal and took another sip of her scotch. She caught a flight attendant's eye and held up her glass indicating she wanted another. She and Morgan had talked about going to Africa. Tears began to well up in her eyes. She thought of that first *chance meeting* at the airport in Austin and then seeing him again at the writer's conference. She remembered the excitement of their first date, the trip to Las Vegas, New York, that Christmas at his place with all her family. Oh, and the time he flew to Tyler—the storm—and the agonizing thought that he had crashed. She remembered that special moment outside her office that day when he first told her he loved her. And she remembered the love making; such excitement, such fulfillment. She couldn't help but wonder if she would ever experience anything like it again? But as much as anything, she remembered the quiet times when he just held her. By the time the flight attendant arrived with her third drink, Clare was crying uncontrollably.

"What's wrong? What can I do to help?"

"Shoot me!" exclaimed Clare, to the shock of the attendant.

The attendant put the drink on Clare's tray and knelt down in the aisle. She hugged Clare and tried to console her. "I'm sorry," said Clare, "I've got to get control of myself." The attendant fetched a small towel from the galley and gave it to Clare. She whipped her eyes.

"A man?" the attendant inquired.

"What else?" said Clare with a sigh.

"I've been there, honey; I know what it's like."

"It's worse than death."

"Right, with death there is closure. It's over."

"Exactly."

"Well, I'm sorry. I'll be back to check on you later."

"Thank you so much. You're very kind. I really appreciate it."

Clare took the fresh drink and downed it. Perhaps the alcohol would ease the pain. "Damn it," she muttered under her breath, "Why did it have to end? We had so much going for us. Why? Why? Why?" For a few minutes she just stared at the seat back in front of her. Then she picked up the journal once more. "Maybe Africa will help."

12:10 p.m.
Border Crossing

The Orange River marks the border with Namibia. The river is a shallow green ribbon that runs at the base of a 1000-foot escarpment. We have to deal with the formality of stamping out of South Africa, then go to Namibian immigration just over the river. Inside the Namibian border station there is a poster of invasive species of plant life to be aware of. It strikes me that we are people linked by the unlikeliest of bonds—weeds.

2:00 p.m.
Namib Desert

It was a carefree game of Frisbee while lunch was being prepared. The desert stretches to the far horizons and we have plenty of room for long distance throws. Marshall jumped and made a bad landing, which brought the full weight of his hefty body down on his right ankle. He appears to have a tennis ball where his right anklebone should be. It could even be a slight fracture, and he's in quite a bit of pain. We'll just have to see how it goes, but it's the worst sprain anyone here has ever seen, and they wince when they look at it. We have about three more hours until we reach camp. We have his leg elevated, and he's taken some anti-inflammatory medication.

March 23, 1997
Namib Desert Camp

Marshall had a terrible night. He was moving around a lot; very restless with that ankle. He's in lots of pain. I let him have the tent all to himself and slept outside. I was the only one of our group to do that.

March 24, 1997

Last night after dinner we all went up to a large shallow pool fed by the hot springs. Marshall hobbled over there with the rest of us. I thought it might help his ankle. The swelling is no longer concentrated in one spot but now envelopes his whole foot and leg to almost his calf. Everyone was in a silly mood, except Marshall, cutting up and telling stories and dirty jokes.

10:30 a.m.
Desert Camp

I had a great hike this morning in the riverbed. I was with Brandon and Tony. It was silent. Occasionally we heard birds. A quarter of a mile in we watched a family of baboons emerge from the saltbush across the stream and amble along for about fifty yards before taking cover again. Soon after we saw something that really got our attention: tracks of a big cat. The prints were probably several days old but well formed and about the size of

Tony's hand. We looked at each other, and Brandon said, "Leopard?" We had all done our homework before coming, and we knew that the baboons are a favorite dish of leopards.

Back in camp now. It's hot, and some in our group complained of dehydration. It's 95 degrees and bone dry. I think the heat feels good; it's a dry heat. And in Austin, Texas, in the summer, we have many days in the 90s and even sustained periods in the 100s. The Europeans are more accustomed to a damper, cooler climate. Marshall's ankle is huge and painful. After lunch we are moving to another camp above the Fish River Canyon.

3:45 p.m.
Camp

We're set up at a camp above the canyon, still in Namib. In the center of camp, looking a bit out of place, is a powder-blue pool with water. So far it has proved to be the most exciting focal point in several days. We spent a couple of hours there. Now we are off on a hike along the rim of the canyon and will enjoy wine and cheese at sunset. Marshall's whole foot is puffy now and turning blue. We still suspect there may be a fracture. Poor guy, he has to stay in camp with Mr. Sacko.

March 25, 1997
Namib Desert

We have a full day of driving. By day's end we should be at the dunes. The desert around us is flat and scrubby with low, purple mesas on either horizon. I am starting to realize just how vast this country is. This morning we passed a single springbok sprinting along and a pair of ostriches. The only vehicles we've seen have been other safari trucks, all self-sufficient. I suspect regular cars would be reluctant to attempt such a vast expanse. Marshall is not quite himself mentally. I think it could be the *medication he is taking. Mandy warned him that there could be some side affects, like depression. He has not been very talkative the last few days. The others are cheerful enough.*

We stopped at an overlook above the Fish River Canyon, which is like a baby Grand Canyon. Couldn't take any pictures, though, because our brand new (and expensive) camera hasn't worked since the first day. Anyway, the idea was to have a wine and cheese party. We did, but the wine was awful. The box tasted better. When the sun went down the sky changed to that desert flame of orange and red. Mandy said it was the best sunset she'd seen here. Will and Thomas started talking about Haggis, for some dumb reason. It made me want to puke.

When we got back to camp, another truck had arrived with about twenty people. They'd been traveling about nine weeks down from Nairobi. They said one day a heard of elephants attacked their camp and did some minor damage. While camping along a river a woman from another safari had been eaten by a crocodile. You just don't think that something like that could actually happen. But we must always remember that we are in Africa.

Chapter 51

March 26, 1997

There was a lot of drinking last night, and Marshall got really drunk. He's depressed from the pain and his inability to do things with the rest of the group. I can understand it. The party went on until midnight.

10:00 a.m.

We're on a paved road for the first time in two days. All paved roads we've been on have been good. As always the countryside and its rest stops have been well manicured and spotless. The Polish couple is a curious pair. She's soft-spoken and amiable. He's completely anti-social and looks remarkably like a human buzzard. When he kisses her I have this overwhelming urge to run at him waving my arms to shoo him away.

11:45 a.m. Bethanie,
Namibia

We just finished grocery shopping in this little one-camel town; maybe a hundred residents. The houses are block with corrugated tin roofs. Except, instead of Indians or Mexicans, these people are Bushmen crossbreeds, according to Mandy. And they are butt-ugly. I'm talking grotesque. The nicer-looking ones have jaundiced yellow skin, and cheekbones like elbows, square teeth, and sparse hair that sprouts in little black dots like peppercorns.

The first store we checked out couldn't decide what it wanted to be. There was hardware, canned food, blue work uniforms, rice, and a lot of animal medicine. No lotto tickets. (Ha, ha) I went with Mr. Sacko to the other store and bought fresh bread, cheese, eggs, some kind of meat and chicken.

March 27, 1997
Sousousvlei, Namibia

The land seems largely untouched and unspoiled. Saw kudu today. We are camped in dune country. Along the Skeleton Coast the dunes that are close to the sea are full of diamonds. The stones lie out in the open and shine in the moonlight. The Bushmen used to collect the stones like trinkets, calling them moonstones. White men came and murdered the little men for the trinkets. The area is off limits to everyone now, except for the mining company.

This was interesting. We were told that at the Skeleton Coast National Park the rangers and research biologists modified a few laptop computers for the Bushmen to use. Instead of letters, the characters were replaced with images of animal tracks and some symbols for numbers. The little men were then enlisted to help researchers by carrying the laptops and recording the migration of animals within the park. The signals were then beamed by satellite to the researchers, and they claim that they have never had more up-to-date and accurate data. Funny, they said, to see little naked men with computers and poison arrows.

These African camps we visit continue to impress. We have no camping areas in America that can match them for cleanliness, maintenance, or amenities. They all have braai (BBQ pits), tile bathrooms, and showers with hot water. This is our favorite camp so far, for beauty and perks. We're camping on the edge of the red dunes. In the center of the camp is a perfect swimming pool with grass lawn around it. Next to the pool is a thatched-roof building that has a bar with South African beer on tap. We were at the bar last night, and while the bartender was mixing our drinks a huge lizard crawled across the shelf behind him. We ask about the lizard and he said it had been around for quite a while—about eight years.

March 28, 1997

This morning we left camp at 5:00 a.m. in order to get deep into the dunes by sunrise. It was one of the most spectacular vistas I've ever seen. This dune is 1000 feet tall. The dunes are a living hell to hike. Marshall is still suffering with his ankle, and there was no way he could do this. He's spent so much time with Mr. Sacko that they may have something going. (Just kidding) We finally managed to make it to the top of a 100 footer. All the dunes have a knife-edge spine that bends and shifts with the prevailing wind. The spine breaks and slides away as we hike. The sand is so fine that it flows down like liquid, the color of cinnamon, and begs to be rolled on. But even after rolling down the dunes you get up clean because it drains off just as easily as it went on. The sand is so heavy and the air so dry that it doesn't stick.

We are all in the pool now, and I'm trying hard not to get water all over my journal. Everyone is crazy to read it, but I still refuse. It drives them nuts. We've got a mixed bag of bathers;

Germans, Aussies, and Kiwis. Our camera *awakened from its mysterious coma and is working perfectly. That's good because we will need it later this evening,*

2:00 p.m.

We went deep into the dunes to hike. The camera went into a coma again. Very aggravating! I'm going to insist that Marshall purchase another one when we are in Swakopmund tomorrow. These dunes are truly spectacular, and it makes me ill that we haven't been able to take a single shot. Not even a shot of Will and Thomas running down the dune naked, while Edra filmed the dueling moons. Aren't I clever?

Chapter 52

March 29, 1997

We've broken camp and are headed for Swakopmund where we'll say for three days. A few minutes ago we passed an oryx walking along the road. I've never seen such a magnificent animal. Big as a horse, with clearly defined muscles moving under his hide. Long spiral horns four feet long that could kill a lion...or a man.

Last night after dinner a group of us were enjoying after-dinner drinks and sitting by the fire. Thomas, in his customary crude way, was undoubtedly showing Mr. Sacko how much he enjoyed the food by letting out a disgusting belch. Carol nailed him when she inquired, "Got a new instrument, there, have you Thomas?" The entire group erupted in laughter.

Marshall is beginning to improve, and we were enjoying some very nice port that he had purchased in Cape Town. Jackals were running around camp, and one of them got within about ten feet of us. Another was outside of the tent where Maggie, Julie, and Edra were bunking. Thomas hollered for them to keep the door zipped. Maggie yelled, "Will he eat us?" Will yelled back, "Not if he gets a good look at you." Maggie reacted immediately. "Jackass!" We all laughed.

We see so many springbok and ostrich that no one even comments anymore. Mr. Sacko continues to impress. We returned to camp last night about eight and were dirty and tired from hiking. He fixed curried chicken, and it was outstanding. I like to talk to him about cooking, and he knows I, too, like to cook. Sacko is from the Shona tribe, and I am learning a few words. Sacko is really a quiet sort, but when he is setting up to cook he gets very excited and hops around, singing in Shona or whistling. The cook teams are supposed to help, but he will tell them the wrong time. Like most cooks he'd rather do it himself. I'm on a different team, but he likes to have me help him.

1:00 p.m.

We got an advanced report about Zimbabwe. The official exchange rate is 50 Zim to one dollar. But the black market rate is 950 Zim to one, so Zim will be unbelievably cheap. We're in the middle of your basic Lawrence of Arabia-type desert. Miles and miles of sand and dunes. Heat waves flutter. But the temp is an unbelievable 75 degrees. We've got about five more hours of driving. I'm going to try to sleep.

March 30, 1997

After thousands of square miles of open desert a town has suddenly sprung up on the coast. We have arrived at a very modern town, a very Germantown called Swakopmund. There is absolutely nothing to indicate we are in Africa. Many of the streets are brick, and the buildings are either contemporary or, more commonly, German-quaint, with flowerboxes and clock spires. Like most places in Africa the town looks like the maid and painter just left.

We're coming back from the Cape Cross Seal Colony with a reported population of 100,000. We saw many huge males, easily as large as a grizzly. But most of the seals were around 100 pounds. Like all critters in cramped areas, they are irritable. If one comes back from a swim he has to hump over a dozen or so sunbathers to get to an open spot.

Tonight we are eating together at a place that specializes in African cuisine. Then for the next three days we are free to skydive, fish, dune surf, quad bike, and drink at the pubs. Believe it or not, I think we will miss camping. But the best part of staying in a hotel is the laundry service.

March 31, 1997
Swakopmund 9:00 p.m.

I'm really too tired to write but it's a good brand of tired. Marshall dropped off to sleep rather quickly. He's snoring like a train. It would help if he'd lose some weight. He gets defensive when I mention it. Anyway, we were up at seven to eat breakfast and off in search of a camera shop. The two crazy Scots tagged along. We found one shop that sold decent cameras, and they had only two available that we would consider. We finally settled on a Nikon with a 300 zoom to go with it and a nice pack. It cost 7500 Namibian, or about 750 bucks American. Of course, when we returned to the hotel the Cannon was working perfectly.

The morning was a complete blast. We went out to the dunes about 15 minutes from town. The dunes were 100-200 feet high. We strapped on snowboards and did some good runs. Sand gets in places I never dreamed possible. The highlight of the day was unexpected. We did some lay-down boarding on pieces of masonite. Marshall actually did this and had a blast. Walking up the dunes was brutal on everyone. Marshall was hurting, but he did it anyway. He said the ride was worth the pain. We'll see how he feels tonight. I did two runs down a 200-footer that had jumps that got me airborne. When I looked up from the bottom they were clapping and cheering. I was pretty proud of myself. Back up on top the guide said my last run was the fastest of the day, and that I was probably doing 60 mph. They got it on video. Later *on we did quad bikes in the same area. That was good because Marshall could do that without pain. Tomorrow we go paragliding and then dancing in the evening.*

March 31, 1997

Last night's dinner was exceptional. We ate at Cape to Cairo in our hotel. Marshall and I had mussels au gratin, crocodile (same as chicken), grilled kudu and several glasses of a very nice house red wine. The total bill was 20 dollars American.

April 1, 1997 Swakopmund

Paragliding is like stripping off all the bed linens and marching up 20 flights of stairs with it so you can jump off the roof. Our instructor took us out to a 150-foot dune but the walk up was more like a quarter of a mile. Walking up dunes with a bad ankle, like I said, is brutal on Marshall, but once at the top he got off well on his first launch and landed about 50 yards from the truck. He was proud of himself. I was happy for him. He needs some good things to happen for a change. I had a good first run myself, and then it was the Namibian death march again. The second flight was better. We had good wind, and after launch I got up about 100 feet and hung there for several minutes, drifting slowly to a perfect landing.

Marshall sat out the second run to catch his breath and rest his throbbing ankle. By the third run the wind was really ripping, and poor Marshall (snake bit I guess), had another bad experience. The German who was supposed to be helping him got his sail too close to the summit, and when the wind caught the sail he got dragged over the crest and down the steep back side to the bottom. The German didn't even bother to check on Marshall. His lines were all fouled and so was his mood when he finally dragged himself back over the top about 25 minutes later. I waited for him. When we got his lines straightened out he got off okay, no thanks to the German, and had as nice a flight as did I. By then we were both worn out.

After we got back to the hotel everyone but Dan and Elsie went to the pub for a beer. Ordinarily, I'm not a big beer drinker, hardly ever touch the stuff. But here in Africa I've kinda acquired a taste for it. Anyway, after the dunes and the German, it tasted like liquid gold and was good and cold. After that we walked down to the camera store; Marshall, Will and Thomas and me. The clerk behind the counter was a really big German, 6 foot 5 inches at least, in jeans and a safari shirt. Thomas needed film and asked for either Kodak or Fuji 400. The German slapped some Fuji 100 down on the counter. No matter what Thomas said, the man wouldn't sell him anything else. With hands on hips he declared, in a heavy German authoritarian accent, "This is sufficient for our country. This is all we use." Thomas was irritated and told the clerk that he'd just wait and stock up on 400 when we got to Zimbabwe. The German shouted, "You can't get film in Zimbabwe! There is no film in Zimbabwe!" Confused, Thomas asked, "Why not?" The German threw up his hands and said, "Why? Because Mugabe is a madman—and they've all run amok!"

Chapter 53

April 2, 1997

We're leaving Swakopmund. Last night was big. We started at a restaurant called Kuki's. The place was very old world and full of stern Germans, who were both large and serious. That pretty much describes the average resident of this town. Even the usually friendly blacks were more reserved. At dinner we were joking around, with Thomas and Marshall doing impressions of the big German from the camera shop. They were getting really boisterous when we spotted Carol waiving her hands at us to tone it down. When Marshall looked around, the entire German contingency was starring coldly at our table.

Marshall and I had oysters au gratin, some excellent grilled fish, some nice wine and coffee. Our bill was 14 dollars American. We love this country!

April 3, 1997

We are camped in an area that looks like south Texas. Yesterday we drove all day, and all of us were tired and quiet. When we got to camp it was close to sunset, and we loaded ourselves into the backs of two trucks to go to the Otjitotongwe

Cheetah sanctuary. The wild cheetahs are fed once a day on a diet of old donkeys and old horses that have to be put down. Marshall got some good close-ups. Before one feeding I was seated on the cab of a truck when a wild cheetah jumped up on the hood and stood within two feet of my face. Mario, the driver, came out with a stick to get the animal away from me, and the animal charged him. That was close. We are reminded once again that this is Africa. Mario told us that Namibia has the largest cheetah population in the world, around 2,500.

For dinner we had traditional African food; mealie meal, stewed chicken, and greens. You roll the mealie, which is white corn meal, into balls and swirl it around in the gravy. All of it we ate with our fingers. Some complained, including my dear husband, but I thought it was great food and great fun.

April 4, 1997 3:45 p.m.
Etosha National Park

Within minutes of entering the park we saw many zebra and several giraffe. Marshall got some good shots with our new Nikon; at least we hope so.

10:00 p.m.
Waterhole

After dinner we all sat around drinking wine. Then someone suggested wandering down to the waterhole just beyond camp. Soft lighting had been rigged up so you can see the animals after dark. There was a black rhino mother with her calf, and she was very defensive. We saw a couple of giraffes who wanted to come in but apparently were intimidated by the rhino. By now some 30 people are watching. Then Thomas, the Scot, became the man of the moment. He leaned forward to aim his telephoto, and with the leaning let out a long, trumpeting fart that raised the snout of the mother rhino from 50 paces away.

Mr. Sacko completely lost it and had to leave the area. Ironically, Thomas probably got the best shot of the evening using a time exposure.

One of the best things about Etosha is the facilities. It's like we are at a four-star hotel, and I know hotels. It has a beautiful pool and an awesome mahogany bar with a bow-tied bartender. The sky is brilliant with stars, and the weather is absolutely perfect. I'm glad Marshall suggested we come on this trip. It is an experience we will remember a lifetime.

April 5, 1997 7:30 a.m.
Etosha

Since the Cannon is now functioning we are both taking pictures. So far this morning I have taken giraffe, springbok, wildebeest, oryx, and a pale, chanting goshawk.

8:45 a.m.

What an incredible morning already. We were watching a waterhole loaded with zebra and kudu when they got really spooky. A female lion had emerged from the bush and had made her way over to the water. We noticed a little later that a young male had come out to the side of the road to watch her. I got some good shots of that bad boy. Then the female ambled back and he chased her, batting at her. She rolled over playfully then got up and played hard to get: evidently a mating ritual. Soon they got it on and then walked off into the bush. I asked Marshall if he was paying attention. He didn't take that very well. He could have a better sense of humor sometimes. We are headed back to camp to lounge by the pool.

7:30 p.m.
Namatoni Camp

The amount of game today was overwhelming. By the end of the day we were passing on shots that would have seemed spectacular in the morning. I've noticed that zebras seem to be leaders of sorts, and I've noticed that the wildebeest seem to follow their lead as to when its okay to enter a waterhole; fascinating. Zebras are also pretty irritable animals, and we see it play out with all the biting, kicking, and snorting. It's also fascinating to see all the different species mixing together, getting along, and even communicating, as when the birds signal the zebras that the lions are approaching.

Marshall tells me he has shot three more rolls of animal pictures today alone: ostrich, kudu, lion, elephant, hyena, jackal, hawk, giraffe, zebra, springbok, oryx and vulture. We happened upon a dead giraffe about ten paces from the road. The carcass was covered with vultures and one very scrappy jackal. At one point the jackal leaped up and bit the ass (if indeed a vulture has an ass) of the vulture above it, and the bird got this hilarious look and flapped and squawked like crazy. I thought Marshall and Will were going to bust a gut laughing. It was pretty funny. We see jackals every night. They are the coyotes of Africa and invade the camps at night to root through garbage cans like dogs. That particular jackal got the respect of our group. Vultures are three times the size of a jackal, but this guy held his own with the dirty dozen.

The Scots are cooking tonight. God help us. We understand it's a dish involving minced beef, potatoes and carrots mixed together in gruel. Next week we'll be in Zimbabwe. We hear stories about it. Now when anyone mentions Zimbabwe either Marshall or Thomas will imitate the big German from the camera shop, and declare, "Zimbabwe! There is no film in Zimbabwe. Mugabe is a madman!" Marshall does it pretty well, but when Thomas the Scot does German, it's hysterical.

With all the talk of Robert Mugabe, we asked Mandy and Carol to clue us in. Between them we got a pretty good rundown. They explained that he was 73 years old and had served as prime minister first, and then was elected president in 1987. He continues to be reelected. It seems he was a leading force in the black population's struggle for majority rule which he said they got in 1980.

Mugabe was born at a Jesuit mission north of the British colony of Southern Rhodesia. He was educated at mission schools and the University of Fort Hare in South Africa. In the late 50s he taught in Ghana, where he became interested in Marxism and African nationalism. After returning to Southern Rhodesia in 1960, he became involved in the National Democratic Party who opposed white rule. After the NDP was banned, Mugabe became involved with a new party, the Zimbabwe African People's Union, or ZAPU, which was also banned due to opposition to white rule.

Like many black political activists he wound up being jailed for 10 years. While in jail he studied law and was awarded correspondence degrees from the University of South Africa and the University of London. His popularity remained, even in prison, and he was recognized by many ZANU members as the leader of the party.

The war between black nationalists and the Rhodesian government began in earnest in 1972. After Mogabe was freed from jail he became active in the ZANU guerrilla army and finally became the undisputed ZANU leader in 1976. They eventually forced a negotiation with moderate leaders. They tried a coalition government in 1979 but later that year agreed to full black-majority rule. Mogabe's government has been plagued with corruption and scandal, but he has managed to hold onto power.

We were up very late, and on the way to bed we passed close to Brandon's tent. We could hear activity inside, and then we heard a breathy female outburst, "Oh, God, oh, God yes!" Marshall looked at me with a sheepish grin and commented, "Sounds like Brandon and Julie are having another prayer meeting."

Chapter 54

"MAY I HAVE your name?" the flight attendant inquired. Looking up from her journal she replied, "Clare, Clare Casey."

"Extending her hand she replied, "Nice to meet you I'm Alison. So how are you doing, Clare. A little better, I trust."

"Thank you for asking. Yeah, I'm better."

"We're serving dinner. Would you like some?"

"'Oh, I don't know."

"I think you should, Clare. It's a long flight, and we recommend it. Besides it's really pretty good."

"Do I have choices?"

"You have two choices, steak or chicken."

"I'll have the steak."

"Coming right up. And what would you care to drink with your meal?"

Before Clare could answer, Alison said, "I don't recommend scotch."

Clare chuckled, "Yeah, I'm with you on that. Uh, do you have Diet Coke?"

"Of course, what kind of airline do you take us for?"

"Enjoy."

"Thanks."

"Incidentally, may I inquire what you're reading there?"

"It's a journal I wrote while on a seven-week trek around Africa a few years back. I haven't looked at it since. I thought it would be fun to read it now and get back in touch."

"Interesting; recording one's thoughts on a trip like that is a great idea. Bon Appetit."

April 6, 1997
Leaving Etosha

Last night after dinner, Marshall, Brandon, Tony and I wandered down to another camp where we'd heard laughter and singing. This is done quite a bit. Marshall and I have no reluctance to do it, and Will and Thomas do it a lot. Those nutty Scots have no inhibitions whatsoever. Marshall and I heard a lion in the distance. The power that comes from their great barrel chests is humbling; a sound like it's coming through an amplifier. Makes us humans seem pretty frail by comparison. Later when Marshall and I climbed into our sleeping bags, stars shining brightly overhead, we could still hear that lion a half mile away.

4:50 p.m.

We're in the north of Namibia, and the landscape is changing, getting greener, with lots of big leafy trees. We've passed dozens of tiny villages with their grass roofed huts. Locals carry bundles on their heads. Cattle and goats are everywhere. All the natives smile and wave, but this is normal. Africa is a very friendly country. The weather is wonderful: dry desert heat with a cool breeze.

April 7, 1997
Rundu, Namibia (along the Angola border)

We camped last night at a spectacular lodge along a picturesque stretch of lazy river. The lodge, of course, had a very inviting bar and restaurant, all in the open with a view of the river. The sunset, and they are magnificent here in Africa, lingered until 7:30. After dinner we all gathered in the lounge for drinks and assorted banter. A guy brought in a dead snake and passed it around the bar. Everyone decided it was a black mamba. The next day I mentioned it to the owner's wife and she calmly said, "I doubt it was a mamba, more likely a spitting cobra." Once again, we are reminded that this is Africa.

The Afrikaners are disillusioned about the politics of their country. Many have lost their ranches and businesses. Some are thinking about moving to Australia. By 1:00 a.m. one of the big Afrikaners had gotten into a bar brawl, and we were kicked out at about 1:30.

Chapter 55

CLARE PUNCHED THE attendant button, and soon Alison was standing beside her.

"What can I do for you, Clare?"

"Do you happen to have some fresh coffee in the galley?"

"As a matter of fact we do. How do you take it?'

"Oh, just black, thank you."

Now, where was I? she thought to herself.

In the morning I woke up to a strange vision. It looked like an ostrich standing outside our tent. It was. Edra got a picture of it and I hope it turns out.

April 8, 1997
Near the Botswana border.

Ngepi Camp sits on the bank of the Okavango River, a private oasis at the end of a sandy road. This place has a beautiful deck overlooking the river. Below the river is a crocodile cage for swimming. What I mean is that you swim, if you are so inclined, in this contraption that looks like a hollowed-out dock. Later we took to a motorboat and rode up river for about an hour before we loaded onto an army truck that took us to the edge of a swamp in the Okavango Delta, a system of waterways and dry islands covering some 1,000 square miles. When we went to bed, there was rustling in the reeds and croaking of one of the crocodiles. Needless to say, we kept our tent zipped. I didn't like that very much.

April 9, 1997

We made it to the Botswana border by 9:30 a.m. The border station is a dusty little building of about 400 square feet. Dan and Elsie, the Polish couple, proved to be a major problem with us getting across to the Botswana side. Apparently the Namibians don't like Poles, and it delayed us an hour and a half while Mandy and Carol worked it out.

We arrived at another camp, and everyone pitched in loading equipment into the boats that would take us up river. Papyrus, cane grass, and reeds choked the river. We saw loads of water foul, crocodile, and hippos. One hippo actually charged the lead boat. We must always remember that it's Africa. The river was like an African Queen-like labyrinth of canals, and I soon lost my bearings, unusual for me. Marshall can get turned around leaving the men's room.

Clare laughed and thought to herself, *Funny, the last two men in my life have each had a terrible sense of direction.*

In about an hour and a half we arrived at a landing. Twenty minutes later we are trucking along to our next stop. We eventually emerged into a broad clearing that revealed a marsh area like the Florida Everglades. We unloaded our packs, and smelly men carried our belongings to dugout canoes called makoros. Native polers navigated us through the Okavango for over an hour until we came upon some big trees on what appeared to be solid ground. This is the most remote camp to date.

Our huge fires burned brightly under the huge canopy of a sausage tree. There is evidence of elephants everywhere. A pile of melon-sized chunks of manure sit three feet from our tent. Behind the camp it looks like a tornado came through; trees pushed over, twisted limbs, bark completely stripped from the trees up to fifteen feet. It was pretty obvious that the elephants had come through and had left their calling cards. There were loads of elephant melons everywhere.

Marshall wanted to go for a hike. We ask one of the polers if it would be okay and he said no. We ask if someone could come with us. He looked at another man, sitting on a buffalo skull, because he had a watch. It was 5:40 p.m. The one with the watch had a serious look. He said, "In Botswana it is illegal to walk after six. It is late now."

We asked what would happen if someone was out walking and couldn't make it home by six. "Would they have to sit down in the road and wait until dawn?" Marshall asked, testing the logic of it.

"Yes, that is right," said the poler with the watch. So much for our hike.

April 10, 1997

Some of our gang have complained of bites, but I have yet to see even a mosquito. It's pretty amazing, a swamp camp without bugs. Works for me. When they are not poling us, they sit by the fire and talk constantly in Kavango.

April 11, 1997

By 6:00 a.m. we were loaded into dugouts, poling through the marsh again. After about 30 minutes we came to dry land and got out. Soon we were spotting Cape buffalo running off to our left. They are huge and dangerous. We also saw warthog, zebra, sable, antelope, and wildebeest. It's still fascinating to me to see all these different animals hanging out together. We wound up walking seven miles in the heat. We were back in camp by noon. We ate, and then most everyone slept for a couple of hours. I had vivid dreams of a man I didn't know. Marshall's feet and ankles are hurting. His ankle is much improved but is still stiff and a bit swollen. That's one Frisbee game he will never forget.

9:00 p.m.

We turned in early. Mandy and Carol came by for a short visit. They are both good gals and very good at their jobs. Marshall sleeps like an anvil and always drops off real quick. And of course, he snores. Between Marshall and the hippos, with their loud incessant grunts, I didn't sleep too well.

April 16, 1997
Victoria Falls, Zimbabwe

Early yesterday morning we went on a driving safari through Chobe National Park. We saw lions with cubs, Marabou stork, and some hippos. Later, after a couple of hours by the pool, we went on a river cruise. Animals everywhere. Got some good pictures of hippo, bull elephant, and crocodile. We crossed the border into Zimbabwe. Official rate of exchange is 50 to 1. Black market rate is near 1,600 to 1, so our lunch was at a good hotel. Marshall and I had warthog with all the trimmings for 4 dollars American. Warthog sounds awful, but it tastes pretty good.

We had dinner at a fun place called Mama Africa where they play live reggae. I had elephant and Marshall had warthog again. After dinner we went to a wonderful air-conditioned casino. Marshall and the Scots played craps. They all think they're high-rollers.

April 17, 1997
Vic Falls, Rafting

On the way we saw the gorge and the green river peeking through the jungle with the mist rising. The rafts were waiting at the shoreline. This was a blast. At lunch we beached and walked about 100 yards upstream to a shady spot where our lunch had been prepared. We were joined by Collibus monkeys. The babies clung to the mother's bellies. A few of them came forward to grab some scraps of bread and ham. One threw down an onion in disgust. They took us back after lunch. It was a real fun deal.

April 19, 1997

Yesterday we went to Zambia for abseiling, which is like repelling. Marshall and I, Will and Thomas, Charlie, Maggie, Julie, and Brandon were in the group that went. We arrived at the gorge that feeds into the main gorge of the Zambezi. The gorge is about 200 feet deep and 200 feet across. We all got fitted with our equipment, but Maggie and Julie chickened out. Unfortunately, Marshall's ankle would not allow him to do it. This ankle thing has knocked him out of so much. I really feel sorry for him. But he is not handling it very well.

Chapter 56

Marshall didn't want me to do this. I don't think he was concerned for my well being. I think he was troubled that I had no fear of it. It's like I threaten his manhood or something. The truth is I was scared. But I was also determined to overcome my fear and continue to show my independence.

Anyway, once we were all checked out we were ready to do it. Thomas was the first off. As he leaped he let out a gigantic fart. It broke us up. Anyway we jumped over the ledge and did standard repelling down 200 feet. Then you had to hike back up, and that's the bad part. It's a challenge, and took about 30 minutes.

The next thing we did was called the "Superman." They put us in harnesses and hooked us to a pulley attached to a main cable. We took turns running down a short ramp and flying across the gorge on a zip line. After that we did face-down repelling. You run face down the side of the gorge while jumping in short leaps. This was fun but the next event was off the charts.

About half way across the gorge there is a line attached to the main cable that spans it. This creates a dead drop with a pendulum affect. Marshall really objected to my doing this. I must admit that I had reservations, but I needed to do it for my own self esteem. So what we did was harness up and stand on the edge. Before we jumped I prayed, "Holy Mary, Mother of God, pray for us now and at the hour when we do stupid things." Then you fell 180 feet. Somewhere in my descent I was sure that the rope was no longer attached, and I screamed involuntarily. When the rope finally goes tight there is no jerk at all but you get a rocket-like acceleration as your body swings out toward the far side of the gorge. You accelerate to about 100 miles an hour in seconds, at which time the laughter is uncontrollable.

Clare remembered thinking, *Marshall was able to do that and it made his trip so far. It was such a relief for me because I'm the one that must endure his pouting about my disobedience, and his little bouts with depression, and the pain of the injury. I could somewhat understand what he's been going through; to a point!*

The highlight of the day was a tandem jump. Marshall and I harnessed together with a safety line between our ankles. What happened next was the most frightening physical sensation I have ever experienced. We stood with our backs to the drop with the instructor holding the rope. We were told to lean back. A second later he dropped us without warning, and we fell head down the 180 feet, and then accelerated to 130 mph. Lots of screaming. With all that speed you get slack in the line and do another free fall at the far end of the arc. We screamed half the way down then laughed the other half. Marshall and I agreed that we would probably never experience anything like that again. Once again, I was so pleased that he was finally able to participate in some of these fantastic activities.

We were tired by evening but wanted to punctuate the day. Brandon and Julie went with us to The Boma. It was sort of a Zimbabwe version of a Hawaiian Luau. It takes place in a picturesque thatched-roof building at the Vic Falls Safari Lodge. The service was incredible. At first a woman comes to the table with a pitcher and basin and says in her culture the man is honored first, so Marshall and Brandon held out their hands to be washed. The boys loved this. The soup course came in a black iron kettle. While we ate, various tribal drummers and dancers would run out and jump around and sing. Another group of musicians sang in harmony like the back up singers for Paul Simon on the Graceland *album*. Then we had the main course of eland, impala and warthog.

During dinner, a fellow who claimed to be a witch doctor came over and said he could tell our fortunes with bones. After we finished eating we went over to his little hut, and Marshall volunteered to have his fortune told. Marshall sat down on a mat in front of him while he chanted and threw down the bones. Then he banged some shells together and threw them down. He told Marshall that he was a strong man and would have many children. He told Marshall that he had a good love life with his woman and pressed him to confirm it. Marshall turned red and naturally agreed.

Chapter 57

CLARE THOUGHT TO herself, *I was a very sheltered young woman when Marshall and I married. I was a virgin with no experience. Mother hadn't given me any information or advice. I suspect that happens with many young women. I was not fulfilled in our love life, but I had not mentioned it to Marshall. I didn't know exactly how to tell him. I do know men have fragile egos, and I didn't want to mess with his head. But he couldn't control himself, and that left me very frustrated. He was satisfied, of course, but he didn't take care of my needs as a woman.* She remembered wondering, *A sex therapist might help us, but that could only be considered if I confronted him with the problem. Anyway, I had to wonder what was going through his head when the witch doctor told him he had a good love life.*

She picked up the journal again and continued to read.

All in all, this has been our best day in Africa. I can't believe I am doing some of the things I'm doing. I am a camper, for sure, and I enjoy the outdoors, but I have never considered myself very daring or up to taking chances. I've surprised myself. I am still pretty young, and I'm growing. This trip has been good for me. I believe I will be a different person when this is over. I already am.

April 20, 1997

We hiked to Zambia this morning and went swimming above Vic Falls. We got some spectacular photos. The normal viewpoint is from the Vic Falls side and that's where tourists go. But we hiked across the Zambezi riverbed, to an area referred to as the "smoke that thunders." There is a series of cascades that fall over 300 feet to the river below. From several miles away you could see what looks like white smoke rising in a cloud. At this spot, near where we swam, the Zambezi plummets 300-400 feet down a narrow gorge.

We hired a porter, who we found eating fish and mealie-meal, and he agreed to guide us and carry our packs, all for 3 dollars American. We headed for the smoke; it was actually the water, to swim in a pool at the edge of the falls. We swam part of the way across while "Roy" carried our stuff over the rocks. About half way across we saw two very large elephants moving toward us. We stopped. Actually we sort of froze. The wind was across us, but they must have seen us because they stopped and flapped their ears. But, they didn't pursue us, so we slowly made our way to the pool at the top of the big fall. The pool eddied at the edge so that we could sit at the lip and look over — 300 feet down. Across the gorge, tourists, no doubt, wondered how we got over here. They pointed at us. We loved it.

. *6:45 p.m.*

When we got back to Vic Falls, I persuaded a reluctant Marshall to follow me to the craft market, and I bought a huge piece of fabric and two elephant hair bracelets.

She thought back, about how it was. *He never wanted me to buy anything unless it was his idea. I did it anyway and enjoyed my show of independence.*

My purchase attracted a persistent pack of hucksters who badgered us relentlessly. Finally Marshall had enough and managed to dismiss them all. After that we decided to join some of the others for "high tea" at the Victoria Falls Hotel. Marshall had introduced me to high tea while we were on our honeymoon in England. Now I am hooked. The hotel is a museum to the Victorian era and a real pleasure to be in. It's a white, palatial thing with red brick walkways and courtyards, expansive lawns, and white-coated staff. Very British—very posh and proper. Marshall commented that he felt like he needed a white straw skimmer and a white linen suit. The lobby is graced by a huge painting of King George V, and across from him is a portrait of Queen Mary. The walls above the spiral staircases are full of stuffed buffalo and kudu heads. There is a Men's Reading Room with a large fireplace and correspondence desk, leather chairs, and papers from London.

Chapter 58

THE CAPTAIN TURNED on the "Fasten Seatbelt" sign, "Clare, it's time to buckle up. We'll be on the ground at Gatwick in about 15 minutes."

"Alison, I've enjoyed flying with you. You've been very kind. I wish I had you all the way to Johannesburg."

"Thank you, Clare. And you take care, okay?"

Clare collected her bags, proceeded through London customs and baggage check and then secured her belongings in two large lockers for safe keeping until she returned. She hailed a cabbie and headed for the city.

"Drop me down by the Thames, please. I want to take a cruise."

"Very good, my lady."

Clare had taken the cruise before when she and her girl friends had come to London from Johannesburg. She remembered it well. It was a wonderful relaxing way to get a perspective of this great city. And you got a good close look at all the wonderful bridges. After the cruise Clare strolled over to Westminster Abby, the great old church with so much history, and quietly stepped inside. She stood for a while, in meditation, viewing the large painting of Jesus knocking at the door. She was as moved by the experience this time as she was before. She prayed before she left and lit a candle.

A cabbie took her to Madame Tussaud's waxwork museum. It was always fun and she wanted to see what was new. Next stop would be the Guinea Grill, one of London's finest eateries, in historic Berkeley Square. She was hungry for a steak and they had good ones. A fortuitous tip from her waiter led to a call to the Dominion Theater who agreed to hold a single for the matinee of *Beauty and the Beast*. On her way back to Gatwick she had a satisfied smile on her face. It had been a most lovely day. She collected her luggage and found her gate. She would read from her journal until departure.

April 21, 1997
Bulawayo, Zimbabwe

This is a city that has courageously stood against Mugabe. People express their dissatisfaction—or contempt—quietly. In many ways Bulawayo is a city like many others in the world. The sidewalks are busy with people walking with purpose, almost oblivious to us. The streets clatter with cars and people. Here in Bulawayo people line up for the grocery store; to get staple goods. There are also lines in front of the bank. Old women sit on the sidewalk outside while guards let people in. Some of our group headed for the museum of natural history. Others, Marshall and I included, rested in a park. We are able to catch a cool breeze underneath some date palms. Think I'll take a little nap before its time to meet Mandy and Carol at the train station.

They are calling our flight, Clare said to herself. *It's time for me to gather up my carry-on luggage. Boarding is always a hassle. People carry on too much, can't find a place for everything, they complain. People bitch about their seats although they've been assigned in advance. And it takes forever. Listen to me complain. I'm always glad when we're in the air again.*

"Do you care for headphones?" asked the flight attendant. Clare had an aisle seat again, the same seating configuration as she did on the flight from Dallas to London.

"Yes, please."

Getting another attendant's attention Clare placed an order, "A red wine when you can get to it."

Clare thought to herself, *Well, the next stop will be Johannesburg. I'll actually be back in South Africa, and I'll see my friend Peter.* She smiled at the thought. *Now back to the journal.* She thought to herself, *I'd really like to finish it before we land.*

April 22, 1997 7:00 a.m.
Matobo Camp, Zimbabwe

We are camping again, which most of us really like. There are monkeys all around the edge of the camp. We went on a walking safari with a local guide. This area is known for rhino. Mandy and Carol had a meeting with all of us. They said the balance of the trip would be less civilized. That's fine with me, as I am getting more and more comfortable with the bush and the wild. We'll be in bush camps most of the time except for Zanzibar.

April 23, 1997
Matobo

Ian, our guide, told us that the penis of a rhino weighs 15 kilograms. The average copulation lasts 30 minutes.

She remembered thinking to herself, *The rhinos did it for 30 minutes. That beats Marshall and me by about 20 minutes. Our sex life was really pretty pathetic, but I just couldn't talk to him about it. You'd think it would have been obvious to him that it was bad. I shouldn't have faked those organisms. I should have been truthful with him and worked to make it better. That's what married people should do. But we didn't. I have an idea that many married couples have trouble with their sex lives. That's another thing I will miss about Morgan. The love-making was fabulous, and thanks to him I know the difference.*

The female rhinos come to estrus only by watching male rhinos fight for their favor. These facts have been interwoven with myth to foster the belief that rhino horn is an aphrodisiac. Ian explained that when the Asian rhino population was all but wiped out, those in the market for horn turned to Africa. So poaching became a major problem here. He said they learned that the horn is worth about $50,000 American, so people are very willing to risk their lives for the money, which is a small fortune in any part of Africa. But the ones risking their lives get only about $1,000. That's still a bunch in a country where the average salary is $4 American a month.

Ian took us out on foot to stalk the rhino. There are 20 black ones and about 80 white rhinos in the Matopo. He said they employ 70 men to patrol the reserve. Their weapon of choice is the infamous AK-47. Marshall told me all about this gun. Ian said we were the only whites on the reserve, and he has no more tours going out for two weeks. Ian is waiting it out; this is home for him. The local paper speaks of the shortage of doctors and nurses.

Ian told us to keep quiet and stay low to the ground. We were down wind of a white rhino mother and her calf. We crept up to within about 20 feet of the big mother rhino. My heart was pumping, and I was squeezing Marshall's hand. Her baby was at her feet. I somehow felt that the mother must have sensed us there, but as long as they can't smell you or see you (they don't see well) they remain calm. We watched her for maybe 10 minutes until she felt comfortable enough to lie down. Marshall mentioned how easy it would be for poachers to get really close. It's the same way for most game in Africa. It's really simple for anyone to get within easy shooting range. I didn't think it was *very sporting, but men pay lots of money to kill these animals. Of course, poaching is not sport. The patrols have orders to shoot poachers on site, and Ian said they kill as many as 20 a month. Unbelievable!*

Sometimes the government orders Ian and others like him to shoot marauding animals. Last week a wild bull elephant killed three people in a nearby village.

Later we crept up on a small herd of white rhino; two large bulls with horns about 18 inches long, two cows, and a calf. It was getting hot, and half of them were dozing under an acacia, so again we moved to within about 10 yards. A great photo op.

We drove to another area and did more hiking. In the hills we came under a huge overhang and a sheer wall of rose-colored rock. We were observing rock art — hunting scenes. Ian said the oldest was about 50,000 years old. He is very passionate about the plight of the Bushman, who he contends are the only civilized people in the world. And they are the only people truly indigenous to southern Africa. Ian told us that years ago when the Harangwe National Park was designated on the border of Rhodesia and Botswana, a plan was instituted to keep the Bushmen on the land to keep out poachers. Ian said they actually let them in so they could kill them. Once a month the park rangers would meet with some of the Bushmen. Bags of salt were traded for human hands. The instructions were to cut off the left hand of a poacher. The elephants were protected.

Chapter 59

April 24, 1997
Gweru, Zimbabwe

We arrived at a place called Antelope Game Park around sunset last night. The lodge and restaurant sit on a bank by a sleepy river. We can't swim in the river because of crocodiles. The major attraction here is the lion-breeding program, which started in 1972. There are 38 lions in the program. Illnesses like feline tuberculosis and feline AIDS, have put the southern African lion population at risk.

This morning we were gladly up at six for a rare privilege of taking two female, one-year-old lions for their morning walk. There are no fences or leashes, just us and the lions. These animals are big enough to kill us, and the lion's play is rough. Will got tackled from behind when his back was turned. They have a wicked sense of humor, these lions, and play incessantly. Their paws are huge—but luckily their claws are not too sharp, but are as big as our fingers. It gives you pause, no pun intended. I'm not strong enough to play with these girls. I hated it but I could only watch.

Though the handlers shout commands, the lions don't always listen and run off from time to time. Sometimes one of the lions will lie down and refuse to move until she is good and ready. The other wonders and paces. This is a tactic they use on us to take us off guard. Then the one on the ground will suddenly charge. They constantly devise ways to play. One time one of them fixed her eyes on Marshall and made eye contact (they don't often do that) then hunched her shoulders into a position to spring. It scared the crap out of Marshall, but the handlers were there and headed off the charge. Not everyone played with them. We got some great pictures.

Later we got to play with some cubs; two to four months old. Everyone got in on this. To my delight a two-month-old really took to me. He crawled up into my lap, chewing on part of a car tire. Then she dropped the piece of tire and licked my arms and legs and then chewed on my thumb. I loved it. You can also ride elephants here, and ordinarily you would be able to swim in the river with them. But the water is too low and the crocodiles are bad.

2:45 p.m. Gweru

We're in town to buy supplies. The town is bustling with humanity, mostly walking. School kids are out. They wear the ugliest uniforms imaginable. Some of the boys and girls are dressed like marching band members in their horrid greens and reds with shiny satin piping on the cuffs of coats, lapels of jackets. We often see women with babies strapped to their backs. The mother makes a kind of sling out of a sheet or towel with the ends tied around the midriff. If the baby ever falls out it's perfectly legal to beat the mother.

April 25, 1997

When we left our tent, Marshall and I were the only ones in our group that were up. The rising sun made little halos over the heads of monkeys in the field next to camp. Trees rattled and shook with them. We walked over and took a look up the field toward the green hills and their big leafy trees. Dozens of monkeys were migrating toward the hills. The guards carry sling shots to run off the monkeys when needed. Mr. Sacko said the monkeys steal his silverware. He doesn't care for them. I think it's funny.

1:20 p.m. Great Zimbabwe

We went in the hut of an old witch doctor and his mother who did readings. He and the mother both wore headdresses of dingy black feathers. The fee for the reading was 100 z (seven cents American), and it was interesting. I was told that I would have a long life, to not be afraid of anything, that I would be healthy and travel a lot, and that I would come back to Africa. Not bad for seven cents. Marshall was asked how many wives he wanted. He said one was enough. The witch doctor said that if his wife ever left him she would be sorry because she would never find as good a man. The old woman grunted and growled some more. It was all coming to an end. Finally the witch doctor told us that our ancestors would protect us.

We went to a small museum. The museum guide insisted on telling us about witchcraft. Said it was hard to bury someone in Zim because you needed permits to enter a mortuary and a release from the police to move the body. He said there was a problem with missing body parts, particularly hearts, because they were used in voodoo. He said sometimes people get possessed. If that does happen, you get a light-colored goat. Then you need the tail of a wildebeest and some beer made from sorghum. The witch doctor you hire will dip the tail in the beer and flail away at the victim all the time shouting for the devil to vacate the body. The evil will leave the human and enter the goat. But if the cured person looks back the evil spirit will reenter their body.

4:00 p.m.

Mandy and Carol have tried three stations trying to purchase gasoline. One place had a 2-hour line and a limit of 30 liters of diesel. We're in another town now at another station with no line and no limit. Will, Thomas, and Marshall went across the street and bought cold beer. We haven't had ice in five days and nothing cold in two days. We all enjoyed the beer while Mr. Sacko worked on a Fanta. There is a lot of Fanta in Africa. The countryside is as green as Ireland.

April 26, 1997 1:15 p.m.
Mozambique Border

Marshall says border crossings are like a visit to the dentist. You always have to wait to get in, and, when you do it's painful. He comes out with some good ones from time to time. Speaking of Marshall, he's the oldest of our group at 35, and Thomas has started calling him the old man. The rest of us probably average about 25 years old. I don't think he minds.

On the way to Harare we got pulled over by the police. They said they wanted money for road tax but wouldn't take it. They claimed we'd have to wait until the following day to pay. After Mandy and Carol negotiated for about 40 minutes we piled back in our vehicle and followed them to the police station in town. On the way in we passed factories and smoke sacks. Harare is a fairly modern city of 2 million people. Anyway, we finally got it all straightened out and found our residential compound where we spent the night.

Chapter 60

CLARE GOT UP, stretched, leaned against her seat, and looked about the cabin of the enormous airplane. Most people were asleep. A few lights aided those passengers who were reading. Since the aisle was clear, she decided to walk a bit. There have been cases of blood clots occurring on long flights when people didn't move about from time to time.

She heard a strange murmur from across the way. Her curiosity was eventually satisfied when she observed an orthodox Jew on his knees in the aisle by his seat praying. It was a bit strange, since that was the first time she had seen such a thing. On her way back from the lavatory she stopped at the galley where three flight attendants were talking. Clare introduced herself. and took a hot cup of coffee back to her seat. The coffee tasted good. She picked up her journal and continued.

April 27, 1997
Mozambique

Marshall and I woke up to find ourselves in the middle of a village soccer field. Here, as in Europe and South America, the game is known and loved as football. Frankly, we were surprised to learn of its enormous popularity here. If villagers are unable to secure a proper soccer ball they make one out of hide or banana leaves. Even in remote areas, like we are in now, there is a flat dirt field with crude goal posts. It brings communities together.

Today we had a little fender bender. It was a matter of settling damages. The police came by but were no help. Mandy showed some hard currency and the negotiations were soon underway. The owner of the little white car we hit was soon happily on her way, as were we, having successfully settled out first $3 car wreck. The crossing experience was the usual; slow, hot, and terrible. As we sat by the fire last night, sipping sangria, we could see the glow of other fires in the villages on either side of camp. They were singing and chanting.

April 28, 1997, 7:30 p.m.
Nkchotakota, Malawi

The proprietor is a 72-year-old character without a single grey hair in his head. He's has owned the place, which looks like it has been expanded over time, for 22 years. Philip K. Banta proudly escorts our group on a tour of his small hotel, which is a labyrinth of rooms and hallways that lead to the courtyard and batteries of showers or toilets. The paint is bright but flaking on the stucco walls. Insects swarm around exposed light bulbs. The whole place reminds us of a guerilla stronghold. Marshall and I have two small beds with blue mosquito netting. For added luxury there is a toilet, and behind that a shower, but no mirror or wash basin. Banta explains that a wash basin can be found down some dark corridor in an odd place with nothing else around it.

After dinner we were sitting out back drinking beer that one of Banta's boys had fetched from town. Will called our attention to a large spider running counter-clockwise laps around the cement enclosure. He ran so fast that he banked high on the steps before hitting the straight-away again. We lifted our feet as he passed. *The spider circled about 15 times, as fast as he could move, following the same route. Then the creature moved inside, down a hallway, past the boy who fetched the beer, and the woman he was talking with. They don't seem too concerned. Marshall asked if they knew what it was. The boy said, "Yes, poisonous."*

Marshall asked, "How poisonous?"

"If it bites you—you die in about 30 minutes." We were flushed as we looked at each other, shaking our collective heads. We must never forget this is Africa.

Chapter 61

I'll never lose my fascination for watching women carry literally everything imaginable on their heads. Men carry nothing. I saw a woman with a large hoe on her head, another with a basket of bananas and a girl with a large bag of rice. Here in Malawi there is red dirt and brown dirt. They make bricks out of it. Even the huts are red brick or mud brick with the usual grass roofs. The hills outside the village are green and thick with trees.

April 28, 1997

I'm not drinking enough water. I swear, the skin on the back of my hands looks like an 80-year-old woman. Maggie is making tea. We had hot dogs for lunch. I love hot dogs. Marshall likes them too and downed four. Even out here, with the heat and exertion, he appears to be gaining weight. I'm going to try to get him to loose it when we get settled in Johannesburg. It's balmy and windblown today. The sky is dingy gray, and Lake Malawi is noisy. Breakers and sets of surfable waves continue to roll in. No boats are going out. Incidentally, they call this Calendar Lake; 365 miles long, 52 miles wide and very, very deep. It looks and behaves like the sea. Most of the world's freshwater aquarium fish come from here, and if the weather clears some of us will go snorkeling tomorrow. Two other safari groups are here at this camp. What an assortment of humanity.

April 29, 1997

Mr. Sacko cooked for two groups last tonight. He does good work. After dinner Marshall and I walked down to the beach and sat in the darkness talking for about an hour. He was very attentive and romantic.

Marshall sleeps like an anvil…and snores…and snores! I was also disturbed last night by drunken Aussie girls who couldn't find their tents. They passed by several times before it was quiet again. The climate here is subtropical. Talked to some of the others in camp who had been attacked by elephants last week. No one was injured but the elephants ate all their fresh produce. We must always remember that this is Africa.

April 30, 1997

Just came back from a tour of a village. In the first hut a really old man made moonshine. We were offered samples of the stuff, and it was really bad. In a second hut a woman was cleaning cassava root. Two men were tightening drum heads over hot flames. The third hut was larger, and we were told to sit. Drumming started, and soon a witch doctor came out of his hut. He began to dance and beat a fly swisher on his hip while the bells on his wrists and ankles jangled wildly. Then, one by one, he invited all of us to dance. After about 20 minutes it was over, and we were asked to fork over 250 kwacha per person.

May 1, 1997

I was awake at 5:00 a.m., which is becoming a bad habit. My bladder seems to be synchronized with the rising sun. I've become a morning person which I hate. Most everyone sleeps until at least 7:00 a.m.

10:30 a.m.,
Malawi-Tanzania Border

Unusually painless stamping out of Malawi. No people waiting. Everyone walks or rides bicycles which are archaic and all black.

3:00 p.m. Somewhere in Tanzania

For the past three hours we have passed through some of the most spectacular country in Africa. The highlands are over 3,000 feet in elevation and are green and lush, with small village gardens and sprawling tea fields. When they catch the light they glow a lime green. Coffee grows well here and is a major crop. Huts are hidden in banana groves. Children walk along the roads sucking mango.

Then we descend into the dusty valley with a couple of small shabby towns. Street vendors sell all manner of the unimaginable. Tailors sit at storefronts cranking out orders on old Singer sewing machines. The stores are like holes in the wall selling such common items as chocolate bars, powered milk, Lifebuoy soap, Pringles, Simba Chips, cooking oil, liquid paraffin, noodles, canned tuna, Vienna sausage, sardines, Fanta, Sprite, Coke, and beer. Everything else is really unpredictable.

May 2, 1997

Marshall and I had a Kilimanjaro beer. I can't believe I'm drinking so much beer and actually enjoying it. But this is not exactly Merlot country.

In Tavzania things grow well. We stopped in the town of Irvinga to buy food while Mandy changed some money. Charlie, Marshall and I went with Mr. Sacko down tiny little alleys with vendors crammed in with no spaces in between. The stalls looked like fireworks stands. The big stores are little more that twice that size. The first butcher shop made me want to become a vegetarian. It was about 10 x10 and resembled a white-tile bathroom with toilet. A dirty, bearded, skinny man stood behind the counter swinging a bloody ax as if standing guard over the three slabs of meat that hung from big ugly hooks. A cascade of entrails swarmed with flies. Sacko walked out, and we gladly followed.

We walked almost immediately into a large open-air produce market under a high thatched roof where we were able to clear our heads and nostrils. Here we were able to choose from excellent specimens of bananas, red onion, hot peppers, tomatoes, lettuce, cabbage, and spices. We entered another butcher shop that looked more like a joint to place bets at a seedy racetrack. A grotesque albino ordered meat from two men in bloody white butcher coats. Standing on a floor rusty with blood they took orders through mesh wire from a dim room that buzzed with huge filthy flies. Mr. Sacko, ordering in a combination of English and Swahili, was handed a bag of meat for 4000 Tanzania shillings. "I may never eat meat again," declared Marshall.

"I'm with you on that, mate," said Charlie. Of course, I had made that decision long ago.

Chapter 62

We've been driving through tropical jungle for a couple of hours. It reminds me a lot of Hawaii. The mountains that surround us are rugged and steep. It's pouring rain. Marshall sweats like crazy and is complaining about the humidity inside our truck. We're still heading for the coast and on to Zanzibar tomorrow.

6:00 p.m.

These locals have the worst huts I've seen in Africa. They make square walls out of broomstick limbs and bind them together to make a grid of 6-inch squares. Into the squares they cram mud, and except for the roof, a shabby mop of palm fronds—that's about it. And they patch the holes with bits of tin. Apparently they are not able to subscribe to Better Huts and Gardens.

7:30 p.m.

We are snarled in the worst traffic jam since we've been in Africa. Mandy is very uptight and hollers back, "Does anyone object if I smoke?"

Before anyone can answer, Thomas shouts, "Does anyone object if I fart?" Mandy was approved, but Thomas was shouted down. Luckily, Thomas was kidding. Mandy mentioned pizza which is sort of a code word for that fact that we still have a long way to go before we reach camp. All I really want is a shower and to claw away the top layer of my skin. Edra suggested that we all burn our clothes.

May 3, 1997
Zanzibar

Someone needs to invent a new word for the kind of humidity found in Zanzibar. We're in Stonetown, the old quarter, staying in the Hotel Karibu. The place looks ancient, but the manager says it's only 100 years old. The walls are four feet thick, and they have external wiring. There are ceiling fans that don't seem to do much good, and mosquito nets. This morning we met Hamid, a jovial little wheeler-dealer in a dark red fez. He is our contact here for various activities. Mandy and Carol just get us from one location to the next, but the local guides show us around.

He led us through brick streets to a waterfront café. Amore Mio is a little oasis of civilization run by a old Italian man who looks and sounds like Anthony Quinn. He speaks very little English. Marshall wanted coffee and blurted out, "Café American?"

Mio disregarded that and countered with, "No!" He threw up his hands and gave us a wry grin. "Expresso! Larga!" I drank some too, and in no time we were very alert in spite of the stale humidity. On a small tray he brought out chocolate and lemon cake, and when he found out Maggie could speak Italian he brought out a selection of sandwiches. We sat contentedly, talking about our various family quirks. We were highly amused at Julie, from Aspen, whose last name was Gay. She had a custom license plate which she readily admitted was a huge mistake. She said it was really a hoot at restaurants when the hostess would call for "the Gay party." The courtyard was filled with sprouts of miniature coconut palms. We watched the dhows with their sackcloth sails, overloaded with men and cargo. Mio looked happy at us enjoying the food and drink; that look Mom always had at Thanksgiving back home. He leaned down to talk softly to Maggie and gave her a brotherly kiss on the cheek.

5:30 p.m.

Marshall and I woke from a nap at to find it pouring down rain. It was very humid. Marshall said, "This place has the climate of a fat man's armpit." That was pretty crude, but the picture was pretty accurate. We got ready anyway and met Charlie, Maggie, Julie and Edra in the lobby. The hotel manager was asleep in his chair by the front door, a Swahili newspaper over his chest. He reminded us of 40s actor Sydney Greenstreet. We asked about food, and he recommended Namaste, an Indian restaurant. When the rain broke the city was cool for a while, and we explored the Casablanca-like alleys, the quaint little shops selling clothing and trinkets, and were intrigued by the carved doors with their brass-studded knobs.

All the buildings are three and four stories, with small Arabian windows and ornate balconies. Tailors work on the streets in little cubbyholes. Down by the water is the fish market, with smells too overpowering to explore. But if you're interested you can get purple octopus tentacles ready to eat; not your usual takeout. But we liked the charcoal smell of the little pots and hand-made grills. The produce market looked okay. Bicycles and mopeds are prevalent, but mostly people just walk. The dress here is from conservative to more western. Most Moslem men wear fez hats. Many wear kaftans, but slacks are more common. The women vary from all black with veils, to black with no veil and a headscarf, to kangas and multi-colored scarves. Zanzibari women love color. Everyone from old people to children say,

"Jambo!" and "Karibu sana!" There seems to be a pathological impetus toward greetings and general politeness. If you don't respond in kind they just continue until you do, sometimes following us as they hurl these greetings rapid fire. We get a bit weary of this given the large number of people, but we really have to make the effort, or it is considered rude. Thomas told us he likes to give them a big fart with his greeting. He's crazy; he really is.

Marshall is shooting black and white film here in Zanzabar, which I thought was a great idea. Can't wait to see how they come out. Oh, I should mention, the people do not like to have their pictures taken. Sometimes when Marshall is scoping out a shot you'll hear someone scream, "Nooo!" It's Ramadan, and will be for the entire time we're here. The Moslems fast all day until 6:30 p.m. We were warned to dress respectfully and to honor the custom of these copious greetings and pleasantries. A sign in the door of a restaurant warned tourists not to eat, drink, or smoke in public.

The men in our group, including Marshall, have spoken about how attractive the Muslim women are. They are slim and lithe, and many have Arab blood, so their features are more refined than on the mainland. Surprisingly, these women are quick to smile and make eye contact. As a woman I notice how they use their eyes, lips, and body language in a very alluring way. They are, for the most part, very sexy. Girls will be girls.

We ate dinner at the Dolphin. We sat by a doorway strung with beads, and next to a parrot that loved to have his head scratched. I mean, this was right out of the movies. Our waitress was a typical sultry Zanzibari, but dressed in western clothes. But I have to say that everything about these women; they way they look, their soft voices, the cat-like way they move, seems to be pure calculated sensuality. Marshall suggested I take notes. We ordered the Ramadan Special—which was the only thing available. It included red snapper, stewed vegetables, a green curry sauce, and flat bread. After dinner we walked the dim alleys and streets again. It is truly safe at night, actually looks better after dark; romantic, more like Hollywood would depict it. I don't know, something about the lighting, the cool pleasant air, and all the people, makes it more exotic after dark. We had a nightcap at an open-air bar at the Africa House Hotel and then turned in.

May 4, 1997

Our first stop this morning was the old slave market. We were told that upwards of 50,000 slaves used to be kept here. We are told that there were sales every day. We went down to the basement where they were kept in darkened, low-ceiling rooms for three days with no food or water prior to auction. The purpose was to weed out the weak ones.

The guide led us into a grove of trees and picked a yellow fruit, cut it open, and removed a big seed with a tan center and a webbing of red rubber over that. Mace was the "rubber" and nutmeg was the seed. He said the locals make nutmeg tea, and it makes them drunk. On our two-mile walk we see cardamom, cinnamon (tree bark), green peppercorns, lemon grass, taro, cassava, apple, banana, jackfruit, and pineapple.

May 5, 1997

Wherever you go in Africa the vendors and merchants seem to be clones of each other, all with near-identical stuff. I mean, from Cape Town to Vic Falls we saw the same carved elephants and giraffes. In Zimbabwe they do a lot of soapstone, but it's always the same three objects. It's the same with street food — except for coffee. It's excellent, and I insisted that Marshall pay the coffee guys double their regular price, but he wouldn't.

This afternoon we drove a hour through the jungle to a great beach; Caribbean blue-green water, sand like white corn meal and warm water. Diving was available, so Marshall, Brandon, and I went out immediately on a dive boat with a German named

Florian. We dove a spectacular reef. Lots of huge multi-colored anemone and numerous species of soft and hard coral. We got within three feet of a huge octopus before he backed under a coral head. Saw giant purple-finned clam, two feet across. We were harassed by remora the entire dive. They kept nipping at us. This really freaked out Brandon, who got certified in Mozambique, and was on only his third dive. He ran out of air in 40 minutes, typical of inexperienced divers, but Marshall, Florian, and I stayed down for over and hour.

Later in the day we went on a dhow sail. It was interesting and pleasant to be on the water. Afterwards we took our first showers since Harare, ten days ago. I'm getting a little tired of being grubby all the time.

Chapter 63

May 7, 1997,
Massai Land, Arusha

We passed Kilimanjaro today. I felt like I was in a Hemmingway novel. The trip will soon be over, and although it's been rough in spots, it has been a great experience, and we'll have some withdrawal when it's over, I'm sure. You bond with people who you will likely never see again. I want to come back to Arusha. It is beautiful, and I like the high-country climate. We are at about 4,000 feet, and it was cold last night. It started to rain about midnight.

6:30 a.m.

We were up early to visit a Massai village. Our Massai guide had taken us to a mud hut with a dim, smoky interior where he told us some pretty fascinating things about his tribe, including polygamy. He told us that he had 15 brothers and 15 sisters produced by his father, now 90-year-old, and an undisclosed number of wives. We learned that boys cannot wear the red cloak or carry a long knife or spear until after the puberty rite. *After the ceremony and six month training they are considered warriors and can marry. Around the age of 14 a boy is taken aside by the men and circumcised, during which time he is not allowed to show any emotion or make a sound. After the ceremony the boy is taken to a special hut where he's fed meat and a mixture of milk and blood to make him strong, During this period he is trained in bush survival and protecting cattle. Not so many years back each eligible bachelor had to kill a lion, but now it's illegal. In Ngorogoro crater, where most of the tribe live, it's permissible to kill a marauding lion in defense.*

When a girl marries her price is 10 cows. Cattle are a source of wealth and are at the heart of the Massai culture; believing that God has entrusted all the world's cattle to their tribe. Only men and boys tend cattle. Women do everything else. Some of the older, wealthy Massai men have six or more wives and dozens of children. They live mostly on mealie-meal, blood-milk, goat, and on rare occasions, beef. All the Massai wear red plaid in one way or another. We have driven through Massai country for two days, and it's amazing how their red forms stand out.

May 8, 1997

After breakfast we found ourselves back in the van from hell, at the mercy of crazy Hassan. The approach to the crater travels up to 5,000 feet, through the most impressive Tarzan-esque jungle we have seen. The air is cool. Then we drove around the crater rim. After a while Hassan slammed on his breaks and declared, "You get out now. Look." It was round as a bowl and dropped 1,000 feet to a grassy floor that is flat as pool table. Water shines in shallow, mirror-bright lakes full of pink flamingos. No animals can be seen from above, but they are there. Descending into the flats we see hippo in the marshes tossing mud on their backs, elephants pulling up the long grass, and big herds of wildebeest. We stumbled into a hyena-lion encounter in progress. Hassan cut in front of other vehicles already on the scene. Four females, one male, in a standoff against ten hyenas. The lions had killed something or run the hyenas off a kill, and the group was upset. Then the lioness casually strolled in the general direction of the hyenas and the pack scattered. When the female came back we saw some movement—a kick of legs, a squeal—and the lioness responded with a bite that stopped the noise and movement. After that we got some great shots of cape buffalo, ostrich, elephant, and warthog. We had lunch at a waterhole, and all in all, it was a good day.

8:30 p.m.

The camp provided a meal that included potato salad, pork chops, sausage, chicken, and mixed green salad. Mandy announced that we would be in Nairobi, Kenya, by tomorrow night. Nairobi is the end of the tour. After dinner we all went to the bar, and it was in full swing. People drink a lot at these bars at the end of the day. But it's rare that anyone gets out of line. Thomas, Will, Marshall, and Brandon played partners in darts, and the feathered projectiles were flying everywhere. It was pretty funny to watch.

May 9, 1997 Kenya
5:15 p.m. Nairobi

This is a big city; what can I say? It's fairly nondescript, with tall buildings, heavy traffic, fumes, and busy people scurrying here and there. Men dress in business suits, with varying degrees of quality or taste. The women dress like they were on the streets in America. Other than being so obviously black, there is really little to indicate that one is in Africa. At 5,500 feet, Nairobi is also cold.

May 10, 1997

Last night was our final group activity: an outstanding meal. At 7:30 our chauffeur dropped us at Carnivore, the most famous restaurant in Africa, according to Mandy. Inside we were greeted by men standing by smoky barbeque pits. The pits were round with coals in a ring that glowed beneath a circle of inward facing swords that rest on iron supports. On the end of each sword there were large hunks of meat. Red lights shine down from above the pits, bathing the men in smoky crimson. It was a bit surreal, quite frankly. It made you think of hell with devils cooking body parts. We were seated immediately. A big black man in a leopard vest took our drink orders.

Following the soup course a long procession of chefs from Hell brought assortments of meat on the end of swords. They would put the sword point on your plate and announce what it was. If you indicated you wanted some he would slice off a large portion with a huge carving knife. We had sausage, ostrich, chicken, lamb, crocodile, waterbuck, and zebra (my favorite). If the flag was up on the Lazy Susan they brought meat. When we got back to the hotel we all said our goodbyes. Some of it was emotional. It's kind of hard after being together so long. And you can't help but bond with some of your traveling companions. There were promises to stay in touch but deep down you know it probably won't happen. You will never see or talk to them again.

Chapter 64

After we got up this morning Marshall found a very large ominous-looking scorpion at the foot of our mattress. As I have noted, time and again, we must remember this is Africa. He killed it rather than leave it for someone else. We were sitting on the back porch, and Marshall was complaining about an insect bite that had been itching since Dar. It looked infected to me. He squeezed around the red area and a worm popped out. That made me sick to my stomach, and he was visibly shaken. I mean, you immediately imagine the possibility of an infection and some terrible African disease. He'll want to see a doctor as soon as we get to Johannesburg. I was a bad morning for bugs.

10:30 a.m.

Martin and I had both read Out of Africa and seen the movie, more than once. Both of us shared a fascination with Africa, but that movie made us fall in love with it. Anyway, I urged Marshall to see if we could find a tour that would take us to Karen Blixen's house. Sure enough we did. A young man calling himself Pogo picked us up at our hotel. We drove through the snarl of Nairobi traffic and finally broke into the countryside; scenic with eucalyptus, Norfolk pine, and bougainvillea. We passed through a suburb called the Bomas, and were finally in the middle of Estate Karen, full of impressive-looking, red-tiled colonial homes with huge pine and cypress trees. Finally we were there, at Karen Blixen's former home. Marshall and I were very excited. It looked the same, just like in the movie. It was cool inside the limestone walls, and the ceilings were 10 feet tall. There's a double fireplace in the central part of the house that opens into the dinning room and the library and office. The house is large but unpretentious, and I could imagine myself living there. We were told not to take pictures on the inside but Marshall did it anyway. The lawn is huge and also impressive. We walked the grounds for quite a while before we decided to leave.

We returned to our hotel, the Heron Court, and sat down in the restaurant for our last dinner on our African excursion. Marshall pointed out the guys at the bar with the unmistakable look of overland drivers. After a while you can spot them easily the unkempt hair, the three-day stubble, and the bracelets made by native craftsmen. They were drinking and talking with strangers. It seems to be a lonely way to live.

Her memory of the ensuing conversation came clearly to mind. "The next time I get this close to African wild life, I plan to have a high-powered rifle in my hands. I would dearly love to bag one of the *big five*," Marshall asserted.

"The big five?" Clare questioned.

"Oh, Clare, I thought you knew that."

"We'll excuse me," she answered curtly; "I don't remember Mandy or Carol talking about that or any of our guides mentioning it."

"Okay, fine," Marshall replied, impatiently. "It's lion, leopard, elephant, buffalo, and rhino."

"They're so magnificent; you mean you'd actually kill one of beautiful animals?"

"In a heartbeat, my dear, in a heartbeat." Clare just shook her head disgustedly. She did not respond. It seemed a waste of time to try and dissuade him. She picked up the journal once more and read the final paragraph.

> *As we sipped our vodka martinis, Marshall asked me what effect this trip had had on me. I told him that the poverty and the living conditions in much of the country were disturbing to me. Some of it I would have trouble getting off my mind. I told him that it would make me appreciate a good home, security and the upper-middle-class life I expected to live. But I also confessed that Africa had gotten under my skin. I felt that I would forever be drawn to Africa. When I asked him the same question he said, "I need to exercise more and drink less." Then he laughed and slapped his sides.*

As Clare closed the journal, her memory of that last night in Nairobi was crystal clear. She always wondered what, if anything, was behind Marshall's question. And after such an experience, she was taken aback by his rather flippant and shallow impression. She had to always remember that Marshall would have access to the journal, and she had to be careful about making any compromising entries. Although she didn't tell him that night, the trip had heightened her resolve to become a less dependent person; to become her own person—instead of the pitiful, obedient, mindless, reticent-to-a-fault person she had become. With that resolve was also the commitment to make their union work in spite of her growing sense that she had made a terrible mistake. And she remembered the excitement and anticipation of seeing her new home, meeting new people, and settling in Johannesburg, one of the great cities of the world. And she remembered that she needed to see a priest.

Chapter 65

December 6, 2001

PETER WAS WAITING when she arrived in Johannesburg. They embraced for a long time. They were glad to see each other. Peter kissed Clare on the mouth but it wasn't a lover's kiss, it was more like from a brother or father. It most certainly wasn't that he didn't want it to be more. But she didn't know how he really felt, and besides, like a fisherman, he would sink the hook before he started to reel in the catch. His first job is to convince her to stay.

Arm in arm they walked over to the baggage claim area. "How was your flight, love?"

She sighed, "Long—but uneventful. I did enjoy the stop over in London. That's one of the great cities in the world, and even for a short time, by my lonesome, it was fun to be there again."

Eventually, the bags were collected, and Peter started the engine of the Land Rover. "Do you want to hit the road or are you hungry? What's your pleasure, love?"

"You know, Peter, I am hungry, famished in fact. I'd love a big African breakfast. We could stop at the International Airport Hotel. We're in the neighborhood, and they used to have good food."

"They still do. That would be fine."

AS THEY LEFT the city, Peter asked about her family and her job. Innocently, just to make conversation, he also asked about her love life. The truth was that he wanted to know if Clare had a man in her life. Clare had said absolutely nothing about Morgan. Clare began to sob and briefly, through the tears, confessed, "Oh, Peter, I have just broken up with a wonderful man, a man I love very much. In fact, I thought we'd be married by now. But it's over, and I'm just going to have to deal with it."

Peter handed her his handkerchief. This news filled him with mixed emotion. He was glad she was free of any entanglements, but taken aback that she felt so deeply about Morgan Mason, a man she clearly loved and expected to marry. He knew that he would have to go slowly. If he could make her trip a happy one then maybe he could convince her to stay permanently. Perhaps the breakup could be a blessing in disguise. Although he had never been married, Peter was not ignorant of human relationships and the ways of the opposite sex. He knew that bruised women often opted for a drastic change in their lives. Knowing that he will need to play his hand carefully, he hoped this might prove to be the opening he needed. Clare laid down in the seat and put her head in Peter's lap. She would sleep now, and she would have plenty of time to do it. It was at least 250 miles to the Petica Lodge, Peter's main camp near the Botswana border.

Chapter 66

CLARE WAS COMFORTABLE in the main house. Although Peter would be under the same roof, he had always been a perfect gentleman. There were servants to take care of her every wish. She was eagerly getting reacquainted with the safari operation. They joined one of Peter's excursions in Limpopo. They road horseback, which Clare truly loved to do, which helped them get closer to the animals. This area was one of the best, most beautiful available for true nature lovers' to get in touch with the African outdoors. The area abounded with fauna and flora and offered a vast area in which to ride. There were a variety of animals to see. Every day was full, Peter had made sure of that, but he hadn't talked business, personal or otherwise. One evening after dinner, at the big house at Petica, Peter sat Clare down and laid out all his promotional brochures which covered the complete scope of the Petica Safari operation. Clare was attentive as Peter explained every excursion and each customer option. Clare asked lots of questions.

○ ○ ○ ○ ○

THEY HAD JUST finished lunch and were enjoying tea on the veranda.

Suddenly, Clare stood up and asked, "Is that promotional material on the company still around?"

"Sure, it's in a drawer in my desk."

She headed for the inside of the house, stopped, turned, and said to Peter, "Well, get it, and I'll meet you at the dinning table."

A bit confused, Peter did as Clare suggested.

"She started looking at the various brochures. Okay, I've been thinking about your operation. Your promotional information is actually pretty good. You've got it at the chamber and at the hotels. The concierges help you, and you rely on word of mouth."

"The outfitters and gun shops all know me, and they recommend us," Peter added.

"Those are good," reasoned Clare, "and you need to keep doing that, but what you really need is to create a web site. I can help you do that. Your excursions are heavily skewed to hunting. That's okay, but I believe you would increase your market and general appeal if you did some other things."

"Okay, like what?"

"Like offering Vilanculo Lodge at the end of the safari. They could combine game fishing, a totally different activity than what they had been doing, with total relaxation on the coast before they go home. I think that would be slam dunk!"

Peter grinned from ear to ear. "Anything else?" he asked. He wanted to discover the depth of her vision.

"Victoria Falls. The falls and the hotel are fabulous. People are impressed, and that in itself is worth doing. We could base them there and then take them across into Zambia for rapelling, absailing, gorge flying, and bungee-jumping. I did all of it in 1997, right before Marshall had to report to work in Johannesburg. It was the thrill of my life, and you don't expect to do these things in Africa. It's a winner! These are the excursions I recommend you add."

"Well, I'll need a marketing director to implement all that. I don't have time to do it. And if you're correct in your assumptions, the marketing director will more than pay for herself; or himself," Peter concluded, laughing. "Clare, this is exciting. You could save me a lot of trouble and make me very happy if you'll agree to take on the project yourself."

She rubbed her hands together, smiled broadly, and asked, "You'd give me a free hand?"

"Absolutely," said Peter.

"Okay, I'll do it!"

Chapter 67

"MOM, THIS IS Clare."

"Oh, hi, sweetheart; it's so good to hear your voice. I can't wait to see my girl. You'll be home soon?"

"Well, that's what I'm calling about. Peter has offered me a position here as his director of marketing. It's an excellent opportunity. I've thought it over, and I'm going to take it."

Marge was silent for what seemed like an eternity. "Clare, this breakup with Morgan has really messed you up, hasn't it? Your decision is not about Africa, or Peter Wilson, or the animals, or the Pope, or my chocolate sheet cake—or an excellent opportunity. It's all about Morgan Mason!"

There was silence on Clare's end of the line. "I never could fool you, Mom."

"Not now, not ever," declared Marge with conviction.

She sighed and then admitted, "Right now, as wonderful as it is, Austin is the last place I want to be. I need a change of scenery."

"And how long do you expect this change to take?"

"Mom, it's way too early to know that."

"Well, I think it's absurd. But you're a grown woman, and I don't have a damn thing to say about what you do."

"Don't get huffy, Mom!"

"You're right, but it's hard to give up my Momma's Card."

"Don't give it up. You'll be able to use it again."

Marge and Clare laughed.

"Listen, you'll tell Burt what I decided. And give him my love. I'll talk to him the next time I call."

"All right, darling, take care. I love you."

"Love you, Mom."

Clare called Arch, and he was completely supportive. But he was always behind any decision Clare ever made. His lack of frequent contact with both the girls made him more prone to go along and get along. The general manager and sales staff at the White House were in total shock. April thought it sounded like fun and agreed to rent out Clare's side of the duplex and ship her things as soon as possible.

Chapter 68

THE PROMOTIONAL TOUR for Morgan's new release had exceeded expectations. The book was certain to be another smash hit and initial sales seemed to bear that out. He was in a joyous mode as the jumbo-jet lifted off the tarmac on the initial leg of his flight back to Austin. It was smooth going until bad weather and severe turbulence causing the captain to turn on the "Fasten Seatbelt" sign.

Morgan grabbed the arm of an attendant as she went by. "Would you ask the captain if they still expect to be on time, or will there be a delay?"

"Certainly, sir."

Morgan watched her as she opened the door and disappeared into the flight deck. In a moment the captain came on the loud speaker. "This is Captain Day. I know that many of you may be concerned about connecting flights, and that makes perfectly good sense. The truth is, we don't know just yet how the weather will affect our ETA. We are in constant communication with ground traffic control and will advise you as soon as we know something definite."

"THIS IS YOUR captain. I'm sorry to say that we will not be able to meet our scheduled time of arrival. I am going to ask our chief flight attendant to give you the status of all American connecting flights."

After learning that he would miss his flight he asked the stewardess to advise him of the next available flight to Austin. "Mr. Mason, I'm sorry to tell you, but we have nothing available until 8:30 in the morning, and no other carriers have anything tonight either."

Perturbed, he shook his head in disgust. "We can put you up at the…"

"No," said Morgan, raising his right hand as if to let her know that she need not continue, "I'm going home tonight."

As soon as they were on the ground, Morgan hurriedly collected his luggage, hailed a cab and headed for Dallas Love Field. A seasoned traveler, he knew he could grab a Southwest Airline flight that would get him to Austin tonight. He hurried in the terminal and up to the ticketing counter.

"You're a lucky man, Mr. Mason. I can get you on this flight. It departs in twenty minutes, but you'll have to carry everything on."

He smiled and signed the credit card charge slip. "That will be no problem, and thank you."

It was a typical crowded Friday night flight, and the plane was full. Eventually everyone was settled, baggage stowed, and the plane taxied into position. Once they leveled off, the flight attendants hurriedly took drink orders. It was only a forty-five-minute flight.

"My God, Morgan, what are you doing on this flight? I thought you always traveled on American."

As he looked up he saw April Collins staring back at him. A smile crossed his face. "Hey, there, good looking! How did I get so lucky as to fly with you?"

"Obviously, you've been living right."

"What can I get you?"

"You have a Corona, by chance?"

"Yes, I do."

April placed Morgan's beer on his tray table and squeezed a lime in it. "I guess I should have asked, but that's the way most everyone likes it."

"Well, I'm not everyone, but I do like it that way."

"Listen, I'm done when we hit Austin. Could we possibly have a drink when we get on the ground?" she inquired.

"Sure, I can do that."

Chapter 69

"HEY MOM, IT'S April, you favorite Austin daughter."

"What's up, sweetheart? Are you doing okay?"

"Well, I lot better lately. Guess who's coming to dinner?"

"Sidney Portier," said Marge, playfully.

"That's very good, Mom," said April, in appreciation. "But wrong. Actually, he's better than Sidney Portier."

"Well, why don't you just tell me? I know you're itching to."

"Morgan Mason."

"Morgan Mason!" she exclaimed with surprise and disbelief. "I don't think that's a good idea, April."

"And why not," said April, challenging her mothers reasoning.

"Well, because he's Clare's…"

"He's Clare's nothing, Mom. They broke up, remember? Clare walked out on the relationship. That's my sister's loss and my gain."

"All right, fine," said Marge, with a sigh, still showing doubts in her tone. "Do me a favor, will you, April?"

"Well—I'll consider it. What's the favor?"

"Don't tell Clare."

April was silent, as if trying to decide whether to agree or not. "Okay, Mom, I won't mention it."

There was momentary silence and then April added, "Morgan and I have gone out several times, but this will be my first time to feed him."

"How do you intend to do that, April, order in pizza?" Marge speculated, with sarcasm.

"Quit it, Mom!"

Still indicating disgust with her younger daughter and wanting to remind her that she was still married, she asked, "What about your divorce?"

"It's final in October."

Chapter 70

"APRIL, THAT WAS an exceptional dinner; it really was. I appreciate the effort it took to pull it off." April had gone to Central Market and purchased an entire precooked meal of impressive gourmet dishes. She didn't see any reason to tell Morgan.

"Well, thank you, Morgan. I'm glad you enjoyed it." She picked up her dirty dishes and headed for the kitchen. Morgan started to take his in as well, but she stopped him. Smiling, she gave him a kiss on the cheek and said, "Stay where you are, I'll do this."

April and Morgan had been taking it easy, keeping the relationship light and casual. But she sensed that Morgan was attracted to her, she was sure of it, but resisted her strong tendencies to seduce him. She knew he was a quality catch and feared that if she was too provocative and aggressive that it might put him off. She hoped that patience would serve her well and she had to keep in mind that he was once in love with her sister. After rinsing her dishes and placing them carefully in the dishwasher, she asked, "Coffee?"

"Yes, I'd like some very much."

"How would you like it?"

"Black, please."

April delivered his coffee and took his dishes. "I'm preheating the oven, and we're going to have some blackberry crisp."

Interested but a bit confused, "What is that exactly?"

"Oh, it's like cobbler except the crust is mixed in with the berries."

"Okay, sounds good. I would never have thought of doing that."

April brought her coffee to the table. She sighed and said, "I never told you what our problem was. You know, why Ken and I split."

"You don't owe me an explanation."

She looked down at the table and then back at Morgan. Her face mirrored the pain and distress that she felt. After what seemed like an eternity she said, "Ken informed me that he was in love with someone else." She stared at him as tears welled up in her piercing brown eyes. Morgan frowned and started to speak but she interrupted. "It's another man, Morgan, another Southwest Airlines flight attendant."

"Good God, April!" he exclaimed with disbelief, "I would have never in a million years…"

"Yeah, me either," she said with a heavy sigh. "Can you imagine what that does to a woman's head?"

Morgan stroked his chin, pondering her question, and his answer. "April, I can somewhat understand, but you need to realize that this is not a reflection on you. It's not really that he chose a man over you; it's more that he succumbed to his latent tendencies. It happens to men, and women, all the time. They fight it, get married, have children, and then realize they can't live a heterosexual life."

"You're right, of course, and thank you for that. But you can surely understand what it's doing to my head."

"Oh, yeah, absolutely. Thank God you didn't get pregnant."

"I've thought about that very thing, Morgan. I've thought about it a lot."

The moment was suddenly interrupted but the buzzing of the timer on the stove. Trying to alter the mood of the moment she forced a smile and said, "Our dessert is ready."

"Ouch," she exclaimed, slightly burning herself while retrieving the hot ramekins from the oven. Using a pad she transferred the bubbling berries into a saucer for serving.

"Morgan, I've got vanilla ice cream for a topping or I've got some heavy whipping cream. What's your pleasure?"

"Oh, the cream, for sure. That's the way I always grew up eating cobbler."

"April, this is outstanding, really excellent. My compliments once again." She had actually made the dessert and was hoping he would ask about the recipe, but he didn't.

"Thank you, Morgan. You know food, and you're a gourmet cook yourself. Coming from you it's quite a compliment."

This time Morgan followed her into the kitchen without any argument. He stood behind her as she rinsed the remainder of the dark residue from the small white porcelain containers. Morgan had enjoyed April's company during their dates, and she was definitely fun to be with. But he had always found her to be a bit crass, a total opposite of her sister.

April and Clare had had many conversations about Morgan and she had been around him on numerous occasions. She knew Morgan Mason pretty well and benefitted from the insight. She was wearing starched white shorts and a pale blue, men's dress shirt, with the sleeves rolled neatly half way up the arm. Her black hair was in a French braid. She looked cute, no doubt about it; and she had a 'major-league' body. None of it had escaped him, let alone the stark similarity of her looks to Clare's. April's sad situation and the way it had affected her delicate psyche had touched his heart. When she finished up, wiped off her wet hands and turned around he was waiting. Overcome with emotion, he took her in his arms—and then to bed.

Chapter 72

April 1997
Johannesburg, South Africa

HER HEART WAS pounding in her chest and the words stuck in her throat, as if searching for an opportunity, any reason at all to avoid the inevitable. The small, inside sliding door opened and she reluctantly began, "Bless me, Father, for I have sinned. My last confession was three months ago."

"What are you guilty of, my child?"

Tears began to run down her cheeks, and he could hear her muffled sobs. "You are in God's house, my child. You can find peace and forgiveness."

"Oh, Father, I have sinned against God and our blessed Virgin. I have broken my marriage vows. I have slept with a man who is not my husband."

"Are you sorry for this transgression, my child?"

"Oh yes, Father; it is tearing me apart."

"For your penitence you shall say ten Our Fathers and ten Hail Mary's. And I want you to perform eight hours of volunteer work at our hospital in the charity section of the maternity ward."

"Oh, yes, Father, and gladly."

"There is one other thing."

Surprised that there was more but eager to do whatever was necessary. "You must never commit this transgression again."

"No, father, never—I swear."

"Does your husband know of this sin?"

"No father, gratefully, he does not."

"Then you must never tell him. It would cause him pain, and it would create mistrust for no reason. You may feel moved to tell your husband in order to help you deal with your own guilt. But your penitence will do that for you, my child. I grant your absolution. Go and sin no more."

She squinted as she stepped out of the church and into the warm sunshine. It was a beautiful day in Johannesburg; a cloudless sky. Clare felt better although she knew she must face another ordeal.

o o o o o

SHE SAT QUIETLY as he entered the room, hoping by some miracle that what her body was telling her was nothing more than a cruel hoax. The doctor sat down, pulled his chair up snugly to the desk and cheerfully gave her the much anticipated news, "Congratulations, Mrs. Splitgarber, you're going to have a baby."

He was taken aback when Clare ducked her head, stared at the floor and blew a nervous breath through her crimson cheeks. The troubled look on her face was unmistakable. She sighed noticeably and gathered herself, "Doctor Van de Mere, you're my doctor, and you must keep the confidence of every patient; right?"

"Of course."

"Then this will have to be our little secret until I tell you differently."

Somewhat confused, but seldom surprised, he assured her that her secret was safe and that her privacy would be respected.

Clare was sadly reminded of the incident in camp, in Rundu, Namibia; the unfortunate situation that was the source of her dilemma. After they were thrown out of the bar that night, she and Tony were walking back alone. As they reached his tent he suddenly grabbed her and kissed her passionately, running his tongue down her throat. His hands were all over her voluptuous body. As he dragged her toward the opening of his tent, he was surprised that she offered no resistance. She thought to herself, *I still can't believe that happened. We were both pretty liquored up I guess, but that's not really an excuse. I don't know, with my situation with Marshall maybe I really wanted him and just wouldn't admit it.* She remembered thinking, *Holy Mary, Mother of God, what have I done?*

In a couple of days Clare recalled that she had a chance to speak to Tony privately. She remembered telling him, *When I see you I'll be courteous, and I expect you to do the same. But if you try to flirt with me, if I hear the slightest sexual innuendo, or you get out of line in any way, I'll make you wish you'd died as a child!* Tony got the message and stayed away. She thought to herself, *I guess we all have a few skeletons in our closet. I still can't believe I did that, a good Catholic girl like me.*

○ ○ ○ ○ ○

SHE WALKED UP behind him, put her arms around his neck, and kissed his cheek. He smiled, reached up and took her hands in his. "Clare, darling, that was a superb dinner." She had prepared all his favorites; lamb chops with mint jelly, oven roasted rosemary potatoes, and asparagus with hollandaise. There was also a nice salad, a complimentary red wine and crème brulee for dessert. There were fresh flowers on the table and the candles had been lit. The great deception had begun, and Marshall would become a willing participant. "I appreciate all the effort it took to prepare such a nice meal," he told her. She patted his shoulder as she pulled away to grab the coffee pot. She poured Marshall a refill and took her seat beside him. She smiled at him warmly as she tenderly placed her hand on his, "Marshall, I've been thinking about your biological clock." He laughed.

Marshall had wanted to start a family immediately after they were married. He had reminded her that he was thirty-five years old and ready to get started. But she was only twenty-three and wanted some time to adjust to being married and some time to play. Even at her young age, she could easily understand that a baby would tie her down; tie them both down. And a child would change their lives forever. She was also mature enough to realize that they needed to find out if this marriage was going to work before they had children. She wouldn't come right out and say so, but that's what see had been thinking.

"Darling, I think you were right. Maybe we should start our family."

Smiling broadly, but still taken aback by her rather sudden change of heart, "You mean it, Clare, you really mean it?"

"Yes, sweetheart, I really mean it." Marshall was beside himself. He could not control his obvious joy at this unexpected bit of good news. And he couldn't keep his eyes or his hands off his beautiful wife.

Chapter 73

DR. VAN DE MERE pulled down his surgical mask when Marshall first noticed him coming down the hall, then walked briskly toward him. He had a serious expression on his face. "I'm afraid she's lost the baby, Mr. Splitgarber." He sighed, having anticipated the disappointment he was certain the expectant father must have felt.

Tears welled up in Marshall's eyes as he shook his head in disbelief. "Your wife is a young healthy woman. You'll have more children. Believe me when I tell you that I understand how you feel. But you must look at this as if it was a situation that was not meant to be. Come with me, now, she wants to see you."

o o o o o

"YOU'RE DOING JUST fine, Clare," said Dr. Van de Mere, smiling and trying to be reassuring. "You are a healthy young woman. You'll have lots of kids."

Calmly, she informed the doctor, "I want you to write me a prescription for birth control pills. And as before, doctor, I'll have to ask you to let this be our little secret."

Chapter 74

At Petica Lodge, near the Botswana Border

"CLARE, YOU MUST know that I love you. I've loved you from the first moment I saw you. But you were the wife of a friend and a client. What could I do?" Peter confessed. Clare stared at him but tried not to react.

"Clare, you've done so much for this company in the six months you've been here. Our revenues are up over 30 percent already, and it's due to the increased publicity and the expansion into the new markets."

"It's been challenging but fun and fulfilling. Frankly, I thought all that talk about needing me to promote your business was a bunch of balcony. I thought it was just a ploy to get me over here."

"Well, love, I wanted to get you here all right, but I was sincere about what I thought you could offer the company."

"I appreciate that, and the free hand you've given me proves it. I mean, you've had a successful business, run your own way. It's not easy to let some outsider come in and want to change things."

"I trusted your judgment and intuition, and I was correct."

"Now, let's get back to you and me. We have a mutual respect for each other, we are friends, we enjoy each other's company. That in itself is a good start for a successful relationship. We have proven that we can work together and you can be fulfilled in a business way, knowing that you helped make this operation what it is today."

"Well, you see, I…"

"Clare, let me finish. I want to get it all out before you respond." She nodded.

"I will take care of you. You will never want for anything the rest of your life. And if you agree to marry me I will leave this business to you, and I'll put that in writing before the wedding. And I know you love Africa. You cannot deny it. I think we have a great basis for a good marriage. And I believe, if not now, you can love me in time. Until then, if that be the case, I love you enough for both of us."

"Peter, that's one of the most…"

Ebenezer interrupted the conversation when he entered the room and inquired, "Do you want more fish?"

"No, thank you, Ebenezer, but it was very good," said Clare.

Ebenezer was smiling broadly, displaying a mouth full of very white teeth. He had trained hard and was making good progress. He was particularly interested in pleasing the beautiful lady from America. He wanted her approval. "The cooking was good?" he asked, seeking reassurance.

"Yes, Ebenezer, the cooking was good."

"I agree with madam, Ebenezer, it was very good," echoed Peter. "We'll have coffee now."

Smiling and bowing, Ebenezer acknowledged the instructions. "Yes, coffee, coming up."

He stopped at kitchen door, turned back toward Clare, smiled and said, "The cooking was good."

She smiled warmly, nodding, reaffirming her approval. He disappeared inside the kitchen and Clare and Peter laughed. It was so important to Ebenezer to get their approval, and he did. He was proud of himself.

Leaning forward, Peter said, "Clare, I believe you were about to give me an answer to my proposal."

No sooner than the words were out of his mouth, than the phone rang. Peter sighed, *another interruption.* "It's closest to you, Clare. Do you mind?"

"Of course not."

"Hello."

"Clare, honey, is that you?"

"Yes, it is. Burt?"

"Yes, darling, it's me."

"I just talked with you guys the day before yesterday. I don't understand; is something the matter?"

"Oh, God! Oh, God, no!" exclaimed Clare. She dropped the telephone, grabbed her hair with both hands and pulled violently at it. She fell to the floor screaming, pounding the hard polished mahogany with her clinched fists. She was hysterical, and Peter was frightened for her. He had never seen her like this. Torn between tending to Clare and picking up the phone, he screamed for help from the head house boy.

"Congorie! Congorie! Get in here!"

"See to madam," Peter ordered.

He grabbed the telephone, "Peter Wilson here. Who is this? What has happened?"

"It's Burt Brown. Oh Peter," he lamented, "it's so tragic, so senseless, so sad."

"What Burt, what is it? You're not telling me anything. What has happened?"

There was a moment of silence and then Burt explained, "Peter, its Clare's mom. She was killed instantly in a head-on collision. Get her back here as soon as you can. I'm depending on you."

"Of course—I'll take care of it. I am so sorry to hear this news."

Chapter 75

Friday, December 14, 2001

IT WAS COLD. The wind was nasty and cutting. It was a bad day for a funeral, and there was the ever present threat of rain. The family huddled together in the first two rows under the green tent. The funeral director thoughtfully invited the mourners, as many as the remaining space would accommodate, to move in around the family. As Father Quigley began to speak, the rain began to fall. Clare caught sight of a familiar figure as he pushed his way under the cover of the tent.

Clare was so distraught she hardly heard a word of what Quigley said. She could not seem to muster an once of comfort from anything. She couldn't stop the pain—and her mind was wondering. "Ashes to ashes, dust to dust, in the certain hope of the resurrection through Jesus Christ our Lord," said Father Quigley. "Amen."

It was over and the family sat silently. Father Quigley spoke to each family member individually and then friends filed by to offer what comfort they could. Morgan Mason was the last to pay his respects. When he got to Clare she fell into his arms and wept uncontrollably. Morgan stroked her hair and held her close. When she was able to gain some degree of composure, he sat down and they began to talk.

"Clare, darling, the cars are leaving now. You must come with us. You must say goodbye to Morgan."

"You all go on, Burt. Morgan will bring me home."

"All right, sweetheart, whatever you say."

Chapter 76

Thursday, May 9, 2002

MORGAN LOVED SPEED. The blue Mercedes convertible had that and more; but one would expect nothing less from one of the world's foremost automobiles. Against a sky of azure blue the warm Italian sun felt wonderful as the breeze mussed his curly hair. His tanned flesh radiated along with his smile of satisfaction.

Now 275 miles from Florence, they planned on taking the Aurelian Way along the Tyrrhenian coast. But Morgan thought they might want an overnight at Montecatini. There was no urgency to arrive in Florence today. As he drove he let his mind wander over the events of the last twenty-seven months, developments that had changed his life.

"OH, DARLING, WE don't have to make it to Florence today, do we? Let's stay overnight at Montecatini. It's so charming I just love it."

"You're reading my mind. I think that's exactly what we should do."

"Then it's a done deal?"

"Yes, a done deal."

She grabbed his arm and squeezed it tight, leaned over and gave him a kiss on the cheek. "I'm very happy, Mr. Mason, in case anyone should ask."

AFTER A DELIGHTFUL breakfast at an outdoor café, they arrived at Pisa, the charming little Italian city with the tower that leaned. They'd both been there before but it was still fun. They spent the night in Firenze, with its numerous unique bridges, colorful architecture and appealing eateries. They both took extreme joy in having lunch, a coffee or wine in a sidewalk café, observing the natives and enjoying the warm Italian sunshine. Their next stop would be Florence, the popular capital of Tuscany. They enjoyed the magnificent Santa Marie Del Fiore, Giotto's Bell Tower, and the sculpture-studded Signoria Square. They stopped in the Gallery of Fine Arts specifically to see Michelangelo's David.

"Old Mike was a right talented sculptor," Morgan observed, with a laugh.

"Yes, wasn't he," she said in agreement, "and can you imagine the size of the mound of clay he started with?"

"You know, we laugh, but David is twelve feet tall. That had to have been one serious mound of clay."

"Sweetheart, if you don't mind, I believe I'll pass on the cathedral. What I'd really like to do is slip into that leather shop."

"That's fine, let's do it."

They looked at bags, belts and boots. In the back of the shop were jackets and coats. As they approached, the clerk said hello in perfect English.

"May I show you a jacket? We've got an excellent variety and some good prices."

She tried on several and although they were all quite nice, there were no bells and whistles. Then James said, "Try this one."

She looked at it from several angles and felt the soft smooth black leather admiringly. A smile crept over her face. "Oh Morgan, I love this one."

"It looks great on you. Incidentally, where are you folks from?"

"Austin, Texas."

"How is the climate?"

"Hot as hell in the summer," said Morgan, "and the winters are mild."

"Then she'll wear this a lot. It's a nice light weight."

"How much is it?" Morgan asked.

James showed him the tag, attached to the jacket that she was still wearing.

Morgan handed James a credit card and the transaction was soon completed. On the street she wore the jacket, admiringly. After a light lunch and a nice red wine they headed across the wooded Etruscan Apennine Hills to the northern tip of the Adriatic Sea.

They took a launch over to picturesque Venice and brought some personal items in case they decided to stay the night. On the way a speed boat passed them with the words, "Heineken Beer," lettered on the side. Morgan joked, "Oh, shucks, the beer boat is gonna beat us to the dock. A cold one sounds pretty good to me right now."

As they exited the launch, Morgan pointed out the large barge unloading produce. "You tend to forget that everything has to be brought in."

They marveled at the Venetian glass blowers, took a romantic gondola ride around the maze of canals and enjoyed a delightful lunch at an outdoor café. After lunch they strolled in St. Marks's Square. "Watch this," said Morgan. He stood alone with his arms outstretched, parallel to the ground. "What are you doing?" she asked with a giggle.

"Quiet," he insisted.

Pretty soon a pigeon landed on his left arm, then two more on his right and another on his shoulder. In a very few minutes Morgan was covered with pigeons as she scrambled to get a photograph before something disturbed them.

Then Morgan moved and they all flew away to the delight of the crowd that had gathered to watch the unusual sight of a man playing like a statue and running a dangerous risk of being treated like one.

"Morgan, you are a nut case," she insisted, gently taking hold of his hand. "I got a great picture." They laughed. After some semi-serious shopping they decided to take a room and a nap, leaving a wake-up call for 6:00 p.m.

At the front desk they inquired about restaurants and had a clerk call ahead for reservations. After dinner they enjoyed a coffee and a band concert in the square. It had been a wonderful day.

Chapter 77

THEY DROVE ALONG the coastline of the Adriatic to Ravenna, then inland to picturesque San Marino, perched atop a mountain peak with a breathtaking view for miles in the distance. They lunched outside at the Trattoria Bar and Grill, in the world's smallest independent republic. Afterwards they departed for peaceful Assisi where the plan was to arrive in time to visit the 13th century Basilica of St. Francis, built above the saint's grave. On the way they stopped for a break at Foschi Café and Inn, frequently used, at one time, by Benito Mussolini and his mistress. The bedroom was now used as a kind of museum to attract tourists to stop and spend money.

On the outskirts of Assisi they stopped on the side of the road to simply take it all in. Sheep were grazing lazily on green grass below with Assisi nestled quietly atop a hill in front of them. They drove into town and to the Hotel Giotto, cantilevered on the side of a cliff. A series of nine suites with large balconies overlooked the city of St. Francis and a breathtaking view of the countryside. Morgan had stayed here before and asked for one of the special suits. Colorful flowers in rust colored clay containers were situated everywhere the eye could see. They embraced as the sun set on the historic city.

Slowly shaking her head in admiration, she said, "Does it get any better than this?"

Morgan, he too in awe of the spectacle, reverently replied, "No, I don't think it does."

It was getting cool now and she shivered slightly as his arms drew tightly around her.

"I'm getting hungry," she explained softly. Morgan glanced down at his watch. It was, indeed, time for dinner in the ornate hotel dinning room. "I can help you with that."

○ ○ ○ ○ ○

BIDDING FAREWELL TO a city they loved so dearly they drove south through the rolling Campagna Romana. They were headed for Pompeii and Morgan suggested she read from a brochure he had picked up at the hotel in Assisi.

"Refresh my memory a bit."

"Okay, let me put my little fingers on that brochure. Let's see, it says, *The Roman city was destroyed and preserved by an eruption of Mount Vesuvius in 79 A.D. See patrician homes, public baths, and commercial districts strikingly recalling day-to-day life when Rome was at the apex of her power.*"

"I remembering seeing a program on Pompeii on the History Channel," Morgan recalled. "It wasn't the lava flow that killed them, it was the volcanic ash falling from the sky. I'm really looking forward to being there again."

"Me too, me too," she exclaimed with childlike enthusiasm.

As they wondered through the ruins they were struck by how well preserved much of it was. "It's very easy to tell the level of opulence in which they lived. Romans lived well all over the empire," said Morgan.

"It's amazing how many buildings are intact along with these courtyards," she observed. "And Morgan, look at these murals that cover the walls, how well preserved they are. And the caliber of art is impressive—but highly suggestive of pagan sex rituals."

"I was noticing that."

As they entered the next house there was a wall painting of a Roman warrior with his penis exposed. "My God, it looks like it belongs on a horse," said Morgan, grinning. As they moved deeper into the house there was a life-size sculpture of a naked man. He had a similar endowment. They looked at each other and smiled broadly. "Morgan," she questioned sheepishly, "what kind of people lived in this house?"

"I'll give you three guesses, and the first two don't count."

As the local guide continued the tour they observed ancient carvings of all sizes and descriptions but the most memorable we the dusty figures of local citizens who had been mummified by the molten hot volcanic ash and now rested quietly in clear glass coffins. The bodies were in various positions, held permanently by death.

Back on the road once more, they made their way toward Sorrento located on the coast by the Tyrrhenian Sea.

"Oh, darling, I think we should stay here a few days."

"Sure," said Morgan, "I thought that's what we'd planned all along."

"Morgan, this is truly one of the most beautiful places I have ever been." She had good reason to be impressed. The coastal waters were emerald green, the architecture quaint, set in a city of traversing narrow streets lined with bougainvillea and other colorful flowers. Cafes and produce vendors filled the streets. Sorrento had long been regarded as a location for rest and relaxation and the happy couple took advantage of that aspect of the lovely city.

Having settled in their hotel they boarded a launch for the short ride across the bay to the Isle of Capri, a royal retreat for 2,000 years. "Baby doll, while we're here, let's go through the blue grotto," Morgan suggested.

"Sure, I'm game for anything—as long as it happens with you."

He gave her a big kiss and hug and then purchased the necessary tickets. The small boats bobbed up and down, as the guides worked tirelessly to hold their position, waiting their turn to enter. Italian oarsmen in dirty shorts with shaggy hair and bushy mustaches hollered back and forth at each other as some of the crafts got a little close while others banged into each other. Finally their boat was next. The oarsmen spoke English well enough to warn everyone to duck their heads as he pulled the boat through the small entrance.

They looked at each other and grinned but they understood and ducked accordingly. On the inside of the grotto, grunts and sighs of wonder came from most of the eight passengers on board. It was cool inside as well and pitch black, except for the beautiful, but eerie blue glow. Soon the experience was over and they ducked their heads again as the left the cave.

"That was pretty neat, Morgan, I'm glad we did it."

"Yeah, I enjoyed it."

Back on land they took a cable car to the top of the island. "My God, it's like a different world up here!" she exclaimed.

"Yeah, it's pretty spectacular at that."

As they strolled around Capri village they were even more impressed. There were spectacular flowers in assorted pots and beds and all sorts of tropical trees, most of which they could not identify. The hotels were opulent five star classics, inside and out. The restaurants were also impressive but all paled in comparison to the truly spectacular view from the top. After finishing their walking tour they took seats at an inviting sidewalk café with a view. They ordered shrimp salads and red wine and decided, then and there, that they would return some day for an extended stay.

That night they dinned at O'Parrucchiano in Sorrento, a restaurant that had been owned and managed by three generations of the same family. They savored a sumptuous four-course dinner in a lush, private garden. "Morgan, isn't this an amazing place? I really couldn't be more pleased."

"I'm so glad you're pleased." He smiled and touched her wine glass with his. They were in no hurry, thoroughly enjoying the moment. After dinner they strolled for a time and later enjoyed a coffee at a sidewalk café with the locals. They slept late, did some shopping and dined later at Il Mulino, at the Roxy Hotel, where they danced until closing. In the morning, they would depart for Sicily.

Chapter 78

THEY WAITED PATIENTLY to drive aboard the ferry. Then they found their way to the upper deck and claimed their seats for the trip across the Straights of Messina. "Do you realize that the Allied forces that mounted the invasion of Italy in World War II had to pass over this same stretch of water?"

"I didn't Morgan, but did you really expect that I would?"

"No, not really," he admitted.

"After all, you've done research for those military books."

"That's true. Listen, I want to stay the day and night in Taormina. Actually, we'll stay at the Ramada Giardini Naxos. It just happens to be one of Europe's most popular beach resorts. Taormina is the town on the hill above the resort and it is a must see."

"I'm with you, Big Daddy. I'm looking forward to it." From their top-level, beach-front room they could observe the well-manicured, palm-tree-covered grounds, the large zee-shaped pool and the beach laden with umbrellas and sun-burned bodies. They swam and played on the beach, enjoyed a light lunch by the pool and napped.

"Hey, time to wake up, sleepy head," Morgan urged, waking her tenderly with a kiss and a smile. "Let's go up into the town."

It was quaint, with its narrow streets, intriguing shops, balconies, and flower bordered steps leading in every direction. Palm trees were in abundance. "Oh, Morgan, the bougainvillea is breathtaking—and it's everywhere. In fact, I've never seen so much of it concentrated in one place. Let's get these people to take our picture." They continue to shop, take pictures, talk with locals and tourists. "I'm getting hungry," she confessed, clinging to Morgan's arm and smiling at him warmly.

"I've got the perfect place. Come with me." They walked a short distance in the opposite direction, and soon they entered the front door of Granduca, Morgan's favorite eatery; their outside dinning area had a cantilevered overlook to the water hundreds of feet below. They were seated by the railing which offered a spectacular view. They ordered wine and waited for sundown; breathtaking. The veal and linguini was outstanding.

The following day was devoted to the scenic beauty and treasures of the island's heart. They motored to Piazza Armerina for a visit to the 4th-century Roman Villa of Casale, its colorful and perfectly preserved mosaics depict mythological themes and hunting scenes. "Morgan, we've said it before, but these villas are a constant reminder of how well the citizens of Rome lived throughout the empire."

"Absolutely," said Morgan.

Their next stop, Enna, was a strategic fortress-town perched high on a sheer rock. "Morgan, this panoramic view is truly spectacular."

He sighed in appreciation and added, "There was a rebellion here. Sicilian slaves went up against the Roman rulers of the city. The Romans were brutal, and their policies toward those they oppressed contributed to constant unrest and rebellion."

"Bad old Romans," she suggested with a laugh.

Back in the car again they descended to the vineyards and olive groves of the south coast. "Sicily is just about the olive oil capital of the world, isn't it?"

"If it's not I don't know who is." said Morgan.

Roman ruins pervaded the landscape as they continued on to Agrigento where they would overnight at the Jolly Hotel. "That pool down there looks awfully inviting. What do say we take a dip?" suggested Morgan. She joined him at the window wearing nothing but a smile. "Do we have to swim right now?"

o o o o o

THE NEXT MORNING after breakfast they joined a group with a local guide for a breathtaking stroll through the Valley of Temples. "I've been to Athens and Delphi, and I'm still impressed with these structures, and to think they have survived 24 centuries," Morgan observed.

"They are awesome and gigantic," she added. Later in the afternoon they visited the Dorian Temples and Acropolis at Selinunte, built on a balcony overlooking the sparkling Mediterranean. Before they continued their journey they lunched at a delightful restaurant by the sea and purchased ice cream cones from a small shop across from the entrance to the eatery. "I don't know if it's widely known," Morgan injected, "but the Italians are also known for their ice cream."

"I'll give them an A+ for this."

Chapter 79

THE DRIVE ALONG the coast was beautiful and they sang and laughed, their joy spilling out the happiness they felt. Tonight they would stay in historic Palermo, where well before the turn of the century, well-dressed men rode carriages over cobble stone streets that wound through the picturesque coastal city. Many of these men belonged to an honored society sometimes called the Costa Nostra. This criminal brotherhood controlled every aspect of life in Sicily. This society had been a law unto itself for centuries. Morgan had learned these things doing research for a book. He explained, "These men had power and money. They were treated like royalty. To many of the citizens, particularly the young impressionable, they had everything. As the young men observed them strolling along the streets of Palermo in their tailored suits and fine jewelry, ordinary men would tip their hats when they met them, and the women would curtsey and kiss their hands. All many of the young males in the city could think of was how to become one of these guys."

He continued, "Extortion was one of the ways the society made money and controlled the populace. In the past, when businessmen would resist, previous bosses would destroy the business. But Don Carmine Garafallo would change things; he was a master of extortion. By charging a moderate fee for protection, the businesses could still flourish, and everyone could make money. And there were enforcers who made sure the protection money was paid, and paid on time.

"In the early 1920s, fascism was growing in popularity. Benito Mussolini had little tolerance for the honored society and made it clear that he intended to destroy the Mafia. Many of the younger members of the society began to question their future, under the circumstances, and those with connections in America used them. Many had relatives and friends already established with crime families in New York City."

"So the Mafia really had its beginning right here in Palermo?"

"That's right."

"Well, that's pretty interesting stuff. Thank you for the history lesson."

They decided to take a city tour with a local guide, which included the ornate Piazza Bellini, the Cathedral, and the Arab-Norman Palatine Chapel in the Royal Palace. Morgan thought for a moment and remembered, "After the conquest of Sicily, Gen. George S. Patton used the Royal Palace as his headquarters."

"You know stuff, don't you Morgan?"

He laughed, "Yes, I know lots of stuff. I'm a regular walking encyclopedia."

They drove up to Monreale for a panoramic view of the Conca d'Oro and a visit to the 12th-century Norman Cathedral with its 50,000 square feet of precious Byzantine mosaics. Finally, they traveled the short distance to the picturesque fishing village of Mondello and back to the port over scenic, history-steeped Monte Pellegrino.

Back at the hotel Morgan commented, "Have you ever seen so many motor scooters?"

"I was thinking the same thing. Oh, Morgan, did you see the basket trading going on back there. An old woman on second floor used a basket on a rope to pull up something she bought from a street vendor. Then she lowered down the money."

"I didn't notice, but I know what you're talking about."

Tonight they would board the overnight ferry for the trip across the Bay of Naples, back to the Italian mainland.

THE TRIP TO Naples was quite nice, a fine cruise ship actually, with cars underneath. The dining room cuisine was superb. After a restful night they disembarked, enjoyed a hearty breakfast in Naples and headed north.

"Sweetheart, I'd like to visit Cassino if you don't object. Being a serious war buff I am interested in seeing the site of one of World War II's most ferocious battles in 1944."

"Sure, I'm with you."

Finally they were at the abbey. Morgan explained, "This is the Abbey of Montecassino. It was rebuilt with private donations, to medieval specifications, after near total destruction by Allied bombers in World War II. He grabbed a brochure. It says the Abby was founded by St. Benedict in 529. Here, you can read about it." From the Abby they could see a beautiful cemetery where more than 1,000 polish soldiers were buried. Soon they were back in Rome where they checked in to the Parco Tirreno Hotel.

The next morning they visited the Spanish Steps, the Piazza Venezia, the Roman Forum, the Colosseum, St. Peter's Square, and Basilica and finally the Sistine Chapel. Later they lunched at the delightful Ristorante alla Rampa. After a nap and a drink at the hotel lobby bar, they had dinner at the Mangrovia Restaurant and threw coins in the Fountain of Trivi.

"Trivi is so romantic," she asserted, "If I didn't already love you, Morgan Mason, I could fall in love all over again."

He kissed her tenderly and held her for a long time.

Chapter 80

THE MASTER PLAN had always been to end up back in Tuscany—where fine food, wine, art and history were in abundance. She had remarked that Tuscany really did look like the photos in travel books, only better. Medieval hill towns like living museums dotted the dusty plains. Their dense protective walls reflected the region's bloody past and the endless wars. Some of the towns were considered new, dating back only as far as the Renaissance. The largest had an upper old town as well as a newer, more modern one. But no matter how old the town, no matter how many gems of medieval architecture they contained, they functioned like towns anywhere. Laundry still hung on 13th century windows, scooters hummed endlessly up and down and around and locals stood on the battlements having smokes and chatting. The fields were rich with grapes, sunflowers and silver-leaved olive trees.

The roads, big and small, were well marked and easy to navigate, each crossing bore pointers with cities and distance. That was a blessing for Morgan, who insisted on doing all the driving, but had the world's worst sense of direction. Thankfully, all anyone really needed was a decent map. Nowhere in Italy was the juxtaposition of old and new in the art of wine-making more pronounced than on the venerable hills of

Tuscany. The contrast between traditional methods and state-of-the art innovation could be found not only with each turn of the road, but often within a single winery.

One fine evening they visited La Grotta in Montepulcian at the foot of the old walled city. They ate in the 15th century garden with its lighted cupola glowing overhead. There they had bisteca Fiorentina, a steak from the increasingly rare Chianina cattle whose texture resembled veal though its flavor was as rich and robust as any beef they ever tasted. They were not surprised to see the accompaniment of white beans.

Except for rustic romance, which they preferred, the simple lunch on a bench in the medieval town of Buonconvento was exceedingly satisfying. Eats for the event consisted of pecorino and sausage along with a nice bottle of Rosso di Montalcino. Spreading their culinary treasures on butcher paper they joyfully hacked off chunks of food, with Morgan's Swiss Army knife, in a park behind a church. The wine was savored from simple paper cups. Pigeons cooed from a nearby steeple. La Doccia would be their next stop. Morgan drove as she read aloud from the brochure.

The original farmhouse was built by monks of the Vallombrosa monastery. It is named after the perennial spring that is considered to have beneficial qualities. The original farm would have been built during the medieval ages when Vallombrosa exercised considerable religious and secular power throughout northern Tuscany. Just over the bridge in front of La Doccia is the old convent where Galileo spent his early formative years under the tutelage of monks. La Doccia is part of the medieval settlement of Ristonchi, which takes its name from Etruscan Ristona meaning the crest of a hill.

Now, La Doccia has been painstakingly restored to an extremely high standard while leaving the original structures largely unchanged. Many features remain such as stone staircases, a mixture of chestnut and terracotta ceilings and much of the original terracotta and brick flooring. Where it has been necessary to improve certain areas, the same handmade or original materials have been used. It is open all year with double-glazing, external glass to all the main wooden doors and full central heating.

Every room is an eclectic mixture of local handcrafted furniture made in the small mountain village of Tosi and family antiques and furnishings brought here from England. Ours is a family home on a lovely small estate into which we invite you to enjoy yourselves in one of our comfortable bedrooms on a bed and breakfast basis.

The newest addition to the house is dated 1632, but it is built onto a much older farmhouse, and the thick walls make the place cool in the summer and warm in the winter. We have superb terraces with breathtaking views of deep valleys and distant hills, perfect for escaping the concerns of every day.

Looking up from the pamphlet she asked Morgan, "Doesn't the old house sound just marvelous? I can't wait to stay there."

Taking his eye off the highway, for a mere moment, he looked at her and said, "I'm anxious myself. I have an inkling that this old house will have more meaning than anyone can imagine." She continued to read.

The accent at the house is on simple traditional pleasures of country living. Spend the day sight seeing, shopping, and visiting vineyards. Return to La Doccia in the late afternoon or early evening and relax over a bottle of great Italian wine. Of course, you don't have to leave La Doccia at all, but are welcome to pass the hours away curled up in one of its many nooks and crannies around the property, reading a book, sunbathing by the pool, or painting or sketching calmly beneath a tree. The substantial main house includes three bedrooms, all with ensuite bathrooms.

In the relaxed atmosphere of a country house party, we like to feel our close attention to qualify menus and outstanding wines gives our guests the best of Italy in a superlative setting. Cena, the Italian evening meal, is served either on the terrace or in the dinning room where guests dine together at one table. Please ask us about this additional dinning option. Our evening meals are intended to be examples of the best home cuisine available here in Italy. Using only the freshest foods available, we concentrate on producing a daily' changing menu that looks not only to Tuscan recipes, but also to those of the many different parts of this country's varied food culture.

"Enough of that," she determined. "I'm sold. I think we should definitely go there."

"Oh you do, do you," said Morgan with a laugh. "Well, then we'll go."

"Did you look at the brochure?" she asked.

"Of course I did."

"Well, if it's anything like the pictures? It really looks inviting."

"YOU ONCE TOLD me that your fantasy was to own a bed and breakfast in Tuscany." Morgan reminded her as he handed her a ring of keys. "Well, my darling, you must learn to be careful about what you wish for. I just purchased this place. You're the new owner. As for me, I'm going to become a wine maker and write more books."

She was truly speechless. Holding the keys limply in her left hand, she stared blankly at a smiling Morgan. Impatient with her silence he urged, "Say something, will you!"

"Morgan Mason, I really can't believe this. It's like a dream come true."

Taking Clare in his arms he hugged her tenderly and then looked into her beautiful face. "Well, Mrs. Mason—I'm the man who makes dreams come true!"

Printed in the United States
73528LV00003B/157-174

9 781424 166121